Stories

From

Wrigley

Marcus Blake

~ The Marcus Blake Collection ~

Stories From Wrigley

A Mavericknes Media / Truesource Publishing book

Stories From Wrigley was edited by
Carol Felder and J M Almgreen

The story is fictional and while certain name of players for the Chicago Cubs and places for the Chicago Cubs are a matter of record and fact the story written by Marcus Blake is purely fiction and any resemblance to actual people, places, and certain facts associated with the characters created by Marcus Blake is purely coincidence.

Mavericknes Media : Dallas Texas

Truesource Publishing : Dallas Texas

www.truesourcepublishing.com

ISBN : 978-1-932996-54-8

Printed in the United States of America
Published in Dallas, Texas

For More information on Marcus Blake go to….

www.marcusblake.net
www.facebook.com/themarcusblake
www.twitter.com/marcusblake
www.thatnerdshow.com

About the Author

Marcus Blake was born in Chicago, Illinois in 1977. He grew up in Chicago and East Texas. His education is in History, Literature, Psychology, and Religion & Philosophy. Marcus Blake has studied at many universities throughout the United States, but his Alma Mater is Stephen F. Austin State University in Nacogdoches, Texas, which is also where he wrote his first book, The Music of Life. Marcus Blake is a Poet, Musician, Comedian, Writer, and Historian. His books are The Music of Life, My Reflections, Returning Home. Sex Game. The Lonely Girl, Stories From Wrigley, 30 Minutes: Trust and Lies, 30 Minutes: Guilty Until Proven Innocent, 30 Minutes: A Soldier's Song, and 30 Minutes: A Badge of Honor. . He has taught in the public school system, served in the Army, and been a guest speaker at Education and Literary events throughout the world. Marcus Blake is also a Radio Host, his current show is Saturday Morning Nerd Show which can be heard on Saturday Mornings at www.thatnerdshow.com. He is a veteran of Rock and Roll shows as well as Political shows on the radio. Marcus Blake makes his home in the Dallas, Texas .

Other Books by Marcus Blake...

The Music of Life

My Reflections

Returning Home

Sex Game

The Lonely Girl

30 Minutes: Trust and Lies

30 Minutes: Guilty Until Proven Innocent

30 Minutes: A Soldier's Song

30 Minutes: A Badge of Honor

Ring of Warriors: Making a Fighter

Stories From Wrigley is
Dedicated to my sister Tina,

The biggest Cubs fan I know!

Our first Cubs game together at Wrigley Field
was the day we became a family
and found something in common.

Table of Contents

"Every player should be accorded the privilege of at least one season with the Chicago Cubs. That's baseball as it should be played - in God's own sunshine. And that's really living."

~ *Alvin Dark*

1

A Baseball Life

When I tell you that baseball is life in my family, it's not an exaggeration. There's no clear-cut line between religion and baseball where I come from. I was the girl that my mother always wanted, but instead of playing with dolls I played with a baseball glove and ball. I guess you could say that I'm a tomboy, but my family is to blame for that and if there's an organization that gets to share in that blame it would be the Chicago Cubs.

I have been a Cubs fan since the day I born - sort of made that way by the baseball gods if you believe in that sort of thing. It was inevitable because I was born into a family that shares a pretty unique history with the Chicago Cubs. My great, great-grandfather, my great-grandfather, my grandfather, and my father have all played for the Cubs. Even my brother plays for them now. That's five generations that have played for Chicago so it's kind of in my blood. And being a fan truly is a family affair. Some people have generations of fans in their family; I have a family with generations of players. It's kind of a given that we're big Chicago Cub fans and why wouldn't we be if the men in your family keep playing for the same team, but we're fans because we've never been able to find any better team to cheer for. Not even the Yankees of old were good enough and to be honest there's no greater faith than being a Cubs fan. And like all fans, we have a love and hate relationship with the Cubs, but no matter what we're still fans and there are no greater sports fans than Cub fans. I figured that out a long time ago covering other teams for the newspaper I work for and when I'm with Cub fans I always know that I'm home.

My name is Amy Larson and I'm a sports writer for the Chicago Sun-Times. I've always loved writing and there wasn't any other kind of news that I wanted to cover other than sports, especially the Cubs. It was probably destiny for me to become a sports writer covering the Cubs, if you even believe in destiny. Then again maybe I just didn't want to do anything else. Why would I, this is a great job and I get to see the Cubs for free, what can be better than that? Maybe sex, but only if he's a Cub fan and looks good in "cubby blue."

People think of me as a super fan for the Cubs, and I'm fine with that. People like to ask me if I've ever had my heart broken because I don't do the dating scene anymore. I tell them my heart gets broken every October and the winter is unbearable because I'm reminded that it's not baseball season. But when the spring gets here and the new baseball season starts my love is renewed with the only true love I have, Chicago Cubs' baseball. To tell you the truth I'm okay with that part of my life too.

I've never written a novel before; never had the ambition to like most journalists, but it's another thing that was inevitable. I have a great story and for me the only thing you can do with a great story is write it. Dr. Fairbanks, a literature professor I had in college once told me that we all eventually write our family story because it's the truest thing that we know. We can write all sorts of stories, but the one that we know best is our story of growing up and the journey of how we got here. For me that story is wrapped up in the history of the Chicago Cubs and what it means to live and die as a fan. The thing is as a Cubs fan I have an extended family because as fans we're all family. I never realized that until a couple of years ago when I walked into a Dallas bar and met some other fans. It was also the first time I realized how important my story was, not only in Chicago Cubs history, but also for me to see how extraordinary it really is. The reason I'm writing this is to share that story – the good, the bad, the ugly, and all the tragic circumstances that happened along the way. But that's mostly within my own family.

In the Larson family we're far from perfect and probably more tragic than other families. I can't even tell you what a fairy tale is because I've never known one like some families have. The truth is every one of us from my great, great grandfather to my brother are broken and battered living with the misguided notion that we're legendary because our family history is wrapped up in the Cubs mythology, if you pardon the metaphor. The men in my family are just lucky to share the uniform of the same professional baseball team. I guess what I'm really saying is that we're nothing special, but everyone of us have been a part of great moments in Cubs history and we did it as a family even if it some of us have only lived through it in the stories passed on by our ancestors. It's not any different than generations of fan that have shared those same moments – my story really is the story of every fan that has watched with passion their beloved Chicago Cubs and then had their heart broken in October.

However, there is one aspect that fans won't get – what it's like living with the men who helped shape the history of Cubs and experienced all the heartbreaks first hand. So for me this story doesn't start with the disappointment of being five outs away from the World Series only to have it snatched away by a bumbling fan. My story starts with a broken down middle -aged man who

threw his career away for too many good times when he was
so close to greatness that he could touch it. This story
starts with my father Steve Larson who pitched for the
Cubs from 1982-1990 and then later finished up his career
with the Texas Rangers until he was kicked out of Major
League Baseball in 1993 for drug abuse.

A few years ago I had just graduated college and finally
took a full time job with Sun-Times in Chicago. While in
college I had been doing some freelance work for them and
it felt good to have a full time job with them especially when
it was my dream job. Unfortunately I couldn't play major
league baseball – it was still a boys sport. After graduation I
decided to spend Christmas with my dad because despite
all of his faults he was always the biggest supporter of my
dream and I knew that he would be pleased that I got a full
time job with the paper as a sports writer. I thought it
would be nice to spend time with him, but I was wrong and
the holidays wouldn't be that Rockwellian scene from the
movies. My dad still liked to drink and he still had a temper
especially when he thought my mother was trying to get
him to meddle in his kids lives. What he should or
shouldn't do when it came to his children was still a sore
point with him and my mother even though they had been
divorced for fifteen years. This time he was being asked by
her through me to help my brother with his career while he
languished in the minors.

I have a twin brother by the name of Ryan, who like
our father is a pitcher and he's in the Chicago Cubs
organization waiting for his call to the show. That's his
dream, to pitch for the Cubs just like our dad did and our
grandfather who pitched for them in the 1960's. Ryan had
played a few of years of college baseball at the University of
Iowa before getting drafted in baseball. He could have gone
straight from high school, but our grandfather convinced
him that he wasn't ready so he waited and got a couple of
years of college under his belt. Ryan also thought that if he
waited and got some experience that he wouldn't have to
wait for very long before getting called up. He thought he

could be another 20 year old superstar like Greg Maddux or Kerry Wood. Turned out he was wrong even though some of us think that he's being held back for personal reasons – not against him but because of my dad. That's where this story starts.

It was the Christmas of 2006 just before the 2007 season and Ryan had been languishing in the minors going on three years now. He still hadn't even been invited to spring training even though he was drafted in the first round back in 2003, which was a little unusual for a first round draft pick, but those things always go by recommendations from other coaches and managers in the system. For three years it had been recommended that he wasn't ready. Of course it was by the same skipper in the minors who made those recommendations and the same manager who had managed the Cubs for three losing seasons. It was a little biased if you ask me, but then again I'm his sister and can be accused of the same thing. While I did want to see my dad that year for Christmas, I really wanted to talk to him about Ryan's situation – I had, had a little prodding from my mother as well.

My father and I had a nice meal and started to talk about things, they were the usual events that family tried to catch up on, but were not always serious. It was typical family small talk. Then I brought the conversation around to Ryan after my father asked how he was doing. They didn't talk much and hadn't since our parents divorced. As the years went by they became more like strangers than father and son and both of them were too stubborn to do anything about it. But of course they would ask about one another through me – some symbolism of how much they really did care for one another even though they didn't let it show. I guess things are like that between fathers and sons.

At some point in the conversation I told my dad that Ryan was still in Double AA ball and probably wouldn't be invited to spring training again. However my father already knew that – he kept tabs on Ryan even though he didn't tell anybody, but he still wouldn't get involved. My father tried to ignore what I was saying about Ryan hoping that he wouldn't have to talk about it - but I asked him in the most honest tone I could find and that's how the real conversation started. It's where this story begins because if this didn't happen then I might not have met the person who inspired me to tell this story. And so this is how it begins.

∞∞∞∞∞∞∞∞∞∞

    Amy looked at her father with an honest look and asked him -"Dad, do you even care what's going on with Ryan?"

"Why would you ask that, of course I do?"

"You act like you don't care, that's why I ask?"

Steve looked at his daughter who now had a disgruntled look on her face and replied. "Just because I don't want to have this conversation doesn't mean that I don't care."

"You know the sad thing is Dad, you could help him."

"What can I do, I'm not the manager, and I don't work in the Cubs system so I really don't have a say."

"You still have connections, you still know people that don't hate you."

Steve smiled at the sarcasm. He said to Amy. "While there might be a few people that don't hate my guts, it's not my place. Besides I hear that they are hiring a new manager. Ryan might have better luck with that one."

"Dad you know that the recommendation will come from Ryan's skipper on whether he should get an invite to sprint training."

"And who's still the skipper of the Tennessee Smokies?"

"It's Jody."

Steve smiled at his daughter with a sarcastic smile. He replied to her. "And you know that he still hates my guts."

[14]

"He could've gotten over it by now. "Do you really think that's likely? Stubborn baseball men don't forget."

Amy sighed and then got up to pour herself a drink from her father's living room bar. Steve has already been drinking scotch and was pretty much lit by now. She liked scotch just like her old man and it was pretty much the only thing that was going to help the conversation at least that was her thinking. She said to her dad.

"You could at least try and do something."

"And you can leave it alone...daughter."

Amy never liked it when he called her daughter in that tone. It annoyed her just as much as hearing fingernails scratch up and down on a chalkboard." She replied in an angry tone. "Look old man, don't be flip about this...he's your son for godsake...that alone should get you to help him."

Steve slammed his drink on the bar counter in his living room that connected to the kitchen area in his condo. He stared at his daughter with a look of rage in his eyes. He paused, not saying anything for a moment. Amy was the first to say something. She shot her father a dirty look and said.

"Say it, you know you want to."

After a long pause Steve replied. "I'm not giving into your bullshit and I'm not going to say what you want me to. You can blame me all you want for what happened years ago, but Ryan is a grown up. He can make his own mistakes and pay for them just like I did. And that also goes for getting himself out the messes he got himself into."

Amy's look turned to sadness instead of anger. Her eyes even started to well up with tears. Then she said. "That's the thing dad; with his current situation he's not paying for his mistakes...he's paying for yours."

Steven Larson, the once great pitcher for the Cubs, didn't say anything. All he did was throw his glass of scotch against the wall in anger, shattering the glass and scaring Amy. She didn't even wait to yell at her dad. She grabbed her purse and stormed out of the condo. Amy got her car and peeled out the driveway trying to reach 60 mph before she was completely in the street. She drove away nearly hitting two parked cars in the process. Steven didn't even go after her. With complete disregard for the shattered glass, he just poured himself another drink and turned on the TV.

Amy drove around North Dallas trying to cool her temper. She was still hot with anger and knew that she didn't need to talk to anyone or it wouldn't be pretty. After an hour of driving around she ended up in Richardson Texas, a suburb north of Dallas. That's when she decided to get a drink and she drove into the parking lot of the first bar she could find. It was a pool hall and Irish Bar all rolled up into one, something only Texas could do. She was also fond of pool. After all, part of working her way through college was hustling drunk guys in pool within the bars around Wrigley field. She was good at pool and most guys never thought a 5 foot 4 inch girl could take them in a game that was mostly played by men. It was the perfect hustle and when you look cute while playing, guys never pay attention to the money that their losing. The place she wandered into was called Lochranns. It was spacious and looked like a Dallas Cowboys bar, the kind of place that nobody would ever talk baseball, but as turned out she couldn't be more wrong.

Amy tried to sneak in quietly and head to the bar, but she was wearing her reversible Cubs Team Jacket and it made her stand out. It was unseasonably cold during Christmas that year and her grandfather, Jack, had gotten her the jacket. She wore it any chance she got, even in Texas where it may not be that welcome As she walked in, Amy made about ten yards on her way to bar before someone recognized the jacket and said "Cool jacket...you're a Cubs fan."

Amy looked over at the guy who said that. He was standing with some other people, a couple of women and couple of other guys. One of the guys was immediately noticeable, not because he was tall, but because he deep blue eyes, which could clearly be seen even in a dim lighted bar. Amy couldn't take her eyes of him. She continued to stare at him while replying back to the guy who made the comment. Amy said.

"Yeah, unfortunately I'm a Cubs fan...doomed to be a lovable loser for the rest of my life."

The guy laughed and said to her. "Just because they haven't won a World Series in a hundred years doesn't mean that it's all bad."

"It's only been 98 years since they last won a world series, but who's counting."

"It feels like a hundred years, I figure we're about due to break the curse."

Amy smiled and replied. "I have a father and grandfather that certainly would agree since they've both been part of the organization and both been close to getting that championship."

The guy reached out his hand and introduced himself. His name was Shane. He invited Amy to sit with him and his friends. They took a seat near the bar and started talking sports. Shane wanted to talk about the Cubs since it was apparent that Amy was a fan. He started asking her questions about the club like what she thought their chances were in 2006. She answered with the best of her knowledge, which was a great deal considering who she was and what she did for a living. The other guy in the group that Amy kept staring at seemed interested in the conversation, but it was also apparent that he didn't know much about baseball. Amy finally asked him. "So do you follow the Cubs at all like your friend Shane?"

He smiled the southern gentleman smile at Amy; it took her breath just looking at it. He said to her. "Not really, never been much of a baseball man."

"What, its America's past time, how can you not follow it?"

"Honey, I'm from Texas, the pastime around here is football. In fact it's pretty much religion in this state."

Amy laughed and then replied "I forgot - I'm south of the Mason Dixon line...football will always be more important here. You at least like baseball don't you?"

"Of course, but the Texas Rangers don't give us anything to cheer about, so what's the point."

"You can become a Cubs Fan – it will change your life."

"He smiled with all the charm of a southern gentleman and again it took Amy's breath away. Finally he said to her. "I think we should introduce ourselves if we're going to continue to flirt with one another."

Amy gave him a laugh and said. "I guess you're right if we are going to flirt with one another."

"I'm Chris and you are?"

Amy just realized that she never introduced herself since they sat down and started talking about the Cubs. She looked at Chris and everybody else at the table and said. "I'm Amy Larson."

Shane's wife, Lisa asked her in her thick Texas accent "So what do you do, Amy, up in Chicago?"

"I'm a sports writer for the Chicago Sun -Times."

Shane gave her a weird look and paused for a moment trying to figure something out. Amy asked him what was wrong and after another brief moment he said in a boisterous tone.

"Man, I know who you are. You're dad and grandfather played for the Cubs. Your grandfather was Jack Larson and your dad was Steve Larson."

Amy smiled at him and said. "That's right; I'm the granddaughter of the great Jack Larson and the daughter of Steve Larson."

Chris gave her a surprised look because he honestly did not know about her family history, but he was intrigued. Shane just got more excited and commented to everybody sitting around them that they were sitting with a celebrity. Amy was a little bit embarrassed because she had this kind of thing happen a lot, but she laughed it off because for the most part the people she was drinking with seemed cool. Shane asked her. "Man, what's it like being in your family, I mean you got to live with two great pitchers for the Cubs."

Amy smiled and said. "It was an experience, I grew up around baseball and lots of people were jealous of me because of who my family was."

"Hell I would be jealous." Shane said to her. "That's so cool. Then it again it must of sucked too considering your dad threw his career away for drugs and alcohol."

Lisa replied to Shane. "Honey, be nice. Don't be rude to our guest."

"What, I didn't say anything that wasn't true. I mean it's not like he got caught using steroids, but he did throw his career away being a coke head."

Chris gave Shane a dirty look and said. "Dude, you're being a dick."

Shane was about to say something mean to Chris, but Amy interrupted trying to prevent a fight. She said. "Look its okay, he's right. My dad did throw his career because of drug and alcohol abuse. He did what he did, but he was still a good pitcher when he was with the Cubs. And he's still my dad and always will be no what matter insults are hurled at me because of him."

Shane had a remorseful look on his face. He said to Lisa. "I'm sorry...I didn't mean anything by it."

"It is what it is. My father wasn't perfect...still isn't."

Chris looked at Amy and asked her a sincere and honest question to lighten the mood. He asked her. "Did you have a cool childhood being the daughter and granddaughter of baseball stars?"

Amy smiled and replied. "Honestly...It was fucking awesome."

"I would imagine it would have to be."

"I had a baseball life and spent my childhood at the ballpark. There's no better playground in the world."

Everybody at the table just smiled at Amy. Shane even had a look of jealousy and what baseball fan wouldn't – to grow up at the baseball park especially Wrigley Field;

it's the purest form of heaven one can find on this earth if you're a baseball fan. Chris asked Amy. "Do you have any other relatives that play professional baseball?"

Amy gave a small laugh and said. "Actually I have more than two relatives who play for the Cubs. My great, great grandfather played for them from 1906 to 1921 and my great grandfather played for the Cubs from 1936 to 1953."

"Really!" Shane said. "You have four generations that have played for the Cubs?"

"Actually I have five. My brother plays for the Tennessee Smokies, Double AA ball."

Shane's draw dropped and then he said. "You're last name is Wrigley, isn't it?"

Amy laughed. Chris had a confused look and then Amy told him that the Wrigley's who started the gum company used to own the Cubs.

"I wish they never would have sold the Cubs. It would be pretty cool to own the Chicago Cubs...greatest dream job ever."

"I think it would be pretty cool to own any sports team." Chris said.

"No, not just any team. Owning the Cubs would be as close to perfect as you can get especially as a sports fan." Amy replied to Chris with big smile on her face.

"It's just a baseball team."

Shane and Lisa gave Chris a dirty look. Amy just stared at him with the most serious look she could find deep down. Then she replied. "They are more than just a baseball team. It's the perfect love of a summer day and the joy of visiting a big baseball park because the Wrigley field is the purest form of baseball. Watching the Cubs play is living poetry and all the joys of the being a kid wrapped up together. And to top it all off cheering for them is the greatest faith in the word because no matter how much hope you have they'll end up breaking your heart, but in the end they'll find a way to give you hope. Not many sports teams can do that. "

Chris smiled and said. "I guess, I don't get it about the Cubs."

"No you don't, but if you get to know me you will."

Everybody at the table just laughed. Chris was an unfortunate soul who just didn't get it about being a Cubs fan, but most people born in Texas don't. For the rest of the evening they all sat at the table drinking beer and telling their favorite Cub stories. Amy told most of the stories and Chris just sat and gladly listened since he didn't have any stories about the Cubs. Somewhere through the conversation Amy found her joy again – she was able to laugh and getting to tell her favorite kind of story, stories about the Cubs. Also through the conversation Christ noticed something; there was something mesmerizing about Amy. She noticed the same thing in him.

The four of them sat and talked until the bar closed down at 2:00am and they had to finally be kicked out. As they were leaving Amy asked Chris, "You know you never told me what you did."

"I'm a lawyer. I take the bar exam in a couple of months."

"Somehow, I can see that in you."

"I like to think that people can't read me that well."

"Oh I just mean that it suits you. So you don't really like baseball, huh?"

"I just never got into it like I did football, but I don't think it's a boring sport."

Amy smiled at him and said. "You ever come to Chicago; I'll take you to a game and show you how fun it can be."

Chris leaned in and kissed her on the cheek. Then he said. "I would like that. In the mean time you should start writing a book about your family. Sounds like to me it's one hell of a story and fans would enjoy it. I would read it."

Amy smiled at him and said. "Maybe one day I will." She kissed Chris on the cheek and said goodbye to Lisa and Shane. She even forgot why she was mad at her Dad. The next day she was on a plane back to Chicago. Pitchers and catchers would report in 6 weeks and that meant for her baseball season was starting. Amy Larson would have plenty of things to write about.

2

The Boy from Iowa

The news room at the Sun Times was a noisy place. People were in a hurry and a thousand conversations were going on at once. It was the typical ambiance of the newspaper office and Amy loved every minute of it. She was engrossed with some reports on the Cubs during the last week of December. Most people would be covering the Bears because it was still football season and the other reporters would be covering the Blackhawks because believe it or not, Chicago was still a hockey town, It was four weeks before Spring Training and all she could think of was the upcoming baseball season – it was an important one, it was 2008 and it would officially be 100 years since the Cubs had last won a World Series. Her phone started to ring on her desk. When she answered, she heard a voice on the other end that she recognized, but couldn't remember. Amy had a puzzled look on her face and asked the gentleman on the other end who he was.

He replied. "This is Chris, Chris Hanes. The guy from Texas you met over a year ago that night at the bar during the holidays."

She remembered and then she smiled. Amy said to him. "This is a surprise. I never thought I would hear from you."

Chris laughed and then said. "I could see that, but you're the only one I know in Chicago and since I'm here I thought I would give you a call."

"You're in Chicago, what are you doing here?"

"I have a job interview at a law firm downtown so I thought I would come up to Chicago and see what they had to offer. Who knows, I might like it up here. "

"I thought you Texas boys would never dare move out of Texas."

"Some won't, but I might if the right offer came along. Hell Kerry Wood did."

Amy Laughed at his amusing statement and replied. "You know how to impress me – keeping up with my favorite team. After all if Chicago is good enough for Kerry Wood then it might be good for you."

"I guess we'll have to see about that. Listen since I'm in town do you want to grab dinner tonight. I know you don't have that much to do because it's football season."

"Yes, you're right about that and sure, I would like to get some dinner tonight."

"Well let's meet at 6:00 somewhere and I'll let you pick the place since you know where the best places to eat are."

"You've got that right. Tonight I am taking you to the best pizza place in town. I guarantee you've never had good pizza before, but after tonight that will change."

They both laughed. Amy's smile couldn't hide her school girl joy. A guy who she was attracted to had called her. Later that night they met at a little Italian joint called Campese's that served the best Deep Dish pizza in the world – this was according to Amy. It was a true fixture of Chicago, just like the Cubs and if Chris was going to be introduced to the Windy City in the right way there was no place better. The two met at the restaurant a few hours later. When Amy walked in she saw Chris standing by the small bar. She smiled joyfully, as if she were a kid again for she was happy to see him. She had to admit to herself that she had a little crush on him. She did a couple of years ago the night she met him and it was still there. Amy walked over and said hi – then she gave him a hug. It was little unusual for her to do that on a first date, but she has never been attracted to someone like this before. And the truth was Chris felt the same way about her; the underlying reason he called her.

They took a table in the back and ordered a traditional Chicago pie with a couple of beers. That's when they started talking. They caught up with their lives over the past couple of years. He told her about working for a small Dallas law firm that was so bad it made him rethink his legal career. The firm represented a lot of the oil companies in Texas and he couldn't stomach protecting them anymore – it wasn't really a Texas quality, but he did have a conscience. Amy started telling about her career over the past couple of years and how she was getting to cover the Cubs a lot more. In the last half of the 2007 season she had started to become the regular sports reporter covering the Cubs for the Sun Times. Amy also told Chris about her brother getting called up in August of 2007. Chris smiled when she told him the story and then he told her that he happened to be at the game in Houston when Ryan got called up from Triple A to pitch for the Cubs. He was at the game with clients of the law firm he worked at and he was also the only one who knew of Ryan Larson. It was a historic game especially being Ryan's first major league game, but also because he pitched a 2-0 shutout and flirted with a no-hitter, allowing only one hit in the bottom of the 8th inning. Amy couldn't believe that he was there and so they talked about the game. Amy was a little infatuated now because being a former college football player he was taking an active interest in her favorite team.

They chatted a little more about their lives, even told a few stories about family. So that's when Chris asked her about the Larson's. He had asked around to a few guys that really knew baseball after he had first met her and every one of them said that the family was legendary in baseball. He had also heard that the tragic history of the family seem to parallel the history of the Cubs organization, but he still didn't know a whole lot about the Cubs and her family. He mentioned what he had heard and Amy gave him a sarcastic smile. She had heard that statement all of her life – in fact she had to live with it being a Larson herself. She looked at Chris and said

"My family has its triumphs and its tragedies and yes, it seems that every major let down in Cubs history, I've had a family member on that team."

Chris smiled and said. "We all have own family demons as my grandfather use to say."

"Have you had five generations play for the same team and suffer every major heartbreak with that team over the last hundred years?"

"No, you've got me on that one, but I know what it means to be let down by family and to feel like you've let down the ones you love."

"You think that's me too?"

"It's a fair bet."

"Maybe you're right, but there are no easy solutions to it all."

"No, there never are, but grandfather used to also say something else that I think fits this particular occasion. Sometimes the only way we truly understand who we are is to tell our story and see it through the eyes of the audience. It sounds like you have a pretty interesting story, maybe you should tell it."

"Well, I am a writer. It's kind of what I do. I don't know where to begin and who would really want to hear it."

"I do. I figure it's a good way to get to know you."

"Oh is that your secret plan with me?"

"You were the only person I called in Chicago."

"It could be just to see if you can get lucky?"

"I'm a guy...of course it is." Chris told her in a sarcastic tone. He then winked at her to let her know that he was just kidding.

Amy smiled at him. She paused for a moment then took a sip of beer and said. "If you really want to know me and hear a little family history then where do you want me to start?"

"Start at the beginning...it's always the best place to start."

They ordered another round of beers and told the waiter to keep the tab open for awhile. Apparently they were going to be there longer than they had anticipated. So Amy started at the beginning with her family history – her great, great grandfather, Paul Larson. He played outfield for Chicago Cubs from 1906 -1921 and was the only member of her family to ever win a World Series. Paul was a large Danish farm boy from Iowa who stood about 6'3" and weighed about 225. The thing is he was about the size of Babe Ruth, but never had his kind of numbers; although he was a great hitter and had a lifetime batting average of .310 with the Cubs. He also came close to hitting over .400 in 1910, 31 years before Ted Williams – he would fall shy of that tremendous feat and end that season with .390 leading the Cubs in batting records that year. Paul Larson was overshadowed in baseball history, but he was always considered a legend in Cubs history and one of the driving forces for the Cubs winning back to back World Series titles in 1907 and 1908. But 1908 would be the last year the Cubs would ever win a World Series. These were just a few of the facts that Amy would tell Chris about her great, great grandfather. Chris didn't really know anything about the Cubs so alongside this family story he was a getting a history lesson about the Cubs.

A surprise visit by a Cubs scout to his home town of Marshalltown, Iowa started Paul's career with the Cubs. The Larson family had immigrated to America in 1899 from Denmark – there were dairy farmers. Paul's father, Paul Sr.

was one of six boys that ran the family dairy farm in Denmark. It was a hard life and he wanted a fresh start for his own family so he moved his wife, three boys, and two girls across the ocean to America and after a year living in New York, Paul Larson Sr. took his family west, eventually settling in Marshalltown where there was an abundance of farm land and, even better, the promise of a fresh start. Paul Larson Jr. was the oldest child and he was 13 years old when they settled in Iowa.

While the Larson family was new to America and trying to adopt the customs of the Midwest while also still maintaining their Danish customs, there was one thing that Larson boys found that was truly American. They found baseball and for them it was the best part of the American dream because even though they might have been different than most of the people in Marshalltown, after all, they were still considered just immigrants, on the baseball field they were looked as equals. Part of that came from the fact that all three Larson boys were better than anybody in town. Paul and his two brothers, Arthur and George, quickly picked up the game, and were playing some kind baseball game when they weren't in school or on the farm.

All three brothers were a year or so apart from each other and they always played on the same team no matter what that team was. Their team also just happened to be the winning team most of the time. Paul played in the outfield most of the time and batted Cleanup – he was the best hitter in Marshalltown and most people said that he was the best in the entire state of Iowa. But that's just what people say. Arthur was a pitcher and he was definitely the best in the state of Iowa – you could tell that because he had more than one scout come and look at him waiting until the day he turned eighteen and could be signed with a big league club. He would turn eighteen in the middle of the 1906 season. George played catcher and although he was not as a good of a hitter as Paul, he certainly would be an above average hitter on any team.

At the beginning of the 1906 season, all three
brothers were playing on the semi pro team in
Marshalltown, the Marshalltown Greys. It was towards the
end of the season when a scout from the Chicago Cubs
came to Marshalltown, and he came to see Arthur pitch.
The scouts name was Frank Seele and he and he had been
manger of the Cubs in the 1890's before having to retire
due to having TB, but he still filled in as a scout from time
to time and that's where his talent really was. He found
everybody that would make up the 1907 and 1908 teams.
He was also the one that put the Tinkers to Evers to
Chance together playing field. His eye for talent was very
good, but saying that would be an understatement.

Stories of Arthur had gotten as far as New York
because even the New York Giants were looking at him.
Paul wasn't on anybody's radar – nobody had even heard of
him in the big leagues. Arthur was known because he had
on more than one occasion thrown a no hitter and a few
complete games, which was almost unheard of back then.
As it turned out the day the scout was at a Grey's game,
Arthur was having an off day, having given up 5 runs and
nine hits in the first two innings of the game. He was not
that impressive, and to the scout all the stories he had
heard sounded more like legend than actual fact. The truth
of the matter was that Arthur had a tired arm. He had
pitched a one hit complete game two days before. He was
far from rested and so he played lousy.

The one brother that had a spectacular day was
Paul. The Greys were able to come back and win the game 9
to 8. All the RBIs were by Paul. He batted six times in nine
innings getting a hit every time he was at bat. The other
team couldn't seem to get him out. He hit for the cycle and
what was more impressive, he hit three home runs, scoring
seven runs on the three homers. What had become legend
in Iowa became fact in front of the scout for the Cubs. In
103 years that feat has never been accomplished again with
any baseball team in Iowa. Not even a Field of Dreams
could match it. That day it seemed as if the baseball gods

ignored Arthur and shined their light a little more on Paul. After the game the scout never even talked to Arthur, he wasn't interested. Instead, he talked to Paul about playing in the big leagues for what was considered the best team in Professional Baseball. In 1906 the Cubs would actually prove it, and what Paul didn't know at beginning of the 1906 season playing for the Marshalltown Greys was that he was going to be a part of it. He may have started playing for the Greys in 1906, but at the end of the season he would be playing or the Cubs.

As Amy got through telling that part of the story Chris looked at her funny. She asked what was wrong. He said. "I thought you were going to tell me about the 1907 and 1908 Cubs teams that your great, great grandfather played on."

She smiled and replied. "I'm getting there, but it's important for you to know how he got there. And to also know how on any given day in baseball the biggest star can be a failure while a little bit of luck can come at the right moment for an average player, and how that's a rare thing that should never be take for granted. That's baseball for you."

So Amy continued her story. After the game the scout from Chicago of course wanted to talk to Paul. He wasn't interested in Arthur anymore. To him everything he had heard about Arthur was a myth – he had seen for himself what the kid could do It seemed to Paul and the rest of the Grey's team that he ignored a major rule to be a good scout; he never thought to himself that Paul could be having an off day. It happens in baseball, more than people realize. As everybody was packing their gear the scout made his way over to Paul asked him one question.

He asked Paul. "Have you ever considered playing pro ball? You hit the ball like nobody I've ever seen?"

Paul replied to him. "No, I haven't. The person you should talk to is my brother Arthur."

"I saw what he could do and I'm not interested. I am however interested in you."

"I appreciate that, but I have no interest in playing pro ball."

"Not if it means playing for more money than you've ever made being a farmer. Not even if it means playing in big cities. Have you ever been to a big city?"

Paul gave him a smile and said. "We traveled through New York when we came from Denmark years ago."

"Yeah, but you've never played baseball in a stadium with thousands of fans that think you're a star. And I guarantee that Chicago is a more exciting city."

"Why Chicago?"

"That's where the club I'm with is located. I work for the Chicago Cubs and they're the best team in baseball. You can be on that team if you want. And the best part, you won't be that far from home."

The last part, peaked Paul's interest about pro baseball. He never thought for a moment he would have a chance to play. He was happy in Iowa, and he was happy playing for the Marshalltown Greys. Paul always assumed that if somebody in his family would play professional baseball and live in the big city it would be Arthur and he was fine with that. After a conversation with the scout from Chicago all of that changed. Now he wanted to live in a big city and keep playing baseball since it was his favorite thing to do. The scout told him that if he really wanted a chance to play pro ball that he would have a seat for him on the train in the morning. Of course Paul needed to talk to his family about the decision because it was assumed that since he was the oldest son he would help run the family farm. While he didn't know it at the time he had already made his decision.

Paul discussed his plans with his parents that night over dinner. His father was less than pleased because he was counting on Paul to always be there on the farm. His mother on the other hand was more understanding and even happy for him. She had always worried that Paul would never know true joy in life and settle for something else that others wanted for him. After Paul's father stormed out of the house and went to the barn to drink his mother simply told him, "Dear you have to follow your own heart and if you can play the game while at the same time make a good living doing it then follow that path. It's your new beginning just as moving to America was your father's and mine."

Paul smiled and hugged his mother. He knew she was right and that Iowa wasn't to be his permanent home. It was just a stop onto the next place in life he had to go. George was also happy for him, but Arthur wasn't. He played the part of the jealous brother and hardly ever spoke to Paul again. He didn't see Paul off at the train station, he didn't say goodbye like George. The silence between Arthur and Paul would last another twelve years. Arthur would be the one to stay behind and it would slowly kill him until the joyful young man that everybody once knew wouldn't exist anymore. But that story is for another time.

The next day Paul would leave on a train heading for Chicago. He was the first Larson to play for the Chicago Cubs and his first season with the team would be 1906. It was also the best season that any baseball team ever had for the Cubs would win 116 games that year and many baseball fans considered them to be the best team ever to take the field. Well, that team had big a lanky blond haired 19 year old kid from Iowa who would perfect the Home Run nearly ten years before Babe Ruth. As the train left Iowa Paul looked out the window at the passing farm land. He thought to himself that he was watching his old life pass him by. When the train entered Chicago and Paul saw the tall buildings and the bright lights he knew that he would never be the same. Paul smiled to himself never being the same seemed to make him happy.

The scout first helped get Paul a hotel and then walked him over to the Cubs baseball park as the team was doing batting practice. He wanted Paul to meet his new manager, Frank Chance. Everybody just called him Chance. He had taken over the manager job when the scout who had discovered Paul retired from the job the year before. Chance wasn't that impressed with Paul at the beginning; he hadn't proved himself yet and the Cubs already had what was considered the best team in baseball that year. Paul was just another scrub in the system and those guys got in the way. None of that mattered to Paul because he was in the big city and he was about to play professional baseball.

The 1906 season had already started, but the Cubs were only about 9 games into the season. They were undefeated and because of that Paul really didn't matter to anyone in the organization - they didn't need him at all. The scout convinced Chance to at least let Paul participate in batting practice just so he could show everyone what he could do. Chance trusted the scout because it was him who moved Chance to first base and made him a star. So Paul grabbed a bat and stepped up to the plate. He took a few practice swings and stared down the pitcher. The pitcher on the mound gave Paul a dirty look because he didn't believe that the kid from Iowa could really do anything. He was about to be proved wrong. Frank Chance decided to let the his best pitchers all take a crack at Paul Larson – he figured that if Paul could hit anything off of his pitching staff then he would be worth his weight as a ballplayer. And that assumption was correct considering the Cubs had the best pitching staff in the professional baseball.

The Cubs rotation consisted of Jack Taylor, who had a streak of 187 complete games dating back all the way to 1901, Mordecai "Three Finger" Brown, Orval Overall, Ed Reulbach Carl Lundgren and Jack Pfiester, who was known as Jack "the Giant Killer" because he was virtually invincible when pitching against their arch rivals, the New York Giants. The Cubs pitchers would pretty much lead the league in pitching categories. And this was who Paul had to face at the plate – it was the ultimate test to see if he was worthy to wear a Cubs uniform. Most of the team bet among themselves that he wouldn't get one hit. They were wrong. When all of the pitchers had pitched to him and after 70 pitches had been thrown Paul had 18 hits and his batting average was well above .200. Everybody was impressed, not at the hits, but because he had made contact on over 80% of the pitches. That alone gave Paul a spot on the roster. He wouldn't start at all throughout the 1906 season, but he proved to be a great bench player and utility man.

After batting practice was over, Frank Chance walked over to Paul and shook his hand with pride. He smiled and said that it was one of the most impressive batting feats he had ever seen, for not even a seasoned player could have done that. Then he told Paul that Frank Seele was one of the best judges of talent he had ever known. That last part was very true because it was Seele who had found most of the team, but what he would become known for was putting together the great defensive team of Tinkers to Evers to Chance. Seele had been the manager of the Cubs the year before, but due to health issues he had to step aside. Truth was he couldn't get away from baseball no matter how much he tried, and he would always go out of his way to find those rare talents that most managers dismissed. Paul Larson would become of those talents that nobody ever thought about. So Paul became a part of the Cubs organization and as he was getting to know his teammates after batting practice Frank Seele started to leave – he had a train to catch back to Colorado where he was living now. He had found the last player the Cubs needed in his mind and now he could really retire from baseball. Even though he didn't want to get away from the game that he loved he had or it would kill him – his health issues were too great. Paul ran over to him and thanked him for what he did. Frank looked at him and said."

"The thanks is getting a chance to watch you play. You're going to do great, son."

Paul smiled and replied. "I don't know if I will see much action on this team...they're pretty good."

"You'll play, maybe not much, but you will. Just make every chance you get count."

And that was it; Frank Seele turned around and walked off the field. That would be the last time Paul Larson ever saw him. He finally did retire, except for letters to Frank Chance about players he was hearing about throughout the country. He was always making recommendations and while scouting for players still wasn't a popular business, Frank Seele was a modern scout trapped in an old fashioned era. He certainly was ahead of his time and what made him better was his rare eye for talent, for if it had not been for him we would never have heard of Tinkers to Evers to Chance. And for the Larson family, well, they might have just been an afterthought in baseball – the story of what could have been as they worked a dairy farm in Iowa for the last hundred years.

In the beginning of the season, Paul didn't see much action. He substituted for players in games that the Cubs won by 9 or more runs, which happened a lot more often than people would think. The Cubs were more than just the best team in baseball – they were simply unstoppable and by August the Cubs had it pretty much wrapped up. They would win 116 games that year; no other team has won more games in baseball history. They finished 20 games ahead of the second best team that year, the New York Giants. They lead the league in batting and of course pitching – they had a team ERA of 1.76, a record that still stands today. They also had the lowest number of runs scored by an opposing team against them – 381, another record that still stands today. To say that the 1906 Cubs were good was an understatement and by many accounts they were the best team ever to play the game. Paul would help with that and he ended up helping more than he thought he would that year.

Paul Larson was the perfect utility man because he could play 7 positions if needed. He could bat and while he never started a game or even played in every game he did end the season with a .276 batting average – not bad for a rookie on that team. By the end of the season Paul had become the regular substitute for the Cubs – if anybody needed to come out, Paul was the man that was put into the game. One day in early August while playing against the Pirates in Pittsburg, he was called upon to replace Frank Schulte after he was hit by a pitch. Paul simply walked up to the plate and launched the first pitch into the right field corner. Because of his speed he hit an inside the park home run and batted in two runs to win the game. A week later after Orval Overall's arm was getting tired by the 7th inning, Frank Chance didn't want to use any of his regular pitchers so they could stay rested. The Cubs were up by eight runs so Chance decided to have some fun – he put Paul Larson in as a pitcher. As it turned out he had a pretty good arm. He had a blazing fastball and a sinking curve – that was all he needed to get the next 9 batters out after allowing only one hit. He struck out 5 of the 9 batters he faced. He may not have had the best mechanics, but he was big and he could over power people with his pitches.

At the end of the season, Paul had become a regular player even if he didn't start. He had proven himself as a professional player and if it had been any other team then he would have been a starting player and possibly an all-star. But more importantly he was the right kind of utility player the Cubs were going to need as they played the Chicago White Sox in the World Series. Everybody expected the Cubs to walk all over the White Sox, and they should have because they were the better team. But as a rule in baseball, what we think should happen in the game usually doesn't happen, after all, the Cubs have gone a hundred years without winning the World Series. Sometimes baseball and the love of a team can be very cruel to the fan. The other rule in baseball, never underestimate the other team because baseball never has foregone conclusions. That was the lesson Paul was about to learn.

The White Sox were very good and in every game they tested the ability of the Cubs. The games were well pitched and every one of them seemed to be a pitcher's duel. In fact some say that the 1906 World Series was the best pitched series ever in baseball ball history and nothing was more evident of that fact than the result of game one. The Cubs would lose the game 2-1 and Nick Altrock of the White Sox edged Three-Finger Brown in numbers and performance to win game one for the White Sox. It was the biggest shocker for the Cubs that year and the worst upset that they had suffered. Paul Larson never made a hit the two times he was at bat in the game, striking out and flying out. The Cubs would come back and win game 2 of the series 7-1 and Paul Larson would get a hit, but game three was a repeat of the game 1 as the Cubs would be shut out for the first time during the 1906 season. Three-Finger Brown would redeem himself and win game four – he single handedly won the game for the Cubs with superior pitching. He was a remnant of his old self. The Cub hitters also came out during the game, including Paul. He would prove again why he was a great utility man and good man to have hitting for your team. He got another hit allowing two runs to score for the Cubs.

The series was tied again. Game 5 would be in the White Sox's favor though as they broke a 3-3 tie to win the game 8-6. This time the one hit Paul would have in the game scoring another two runs for the Cubs wouldn't be enough. So it came down to game 6 and everybody just expected the Cub to win it, tying the series and sending it to a deciding game 7. It was not to be, however, because the invincible Cubs proved to be the opposite and the White Sox were the better team that day. Frank Chance wanted "Three-Finger" Brown to pitch game 6 and he told him that since he was the best pitcher on the team it was up to him to even the series. But that's not the way it happed; Brown would give up seven runs in the first two innings. It was practically over by then, but the Cubs tried to rally. They scored one run early in the game. The score was 7-1 by the fourth inning. That's when Paul Larson came up with a little magic of his own. Just like he had done before he would get a hit and the Cubs would score two more runs. Paul would get a triple, but nobody could hit him home. The score would remain 8-3 until the eighth inning when the Cubs would start hitting again. One man got on base and the next hit would end in a double play. Frank Chance told Paul to do whatever he could to get a run before he walked to the plate.

Everybody knew that Paul was hot and one of the best chances they had to come back. Paul did get a hit in the right field corner, so he did what anybody else would have done in that situation. He tried to stretch a double into a triple, but he was tagged out at third to end the inning. It was close and of course Frank Chance argued the call, but the call stood. The ninth inning was the Cubs' last chance and with three outs away they never hit the ball out of the infield, and the White Sox would win the game and the series. Nobody wanted to talk about it as the Cubs clubhouse was silent. Even Paul had never felt such sadness. For Paul, it hurt because he absolutely believed that they would win and he would do great. But he learned the hard way that there are no guarantees. Even in baseball, despite how well you play the game.

The only thing ever said about the series was by Frank Chance. He told the team in the Club House. "Maybe now you sons of bitches have learned a lesson as to what happens when you underrate the other sons of bitches." What Frank said to the team was all that needed to be said and for Paul Larson he would take it to heart. Paul would go back home to Iowa during the off season and work on the farm. It would be a good off season and a tragic one. First he would get married to a woman that he had grown up with and loved since he was eight years old. Her name was Sonja and she was of Swedish descent. The tragedy that would happen was the death of his brother George. It was freak farming accident, something that hardly ever happens, they say, but it did. Paul would be forever changed by it and it would divide the Larson family.

3

The Last Great Championship Team

It was February 1st, 11 days until pitchers and catchers reported to spring training. The 2008 baseball season was about to start and for most fans winter had been too long. Amy was sitting at her desk smiling, but she wasn't smiling at the fact that baseball season was around the corner – she was smiling because of him. True, they weren't officially dating, but both of them weren't seeing anybody else and most of their evenings had been spent with each other. Amy was the only friend he had in the city after accepting the position at the law firm and moving to Chicago and he was the only person that she wanted to spend time with. Of course they were attracted to one another, but they had really started to like each other as well – it was the beginning of as romance even if they couldn't see it.

The sports editor walked over to Amy's desk and commented on her smiling and the fact that she was happier than usual. She said it was because of baseball season and her brother would get a chance to be on the team, but he knew better than that because he knew her way too well. They were good friends and good friends always know if you're hiding something, but he didn't press the issue. He said to her.

"Well I guess you know what time it is?"

"11 days until pitchers and catchers report and spring training starts."

"Just making sure you can still keep up with a calendar."

"Jim it's me Amy Larson...I would know when baseball seasons starts without a calendar. I'm like an Indian; I feel it in my bones."

"Fair enough! You already know that we'll be sending you down to spring training in Arizona for a few days, but I have another assignment for you. I want you to write a piece about your Great-great grandfather."

Amy gave him a serious look and said. "You've never asked me to write something about them before, why now?"

"Because it's the hundredth anniversary of the Cubs last championship and he was on the team. I thought it would be nice to write a human interest piece on it."

"You don't think it's a bit of bad luck for me to write about him and that team?"

"For god's sake this is not going on the cover of Sports Illustrated. Other news outlets will probably be writing about it as well.   Anyway we're the news, not a sports team; we shouldn't have to believe in superstition."

Amy smiled at the comment and said. "Alright, but if we jinx the Cubs this year, I'm hunting you down."

He smiled at her and said. "Ok, that's fair. By the way I already have a title for it...*The Last Great Championship Team.*"

"Somehow I'm not surprised."

Amy thought about it for a while. Normally she wouldn't do something like this because it was considered taboo for a family member to write about their own family in the news – they wouldn't be objective enough. But the thing is there was nobody better to write this story and she knew the history of the team better than anybody. So she started to try and write it. All she had was a title on a page and it wasn't even her own. After staring at the blank word document for an hour she finally gave up and went home. Chris was cooking her dinner anyway and it was a good way to get her mind off the subject. Then again it was good to tell this story to someone that had never heard it and or didn't know anything about the subject seeing as Chris was a Texan who loved football. Later that night as Chris was cooking dinner, Amy was staring at a blank page on her laptop with only a title on the page. She still couldn't figure out what to say. Chris asked her what she was supposed to be writing about. She replied.

"I have to write about the last great championship team or better put the last time the Cubs won a world series."

"That was a hundred years ago," he asked. "This year to be exact, right?"

"Ah, you've been paying attention." She smiled and winked at him. "Yeah, this is the 100-year anniversary of their last championship and my paper wants me to write about it or to be more exact to write about my great-great grandfather being on that team. I don't know where to start."

"Well, why don't you start at the beginning? After all I don't know the story and maybe telling me will help."

Amy smiled. She knew he was right. She had to go back to 1907 and start with the facts. The same team that played for the Cubs in 1906 returned and they were just as good. Paul Larson had gotten better after his rookie year. The season was no contest – the Cubs pretty much rolled by everybody. While they did not win 116 games again, they did win 107 and finished 20 games ahead of the New York Giants. They were just as superb at defensive play. The pitching staff was just as dominant and in fact had four of their pitchers go 1-2-3-5 in pitching categories when it came to numbers in all pitching categories. There wasn't any team that could really compete. Paul Larson started playing regularly – he played in 120 games that year batting .290 for the season. He was a star and would be considered the best hitter on most teams in the National League and American League. There were even some other teams that inquired about trading for him, but no way was Frank Chance going to let the young kid go. He could hit cleanup in the bottom of the lineup – not an easy feat. Paul also had a rocket for an arm and could throw anybody out from the outfield if they were heading for home, which he had done 18 times during the season...another great feat in baseball.

At the end of the season the only team close to being as good as the Chicago Cubs that year was the Detroit Tigers who the Cubs would face in the World Series. The Tigers were led by the virtually invincible Ty Cobb who led both leagues in batting – his average was .350 for the year. He also led the American league in defense, but none of those same numbers appeared in the series with Cubs. The Cubs would shut the tigers down with pitching. The first game of the series was the only time the Tigers even gave the Cubs some competition in the series. The Cubs scored three runs and then the Tigers came roaring back and tied the game - it was eventually called on account of darkness. They didn't have lights back then and when it got too dark to see the ball baseball games would be called because of darkness – sometimes they would be replayed if there was a tie and sometimes who was ever leading at the time would win the game. Amy looked at Chris with a serious look and told him that this was before they started putting lights up at sports stadiums so they could play night games. Chris gave her a sarcastic smile and replied.

"Yes I know the history of outside lighting when it comes to playing college or professional sports. We do have history books in Texas."

"I just wanted to be sure; I never know what you may be lacking below the Mason Dixon Line."

"Hey we've had electricity for a long time, at least forty years...Civil Rights saw to that because we just couldn't be a bunch of rednecks living in wooden shacks."

"Sarcasm...it's a little attractive even in a Texas boy like you."

Chris laughed, walked over and kissed Amy as she was still sitting at her desk in front of the laptop. It was still on the blank page with the title on it. He said to her. "I hear Danish Girls are quite devilish."

Amy smirked. She replied. "We can be but only in certain areas...maybe one day you'll find out."

Chris smiled at her and then she continued her story. Amy and Chris were already getting into that playful banter that comes with a new relationship – the trick is can two people keep it or just get annoyed at each other. Most often not it's the latter, but for Chris and Amy there was a connection. They didn't know what it was exactly, but they knew it was there and for now that was good enough.

Although the first game ended in a tie the Cubs completely dominated the Tigers for the rest of the series. It was all done by pitching and even the great Ty Cobb batted only .200 for the series. The Cubs would win the next four games with scores 3-1, 5-1, 6-1, and 2-0. Three-Finger Brown shut the Tigers out in the last game using only one pitch most of the time – the "screwball" and the Tigers would later claim that it was the most devastating pitch they had ever seen, so the legend goes. Baseball is full of those and it's what adds to lore and mystery of the game, but the one thing that never lies are the numbers. With all the stories and all the tall tales, they can never make the numbers in the game a farce and that's also what makes it beautiful because the numbers in the game are a beautiful symmetry between man, stick, and ball as they point to the truest object of the game – to get home.

Chris smiled at Amy as she finished the last part. She was being poetic. He said to her. "You just had to throw that last part in didn't you?"

"Maybe I did," she replied. "A story like this deserves a little fairy dust on it."

"It kind of does, actually."

Amy was about to continue the story when Chris spoke up again and asked. "You told me one time that Paul almost never came back after the 1906 season, why was that?"

"There was a family tragedy back in Iowa and for a while he didn't think that he was going to play baseball again."

"What happened?"

Amy began to tell the story almost forgetting that the back story even existed. After the 1906 season was over Paul went back to Iowa. He was getting married to his childhood sweetheart Sonja, but before he got home he got word that his brother George has been killed in an accident. Part of the barn had caved in during a terrible storm. He was caught in the barn trying to get the animals settled when lightning struck the roof and caved it in – part of the roof fell on him and crushed his skull. When Paul got home he wasn't just returning home to get married, he was coming home to lay his brother to rest. After the death it was only Arthur that was left to work the family farm and he had taken to drinking more than usual since Paul got called up to the big leagues and he hadn't. The drinking was his way of forgetting and he was well on his way to being a full blown drunk. Paul and Arthur's parents needed help on the farm and so Paul was asked to stay.

He almost did, but it was a conversation with his brother Arthur that changed his mind. Of course the conversation is just hearsay, being passed done through the generations, but this is what was said. It was about a week before Paul was to leave for Spring Training. He had been married for about a month and was settling in nicely for a quite life on a farm and was having to deal with the fact that he had given up his dreams for family. He and Arthur were working on the new roof to the barn. Arthur said to him as they were working.

"It's getting close for you to leave, or least supposed to leave. You may feel sad now, but you'll get over it. You'll see that you made the right decision."

Paul looked at him angrily and replied. "You don't know what the right decision for me is. You're usually too drunk to know anything."

"Bastard...you don't need to be playing baseball anyway. Family's more important. You should have never gone last year anyway."

Paul stopped what he was doing and grabbed the Arthur's arm. He said. "You're still jealous that it was me that went and not you."

"You're right...it should have been me. I'm the better player anyway."

"Maybe, but they didn't choose you. I'm the one that got the shot and if you were half the man you're supposed to be then you would be happy for me."

Arthur hit Paul with the back of his hand cutting open his lip. Paul wanted to hit him, but stopped. He knew Arthur was mad and throwing him off the roof wouldn't settle anything. He just looked at his brother and said. "You're a no-good drunk. You don't deserve any chance you could get at the big leagues. You're not good enough." Arthur tried to hit Paul again and Paul caught his arm stopping him from making contact. He stared at his brother and said. "I'm done with you and this farm."

The next day he and his wife Sonja left. He wasn't going to retire, he still wanted to play baseball and it was the fight with Arthur that in some strange way showed him that he couldn't stay home anymore. Paul had gotten a taste of the big city and Iowa wasn't what he needed anymore. That would change in the years to come, but he was only 20 years old and a world that he had never seen was waiting for him. Paul Sr. wasn't happy about the decision, but his mother simply hugged him before he left and said that she loved him. So that was it, Paul returned to Cubs and he would play professional baseball for the next 14 years.

Chris being curious about her family, believed there was something more to the story so he asked if there was. Amy said that was all that she knew, but she reckoned there were deeper reasons for leaving Iowa. Maybe he felt guilty or ashamed that he wasn't there when it happened. Perhaps Iowa and the family farm served as a reminder of the tragedy and that's why he left. But Paul never forgot about his brother George. Paul would have a son in 1916 and he would be named George Larson II. Also, Paul would never return to the family farm after that day. His parents would die a few years later, both getting sick from a disease that most people didn't know anything about. Today we call it cancer. Arthur would sell the dairy farm and move away playing for whatever semi-pro team would have him. Paul was the luckier one – he would go on to be a star during the 1907 season. That's where she ended since dinner was ready.

Chris and Amy ate dinner and talked about other things. Because Chris saw her more than a huge Cubs fan with a unique family history – he saw her as a beautiful woman that could make him laugh and have an intelligent conversation with. And while all of that was fine with him her story was still very much a baseball story, but it was also family story. After dinner Chris asked Amy about the famous 1908 season. He had read a little bit about it on the internet. So Amy picked up right where she left off.

1908 for the Cubs was a tough and unusual year. They weren't as dominant as they were the previous two years. All year long it was a tight race in the National League between the Cubs, New York Giants, and Pittsburg Pirates. In fact the National League wouldn't be decided until the last day of the year. For the entire season the Cubs, Giants, and Pirates stayed a game or two within each other as all three teams battled for first place. However, for the Cubs, a controversial game on September 23, 1908 against the Giants at the Polo Grounds in New York would be the reason why the season ended the way it did that year. The Cubs had not been that dominant during the year because of injuries. Paul Larson, however, had a great year as a starter in the outfield and batting .290 for the year, second place in batting behind Frank Chance for the 1908 season.

The game in question on September 23, 1908 became known as the "Merkle Game" or "Merkle's Boner." The game was tied in the 9th inning 1-1. There were two outs in the bottom of the 9th and the Giants had two men on base – one on first and one on third. Merkle was on first. Al Bridwell hit a single into the outfield and the runner on third scored ending the game with a Giants victory. The only thing is as 10,000 New York fans rushed the field Merkle forgot to touch second base; he just stopped, turned around and headed into the dugout, which was customary at the time. But the rule book said different, the runner on first had to touch second base for the run to count or he could still be counted out therefore making the scoring run void. Johnny Evers, the Cubs second baseman, saw that Merkle had not touched base and called for the ball from the outfield. In all fairness, it was the first game Fred Merkle ever started and it would be the one game he would never live down.

It was Paul who saw what was going on alongside the other outfielder, Steinfeldt and got the ball from spectators who had rushed the field to throw to Evers and then Evers, after catching the ball from the outfield in the middle of Giant's fans swarming the field, touched second base getting Merkle out. But before he did that Evers was able to get Hack O'Day, the umpire, over to second base so he could see what he was doing. O'Day counted Merkle out. Normally the game would have gone into extra innings, but since the field was filled with fans the game could not continue. Also by that time fans were fighting with Cub players – the rivalry between the Giants and the Cubs was a brutal one. Paul had to punch many fans in the outfield to even retrieve the ball and get it to Johnny Evers. Then he had to punch fans again just to get off the field. This was the same for all the Cubs as the field was turning into a mob scene.

The game would end in a tie and would later have to be played again if the Cubs, Giants, or Pirates ended the season in a tie. The controversy was just beginning for the Cubs because John McGraw, the manager of the Giants would contest the game and a decision over the result of it would have to be made by a meeting of the owners in the league. The controversy surrounding the game actually became a nationwide controversy as people all over the country picked their sides, Cubs or Giants. The Sporting News which was coming into its own at that time had a field day with the events and blew the story up to where it gripped the nation. John McGraw would say to reporters in New York that the Giants were robbed and Frank Chance, adding fuel to the fire, would go on to say that the Cubs really won the game by forfeit because the Giants refused to take the field in the 10th inning. Technically, Frank Chance was right. The Owners of the leagued decided to stand behind Hack O'Day's decision and if the Cubs and Giants ended the season with a tied record then they would play one game to decide who won the pennant. As luck would have it the Cubs and Giants ended the season in a tie and they replayed the Merkle Game October 8, 1908.

Amy commented that Paul had said in later years that the championship game for all the marbles was never the World Series against the Tigers – it was that one game against the Giants at Polo Grounds in New York. Paul would also say that the team felt like Daniel walking into the Lion's Den and it wasn't exactly untrue. There were 25,000 fans who attended the game that day in a stadium that only sat 10,000. The New York Giant fans were loud and violent, much like Yankee fans. There were even death threats by fans on Cub players if they scored so New York police officers were called in full force as added security for the game. In fact, it was the first time that a baseball game would be played with security present. Frank Chance commented to his players that having New York police didn't make him feel much better –they could still get beat even if they won the game on the field. New York fans have never been known to be the friendliest of fans, even back then.

Now, the game should have gone in favor the Giants that day, but it didn't work out that way. It did start off that way after Jack Pfiester, who was the Cubs starting pitcher, gave up a first inning run. The Cubs started the third inning off of with a Paul Larson double scoring the first of four runs that inning. They would never lose the lead after Three-Finger Brown came in to relieve Jack Pfiester in the first inning. Brown simply shut the Giants down, masterfully pitching the game and allowing only one more run. The Cubs won 4-2 and won the pennant the third year in a row. It was the greatest game they played all year and as the Cubs ran for their lives off the field before a swarm of angry Giants' fans could hurt them, they celebrated the victory as if they had already won the World Series. It was already evident who would win the Series as the Cubs faced the Tigers again three days later. Unlike in 1906 against the White Sox, this time it happened to be true. The Cubs won the World Series in 5 games. They shut the Tigers down just like they did the year before with superb pitching and great defense. The only game the Tigers could muster a win in was game 3 when Ty Cobb had four hits that game, but in game 5 Orval Overall shut Cobb down along with the other Tigers with his flawless pitching. The Cubs were champions that year, but it would be the last time they would ever win the World Series. Paul once said to his son George and grandson Jack before he died that those years from 1906-1908 were the greatest teams that he ever played on.

Amy looked away after saying that and then smiled. She told Chris that it was from her grandfather Jack that she heard the 1908 Cubs described as the last great championship team -he had heard that description from Paul. Then Amy commented that perhaps her boss was right; it's the perfect title because it was true about that team. If there was any better way to describe the great defense of that team then maybe it was best said in a poem

– the one about Tinkers, to Evers, to Chance. Chris had
never heard it before and he asked Amy to say it out loud.
She recited it by heart, like every Cubs fan.

"These are the saddest of possible words:
'Tinker to Evers to Chance.'
Trio of bear cubs, and fleeter than birds,
'Tinker and Evers and Chance.'
Ruthlessly pricking our gonfalon bubble,
Making a Giant hit into a double –
Words that are heavy with nothing but trouble:
'Tinker to Evers to Chance.'"

Chris smiled, for he had never heard something like
that before. Someone once told him that baseball was
poetry in motion and after hearing that poem and the way
Amy described the Cubs and their players for the first time
he believed it. Amy leaned back on the couch smiling; she
knew the words to say for her article. Chris saw her smiling
and said.
"Your writer's block is gone now isn't it?"
"Yeah, it is."
Chris chuckled to himself and then said. "You know
my grandfather used to say that best way to know the story
is to tell someone else because that's when we know truth."
"It's funny you should say that because my mother
had a saying too. The only way we know the truth about
our family is when we tell their story."
"Well, there you go...I guess if you continue telling
someone like me the story of the Cubs and your family
you'll start to see more truth than you realize."
Amy smirked at the comment and then replied.
"That's what I'm afraid of."
"It won't be as bad as you think. When we come face
to face with the sins and the lies wrapped up in the
hypocrisy that is our family, that's when we finally get set
free."

"I think I heard something like that about truth before, but what they never tell you is how far you have to travel down into the abyss before you can be set free."

"No one said it would be easy...It wasn't for me with my father, but I am the better man for it. Going through what I did with him has made me the better man."
Amy leaned over and kissed him. Chris asked her what it was for. She said it was for listening. Amy knew that what he had said was right. In telling any story about the Cubs she would have to tell her family story and it wouldn't be easy. There were things that she would like to forget and then there were things that she didn't want to know. Perhaps finding out would make her a better person – maybe she would finally understand all of the "whys." Why hadn't the Cubs really won a World Series since 1908? Why did her father throw his career away when he was so good? Why did her grandfather, as great of a pitcher as he was, never get a World Series Ring when the teams he was on were so deserving of one? Why could the Cubs come so close only to have it end in failure? But perhaps the most important "why " for Amy was, why she was afraid to tell this story. She wondered, could it really have a happy ending?

As Chris started to clean up the kitchen Amy went back her computer. She stared at the white piece of paper on the computer screen with the title *The Last Great Championship Team* and then she started to write. The first line of the article read, "Will there ever be another great championship team like the Cubs of 1908?" As fans we have been asking ourselves that for a hundred years and we could very well be asking that for another hundred."

4

Mr. Wrigley and the Field of Dreams

ESPN Sports Center began to play and two announcers were smiling behind the sports center news desk. The first announcer began to speak.

"Well, its baseball season again, spring training starts today. It's a new season filled with new hopes and dreams. This year, some teams have a very different look, trying to improve their chances at a spot in the postseason. The most aggressive changes to a roster had to be the Chicago Cubs. After last year's collapse in round one the playoffs, can you really blame them?

The second announcer replied. "No you can't. After winning 97 games and having the best record in baseball they should have won the World Series, but it wasn't in the cards for the Cubs."

"Last year was supposed to be the year. I think everybody expected to win it after the regular season they had. A 99-year championship drought could have ended, but the Cubs of the regular season never showed up during the playoffs. Well, their off-season moves prove that they're serious about redeeming themselves, and let's face it, they are a heavy favorite to be a World Series contender and this year would be the perfect year. It's 2008, a hundred years since their last championship."

"I think they can do it," The second announcer said. "It looks like they made the right moves. They got two more starting pitchers and actually have six pitchers that can pitch in the post season."

"Let's not forgot the emergence of Ryan Larson. He got called up in August and started for them at the 5th man in the rotation going 7-1 for the season. He's got the makings of a good starting pitcher."

The second announcer looked at his co-anchor and said, "I don't care if he is the son of Steve Larson and the grandson of Jack Larson, two great pitchers for the Cubs. He's still a rookie and all six starting pitchers that the Cubs have are more experienced than Larson – if he stays with the team and doesn't get sent back down to Triple A he'll be in the bullpen."

"Maybe, but he's definitely someone that the Cubs need because let's face it the kid can pitch, and look who he was taught by, probably since birth. Coaches are already saying that he's just as smart as his grandfather on the mound and ever deadlier than his father on the mound. That's a hall-a-fame combination and this kid is going to win ballgames for the Cubs."

"Well the other guy that's going to win ball games for the Cubs is Milt Bradley, the switch hitting right fielder that the Cubs acquired from Texas." The Second Announcer said. "The Cubs need that solid bat in the line-up, especially a good lefthander. This was a smart move by them and Chicago is the perfect place for him."

"You're crazy just like he is. Last year batting 320 with 40 home runs was just a fluke. He's had problems with every team he's played and in his 9 year career he's played on 7 teams. He will be a problem for Cubs, mark my

words. If Chicago is the right place for him, then he belongs
on the Southside with the White Sox. They have a crazy
manager – he'll be perfect for that team."

"I guess we'll see," the second announcer said. "The
season is just beginning and we're two months from
opening day. So we'll see what happens. In the mean time
my prediction is to see the Cubs in the Series playing the
Angels – they're the two best teams in baseball and they're
destined to meet in October. "

"You're only saying that because they were the two
best teams in the league last year. I guarantee it won't be
the same this year. My prediction is to see the Dodgers and
Yankees. The Cubs and Angels may get to the postseason,
but the World Series is not where they will be at the end of
the season. They'll be watching the fall classic at home."

The second announcer laughed at his co-anchor then
he said. "I guess in 7 months we'll see who's right. Spring
training is here and we'll bring you all the news, stats, and
funny stories in the baseball world."

A week into Spring Training Amy was assigned to
Arizona, where the Cubs Spring training camp was located,
by the Sun Times. She had done this every year for the last
three years because she was the baseball expert among the
staff, and with good reason. Her first year with the paper
she went to spring training with one of the other sports
reporters who had been at the paper for over ten years. But
after 1 day it was clear she was more knowledgeable about
the Cubs and baseball. She proved to be the better reporter
and ever since then she was assigned to Spring Training by
herself. Besides, she knew everybody down there from the
players to the staff and the organization – she had
relationships because of her family connections. Of course
she was the best reporter to have assigned to spring
training. This year was a little different because it was the
first year that her brother had gotten invited. The last time
she was at spring training and a Larson was playing was

the last year her father Steve played for them so this year was exciting to say the least.

The first day she was there she made the rounds and talked to the staff and some of Cubs legends from when her father and grandfather played who were there helping out during spring training. She got some interviews and did a couple of stories about the Cubs' new look – mainly about the new players the Cubs had gone after and the money they spent to acquire them. It was the important news for the paper, but there was another story she was interested in even if she would never write about it for the paper. The story was her brother Ryan Larson and his first year at spring training. On the second day she found him doing warm-up drills with other pitchers. She watched him for awhile and noticed the control problems he was having. She finally yelled to him.

"You're not bending your leg enough."

Two of the other pitchers including Wood, the seasoned veteran and new closer turned around to see who was yelling that. Rothchild, the pitching coach, who was nearby watching all of his pitchers, also turned around and then smiled. He shouted back to Ryan, "She's right, you're not bending your leg enough."

Wood looked around confused thinking that everybody was talking to him. Ryan looked at him and said. "Don't worry, they're talking to me...my sister is just giving me a hard time."

"Oh good, I thought my wife was here yelling at me...I come to spring training to get away from that you know." Wood said to Ryan. He smiled at Wood's comment and walked over to his sister.

He gave her a hug and said sarcastically. "Quit trying to get coaches onto me."

"I'm only trying to help you make the team. Grandpa would have been yelling at you by now anyway."

Ryan laughed because she was right. "So how are things with you?"

"Good, baseball season is here again so I won't be bored anymore."

"Glad to see we can entertain you. Mom told me that you have a new boyfriend and that he's a lawyer from Texas."

"We're not serious or anything, I don't know why she told you."

"Because she's mom and she can't keep a secret."

"That's true."

"You've been seeing him a lot haven't you?"

"Yeah, so what?"

"Sounds serious to me."

"Whatever, think what you want."

Ryan laughed and said to his sister. "I read your article, *The Last Great Championship Team*; it was good; Very fitting for our great-great grandfather. You had a lot of detail, what brought that out?"

"I'm a journalist...it's my job to have that much detail."

"No...there was something else to it. You wrote it as an inspiring story like you were trying to make somebody believe in the Cubs...you've never written in that style before."

Amy gave her brother a dirty look because it sounded like he was insulting her talent. She replied. "I am good at what I do... I have that kind of talent you know."

"I didn't mean it in bad way, I was just pointing out that there was a different flair to your writing and it was very good. So whatever is doing that for you keep doing it ...it's a good thing."

"I have been telling Chris, remember the guy I told you about, a lot about our family and the history of the Cubs. I want him to understand what it means to be a fan and what the team means to the city of Chicago."

"Well that's a good thing. If he's going to live in Chicago then that's something that he needs to understand. It's part of being a Chicagoan."

"Yeah, not many get that unless they're from the Windy City."

"We'll there are a lot of good stories and it sounds like you've found some inspiration. Keep it up. Have you told him about the first time our great-grandfather met Mr. Wrigley?"

"No, not yet." Amy replied.

"That's a good story...its one of my favorites."

"I'll have to tell him." Amy smiled again at her brother. "So before you have to get back do you have any juicy tips for me...any predictions for this year?"

"Ryan gave her a sarcastic look and replied, "No comment." The he walked off and went back to practice.

Amy got a nudge on her arm, she turned around to see Randy Hundley, the Cubs' old catcher from the 1960's He also happened to be the catcher that was behind the plate for her grandfather Jack during most of his career. Randy and Jack had been great friends ever since their days with the Cubs and it happened to be that he held a special place in his heart for the grandchildren of Jack Larson. Amy always made a point to see him at spring training and say hello. This time he found her instead.

Randy said to her. "I was wondering when you were going to get around and say hello to me."

"First things first...got to see how my brother is doing so far. You know I want to see him make the team this year."

"I don't think you'll have much to worry about. He's doing fine. All he had to do was get here to spring training."

"Well it took him a little longer to get here than the rest of my family."

"Maybe, but he's where he belongs and that's all the matters."

"So tell me straight, how's he really doing?"

"He's a little nervous and will have to settle down over the next few weeks, but his control looks good."

Amy sighed. Then she said. "Is that going to be enough though! He's just as wild as my dad was."

"Of course he is…he's a little better than your dad, he's also just as smart as your grandfather. He'll make it this year and I guarantee you that he'll get the 5th spot in the rotation. He's a Larson…you're brother's going to do just fine."

Amy gave Randy a hug, he was being encouraging like a grandfather, and she knew he was right. Randy knew pitchers. He had helped Jack be the best he could be and he made Steve better than he should have been by working with him during spring training 25 years before. He would help Ryan too and someday Ryan would be an all-star because of it.

∞∞∞∞∞∞∞∞∞∞∞

After a week at spring training Amy was back home so of course Chris cooked her dinner when she got back. Chris wasn't a great cook, but it was the gesture that counted. Beside she needed someone there for her after a long week. He was the perfect choice. After dinner they started talking about the Cubs and spring training. She was filling him in on all the details – it was like he was getting the inside scoop for his fantasy baseball team. Chris was basically learning about the sport and of course the Cubs. Amy started laughing at one moment and was reminded of what her brother said. She told Chris that Ryan wanted her to tell him about the first time George Larson met Mr. Wrigley, but in telling him that story she also had to tell him the back story. He sat on the couch with her feet propped up on his legs listening intently. Some might have said that he was doing the good boyfriend thing, but truth was he was interested in the story just like he was interested in the Cubs now.

[59]

By 1918 the Cubs from 1908 were pretty much gone. Most of them had retired or traded somewhere else. Frank Chance wasn't even the manager anymore. The Cubs had a first-time manager that year in Fred Mitchell and most of the big league stars were gone that year, serving in the military during WW1. Paul Larson was for the most part the only one left over from the 1908 team. He had, had a great career over the past 12 seasons, a hall-a-fame career to be exact. He was playing third base now regularly for the Cubs and he could still hit. His career average up to that point was .307. In 1910 he came close to hitting .400 but he ended the season with .390. The Cubs had a great year in 1918 and it was the first time in 8 years that they had made it back to the World Series by winning the national league pennant over the Giants. Paul was the superstar for the most part on the Cubs that year, but winning the World Series was not to be.

They faced the Boston Red Sox and the best pitching staff in both leagues led by none other than Babe Ruth. The pitching staff of the Sox that year reminded the Cubs of the staff they once had in 1907 and 1908. The Cubs would lose the series 4 games to 2. It would be the last time Paul would play in post season. The Cubs were not that good for a few years and the team would have to be rebuilt, but by the time it happened Paul would retire.

After the last game of the series Paul got a visitor. It was his brother Arthur and he was waiting for him outside to clubhouse. It had been 11 years since Paul had seen him. He got a few letters from Arthur over the years, but that last letter came about three years ago after Paul's son, George, was born. Seeing Arthur was a shock to say the least, but it was good seeing him as well. Paul walked outside the clubhouse and saw Arthur. He walked over to give his brother a hug, but Arthur only reached out his hand to shake Paul's. Paul was disappointed that his brother was distant from him as he shook his brother's hand. He asked Arthur how he was. Arthur answered him by saying…

"I'm fine. I was at the game today. Sorry that you guys lost."

"What are you doing in Boston," Paul asked his brother. "Are you living here now?"

"No, I'm leaving the country. My boat is in the Harbor."

"Leaving…leaving for good?"

"Yeah."

"Where are you going?"

"Back to Denmark. I've had enough of this country."

"You know they don't have baseball in Denmark," Paul said to his brother with a concerned tone. "It won't be the same."

"I'm done with baseball…have been for a long time."

"Is it because you never made it to big leagues?"

"Something like that. I wanted to thank you for getting me that tryout with the Cubs years ago. Sorry I didn't take you up on it, but it was just as well. You were always the big star."

Paul walked closer to his brother and gave him a sympathetic look. He told Arthur not to do that to himself. He knew Arthur had never forgiven him for going back to the Cubs in 1907 and having a big league career – he had never forgiven himself for not making the Pros. By the time he actually had a tryout for the Cubs the drinking had destroyed his life even though he could never admit it. Paul never wanted to admit that either. So it came to be that Arthur had spent the last ten years wandering from town to town that had a baseball team trying to have a career and when it never happened he decided to go away, far from the United States, and Denmark was the only other home that he had known. Arthur would disappear forever after that day. Paul said to him.

"Don't leave just yet. Come back to Chicago with me and meet your niece and nephew."

"I got your letter that you had a son a few years ago. It was nice that you named him George, but I can't. I wanted to see you once more before I left so that you knew I was all right and so that I could see that you were too. "

"I'm going to miss you Arthur, but I can't stop you. If you have to go, you have to go."

And that was it. Arthur shook his brother's hand again and looked at him a little longer this time just to get a good clear picture in his mind of what his brother looked like. Arthur knew it would be the last time that he saw his brother. Paul hoped that it wouldn't be the last time they saw each other, but he didn't kid himself either.

The 1918 World Series would be the last time Paul would ever play in the post season. The next year the Cubs had a new owner and it would be the man who changed everything for the franchise. William Wrigley who had a small interest in the Cubs finally bought out the previous owners. Now the Cubs had been playing in a new ball park since 1916, but they never imagined what it would become when Mr. Wrigley took over in 1919. At first was it was called Cubs park, but it eventually became Wrigley Field in 1926.

Mr. Wrigley was the son of soap salesman, but he never liked working for his father, although he was a hell of a salesman and he knew how to market a product. He knew how to sell the Cubs during a losing season, which they would have from 1919 - 1925 and part of doing that was making the ballpark that his team played in the best place to be even when the team was losing. It was a magnificent park even back then and the ballpark was kept almost spotless – most sport stadiums were dirty and not a very desirable place to be. That would not be the case with Wrigley Field.

William Wrigley became rich by having a stick of gum in with the soap as an added bonus. It turned out that customers were buying the soap for the gum and so another company was born from that – the Wrigley Gum company or Wrigley's Spearmint Gum. The fortune made from the gum company allowed him to buy the Cubs. And as it turned out Mr. Wrigley was a huge baseball fan and it made him one of the best men to own a baseball team , especially a team like the Cubs.

He was even smart enough to recognize that he did not know how to run a team so he found somebody that did. William Veeck Sr., a sportswriter in Chicago, had given Mr. Wrigley a lot of criticism on running the Cubs. One day Mr. Wrigley wrote Mr. Veeck and told him that if he could do it better then he could have the job of running his baseball team. Mr. Veeck took the job and he and Mr. Wrigley would revolutionize how a baseball team would be run. It was these two men who came up with the idea that baseball should be broadcast on the radio and when most owners scoffed at that notion, Mr. Wrigley and William Veeck proved all of them wrong because the Cubs started to gain more fans from out of state, much like they would with WGN as a super station broadcasting the Cubs' games all over the country in the nineteen eighties.

The first time that Paul Larson met Mr. Wrigley he instantly became very fond of the man. He was impressed at how well he could manage this ball club and make the team profitable, but more importantly he was impressed by the fact that Mr. Wrigley was the ultimate fan. Being a huge fan also helped when it came to the level of energy that Mr. Wrigley applied running the ball club. Mr. Wrigley became very fond of Paul as well because he was the working class ballplayer and not a huge superstar even though he had the numbers to be a superstar, but because he played hard every day. Paul wanted to retire after the 1919 season, but he was convinced by Mr. Wrigley to keep playing because the team was heading in a new direction even though they didn't have a winning season that year. He convinced Paul to stay on and play another two years. He was the senior member of the team now and unlike most superstars a lot of his skills still hadn't diminished. Paul became the guy to show the younger players how to be better ball players in the pros.

However in the middle of the 1921 season Paul decided that it was time to retire. That season would be his last and is why Sonia was glad. She had had enough of the baseball life and didn't want to be a baseball wife anymore. Part of it was that she was homesick for Iowa and Paul even though he would not admit to it was a little homesick as well. The Cubs finished in third place in 1921 and although the Cubs were starting to improve there was no reason to stay on and try to get to the postseason one last time. Paul had had enough and of course Mr. Wrigley did try to convince him to stay one more season because he could still play the game. Paul simply declined. Not even a raise in salary could get him to stay.

The next day after the last game of the season Paul took his five year old son George to the Cubs ballpark. It was more sentimental because it would be last time he would play on the field. He wanted to walk around it one more time. Paul also wanted to play a little ball with his son and there was no better place to play than in Cubs Park. Mr. Wrigley happen to be in his office at the ballpark and saw Paul playing with his little boy so he walked down onto the field and said hi to Paul. Then he asked him a question.

"Can you really walk away from all this?"

"Yes I can and with no regrets." Paul replied.

"So what are your plans Paul Larson?"

"Going back to Iowa sir...bought a farm."

"A farm is a good place to raise a family."

"I agree... that's why I'm taking my family back to Iowa where I'm from."

"I always wondered if I would've been a good farmer...perhaps I should have bought a farm instead of this ball club."

"There is no better place than a farm, but I think, sir, you are exactly where you belong. This club needs you and you probably need it."

Mr. Wrigley smiled at Paul's comment and then he said."You're probably right Paul, just like you probably belong on a farm."

"That's what my wife keeps telling me and she knows me better than anybody."

"The women in our lives always know us better. That's why we need them."

"I quite agree, Mr. Wrigley."

Mr. Wrigley looked down at George and smiled. George smiled back and then he reached up to shake Mr. Wrigley's hand. Mr. Wrigley obliged the young man and shook his hand. Then William Wrigley did one of the most memorable things that Paul had ever seen and it was a story that he would pass on to his family throughout the generations. Mr. Wrigley looked at George and said. "You learn everything you can about the game of baseball from your dad. When you're older and if you want a career in baseball you come see me and I will give you a tryout with the Chicago Cubs." George smiled and replied. "You got it sir."

Now of course most men would have said that just to be polite and to amuse a little, but Mr. Wrigley was a true man of his word and he meant what he said. If George ever showed up and wanted a tryout with the Chicago Cubs he had it. Unfortunately, George would never get to see Mr. Wrigley again because he died in 1932. Although that did not stop Mr. Wrigley from fulfilling his promise, when he died he left a letter with his own son P.K. Wrigley that said if any son of a former player wanted a tryout with the Chicago Cubs he would automatically have one. This was in honor of the father that had once played for this team. In 1935 George Larson would get a tryout and he would officially be playing for the Chicago Cubs' professional team in 1936.

5

A Father's Pride

It was Ryan Larson's first game of the 2008 season as a starting pitcher. There was excitement in the air and on his part there was a little bit of nervousness. Ryan thought to himself as he was getting ready in the locker room that he was probably more nervous today than he had been on the day he pitched his first big league game the year before. He was also nervous because his entire family was there at the ball game except for his dad – Steve Larson was the acting pitching coach for the Texas Rangers. As he walked out of the locker room, the warm up to the pregame on WGN had started. There was a small thought in the back of Ryan's mind as he went to the practice pitching mound, the thought of what would people be saying about him. How would they compare him to his dad and grandfather as a pitcher? Let's face it, he had big shoes to fill and it wasn't easy being in the shadow of two great hall of fame pitchers for the Chicago Cubs.

Len and Bob had started doing their pre-game announcing saying, "It's a beautiful day here at Wrigley Field as we bring you the fifth game of the 2008 season for the Chicago Cubs. The Cincinnati Reds are here in town and today we see the first game for Ryan Larson. He is coming off a great year going 7-1 the last quarter of the 2007 season since being called up in the middle of August last year."

Bob started talking. "I think everybody remembers his first game last year, he got quite a surprise when he was with the AAA club. They were down in Round Rock, Texas and instead of pitching for the Iowa Cubs he got called up to the big leagues. Ryan Larson started the game for the Cubs against the Astros that night and for those of you that still haven't heard the story of his first game, he pitched a one-hit shutout while striking out thirteen batters that night."

"And let's not forget, Bob, but some say he would have had a no-hitter that night if it weren't for a bad call by the third base umpire. He was pitching a perfect game into the eighth inning when the umpire ruled what was obviously a foul ball fair and an Astro got a hit." remarked Len.

Bob answered. "Well no matter what the outcome with the call by the umpire, he still pitched a hell of a game and it was history in the making. He proved in one night that he was an All-Star and that he could pitch just as well as his father and grandfather. So today we bring you the first game of Ryan Larson for the 2008 season. It should be a special treat for him as it looks like most of his family is here including, Jack Larson."

"You know Bob, I just want to point out as we start his first game of the season that many weren't quite sure that he was going to make the big league roster this year, especially as a starting pitcher." said Len. "He entered his first spring training with some control issues. And the Cubs had acquired two other potential starting pitchers to give them what most people think is the best rotation in major league baseball."

Len continued. "But just like his father who used to have control issues at the beginning of every season until he got into his groove, Ryan was able to work them out. He ended up pitching a lot better than most people would have thought. It should also be noted that one of those starting pitchers that the Cubs acquired during the off season ended up being released by the end of Spring Training and that helped the young Larson get a spot in the rotation. So today we get to see what the young 25 year old starting pitcher of the Chicago Cubs can do."

Bob responded, "And one more piece of trivia that we should tell our viewers and those Cubs fans that may not know their history, Ryan Larson is the fifth generation of the Larson family to play for the Chicago Cubs. His great-great grandfather Paul Larson played on the 1906, 1907, and 1908 championship teams. His great grandfather George played in the forties and was on the 1945 World Series team. Of course most Cub fans know Jack Larson, Ryan's grandfather who pitched all through the sixties and was on the infamous 1969 Chicago Cubs team. And we all know his father Steve Larson, the wild man, as they used to call him, pitched from the end of the 1982 season until 1990 when he was traded to the Texas Rangers where his finished his career in 1993. And today we get to see the fifth generation starting pitcher take the mound in his first full season with the Chicago Cubs so stay tuned for the start of the game, it is right around the corner."

The game started and Ryan got off to a great start – he struck out the first two batters and the third grounded out. Then the game got off to a better start when the Cubs got on the board early in the first inning scoring two runs. Ryan got into his groove allowing only one hit over four innings. The crowd was excited and by that time the Cubs had four runs against the Reds. Chris leaned over to Amy and asked about how Ryan got to the major leagues. He told her that he had heard a story about their father being involved and it had to do with three pitches. Amy laughed because the story was one of those legendary stories that gets retold over and over in baseball and then of course gets embellished over time.

She looked at Chris and said. "Well there are three pitches involved in this story but I'm sure you haven't heard the story of how my father helped Ryan get to the majors."

"Somebody just told me that your father made a bet with the manager at Tennessee that he could get one of the batter's out with only three pitches. If he succeeded then the manager had to recommend Ryan for AAA baseball and get him an invitation to spring training."

"That's sort of how it happened. The truth is the manager down there; Jody used to play catcher for the Cubs in the 1980's and caught for my father when he was a pitcher for the team. They were on the 1984 team together. Any way they used to be great friends but there was a lot of bad blood between them over a game that was pitched in 1984 during the playoffs."

"Is that the game that your father pitched during the playoffs that year and he gave up the game-winning home run to Steve Garvey?"

"Yeah."

"I heard something about that too."

"Well what happened was my father in the ninth inning started shaking off the signs from the catcher and tried to get every batter out with a fastball. It was a big no-no on his part and he would give up the game-winning home run. If he had pitched like he was supposed to then the Cubs would have won the World Series that year. That's what most people believe and of course Jody always blamed my father for what happened because if they had won that game then they would have played game five. As it was, Steve Garvey's ball went through Leon Durham's flags allowing the Padres to score two runs and eventually win the game."

Jack Larson heard part of the conversation and leaned over to say something. He said, "Chris, son, you never shake off the signs and then try to get everybody out with your fastball, no matter how good it is, when you've got men on base and a potential home-run hitter up at the plate. That is the cardinal rule of the pitcher."

Amy chuckled a little bit and then replied. "That's also why my father gets most of the blame for the 1984 World Series, at least by pitchers, because a good pitcher knows better."

Chris looked at her and said, "Then it really happened, because I've also heard there a lot of Cubs fans that never forgave your father for costing them the 1984 series."

"Yes, it did, and no, I don't think the fans can forget after 24 years, we have very, very long memories."

So Amy proceeded to tell the story of what really happened when Steve helped Ryan get to the big leagues. After that Christmas when Amy and her father fought about Ryan, Steve didn't really think about it too much until the middle of spring training. He was working for the Texas Ranger organization at the time and knew that Ryan did not get invited to come to spring training that year, but he figured there wasn't anything he could do about it. And so the 2007 season started, but after a couple weeks into the season Steve decided that he could at least have a chat with Jody even though he hadn't seen him for fifteen years. Steve took a day off and flew out to Tennessee where the Cubs AA affiliate was located. The Tennessee Smokey's had a game in the evening. When Steve arrived it was later in the afternoon when batting practice and warm-ups were going on. He wandered into the clubhouse when he didn't see Jody on the field. Steve didn't even stop and say hello to his son for trying to find his old friend. Some of the other personnel that were in the clubhouse didn't even tell him to get out. One of the men said hello and told Steve that Jody was in the office. Most people figured that after four years with the Tennessee Smokies and never getting an invite to spring training that somebody in the Larson family would wonder down and talk with Jody about Ryan's situation. Most people thought that it would always be Jack Larson that would show up and talk to the manager, but it Steve Larson, a man Jody hadn't spoken to in over 20 years.

The door to the clubhouse office was open and Steve stood at the entrance. He spoke in a quiet tone. "Jody, how are you?"

Jody turned around and had a surprise look upon his face. He replied. "Steve…never figured I would actually see you here. Always figured your dad would be the one to come talk to me. So what the hell are doing here?"

"I wish that I could tell you that I came to buy you a beer, but we both know it would be a lie."

"Well if you're here to talk about your son. I have nothing to discuss with you. You're not my boss here and the last person to tell me how to coach."

Steve gave a small laugh and said. "I'm not here to tell you how to coach, you're right, I have no room to talk, but I do want to know about Ryan."

"I can assume it's not just a friendly visit to see how he's surviving in AA ball?"

"That's right."

"Look, he's not ready to move up yet. He still has control issues; he can't keep his pitch count down."

"That's bullshit Jody, I've seen what his numbers are, and he's got the best numbers in the club. There enough to get him an invite to spring training?"

"There's more to it than numbers and you should know that."

"I know that your recommendation is being withheld. What I want to know is it because of me or is it really because of Ryan."

Jody slammed his notebook on the desk and said. "How dare you, you son of a bitch? To think that my coaching decisions are personal is a fucking insult."

"I'm not trying to insult you, but he's been here for 4 years and it's time to see what he can really do instead of wasting his time here in AA ball. He deserves an invitation to spring training and his numbers are good for it. I don't care if you like me and I certainly don't care if you want to still blame me for 1984 but give my son a chance."

Jody looked at Steve for the longest time and then replied. "I don't have time for this shit, Ryan is not ready yet."

Then Jody walked past Steve in the doorway and headed for the ball field. That's when Steve said something that Jody had not heard in twenty years. "Three pitches, Jody."

"What?"

"Give me three pitches and I'll strike out the best hitter you have on the team."

"So what if you do?"

"You recommend that Ryan goes to the Iowa Cubs this season so that next year he will actually get invited to spring training And let's see if he can make the big leagues next year."

"And what if you can't do it, then what do I get?"

"I will admit on the record to a journalist in Chicago that I'm the one to blame for the Cubs losing in 1984."

"While I don't really think you're gonna do that, I'll give you your three pitches just to see if you can actually do it, but you don't get any warm up, you have to go out there and just pitch."

"Do I least get to stretch, hell I'm 46 years old, I can't pitch like I was nineteen anymore."

"Fine, old man, you can stretch."

"Do I get a baseball glove?"

"Borrow Ryan's, you're about the same size and for the record this is gonna be the best entertainment I've had in a long time."

Steve walked with Jody out on the field and laughed a little bit. Then he replied back. "It's going to be more fun when I actually do it."

Steve Larson walked down with Jody onto the field and that's when Ryan saw his dad. He walked over and asked him what he was doing there. Steve simply replied that he was doing something that Ryan's mother had asked him to do...try to help Ryan if he could. Ryan gave his father an angry look and replied. "I don't need your help; I can make it in baseball without you."

"I'm sure you can," Steve said to his son. "But this isn't about you; this is about your manager being asinine about something that happened 25 years ago."

"I don't understand; what are you doing?"

Steve smiled at Ryan and said. "Three pitches."

After that Steve took the mound and started stretching and that's when the best hitter on the team walked up to the plate. Ryan started shaking his head and then he said out loud. "You've got to be kidding me, you're gonna pitch at your age?"

"If I get this guy out in three pitches you get to move up to AAA ball."

Ryan just walked away thinking that his family always interfered with his life. While he was walking away Jody was giving some instruction to the batter. He told him. "This guy may look old but he can still get you out. I need to make sure that doesn't happen so I'm going to tell you what pitches he's probably going to throw...he's a little predictable."

"Skip, I don't need to know," the batter said. "I can hit the ball off of this guy."

"Maybe, but you still need the instruction. First he's probably gonna start you off with a slide inside, trying to get you to swing over the top of it or hook it foul. The next pitch will probably be his curve. That pitch will embarrass you. The last pitch that he will play will be his famous sinking fastball so if you swing low you should get a hit into the outfield."

The batter gave a cocky smile back to the manager. His mistake was thinking that Steve Larson was too old. Nobody ever thought that Steve could be just as smart as his father when it came to pitching. The fact is he was.

Steve was wilder as a pitcher than Jack Larson and that overshadowed how intelligent he really was on the mound. Steve picked up the glove that was lying on the mound. He did not know whose it was but it fit perfectly. He waited for the batter to go through his practice swings and then he went into his windup. The first pitch was a slider to the inside and of course it had just enough move on it to make the batter hook it foul. Jody said to the guy standing next to him in the dugout. "He's predictable as always...always throws in sequence thinking that he can get the batter out with his pitches." That's when Steve was about to prove his old catcher wrong.

Steve would wind up again and his second pitch would be a breaking ball, and the batter, looking for a curve low and away, swung too early, going right over the top of the ball for a strike. Ryan was standing next to the other pitchers who cheered out loud for Steve Larson throwing such a great pitch. Ryan said. "Uh, my father really is trying to mess with everybody's head today. He's throwing out of sequence." The pitcher standing next to him asked. "What does that mean?" "It means that my dad is about to embarrass the batter and make our manager look like a jackass. Watch the next pitch because the bottom is going to drop right out from underneath it for a strike."

Nobody really knew what Steve was going to do next except Ryan because Steve was doing the same thing that he taught his son to do – mix up your pitches and confuse everybody. Steve seemed a little slower as he went into his windup. He reached back to the last reserves he could muster and threw the Larson sinking fastball and it looked like a knuckle ball with speed as soon as it got to the plate. It would be around the batters knees when the bottom would drop out from underneath and land at the bottom of the catcher's mitt where the batter would swing right over the top of it. And that's exactly what happened with this batter. The entire team erupted into loud cheers for Steve Larson as he struck out the best hitter on the team with three pitches at the age of 46. They actually had the gun turned on for the last pitch and the clock showed the pitch to be 94 miles an hour. Jody wasn't exactly happy, but he did walk over to the mound as his players were congratulating Steve and shook his hand. He said to Steve. "You looked like a pro today by throwing out of sequence."Steve replied. "Couldn't have you thinking that I was predictable!"

"Looks like you still have a fastball...didn't think you could throw your sinker anymore."

"Trust me, I will be feeling it tonight. So you will give the recommendation for my son?" "I'll make sure Ryan is moved to AAA ball before the year is out...after that he has to make it on his own."

So that was it, Steve and Jody shook hands, something they had not done in a long time. Ryan actually walked up to his father and congratulated him. They were probably the kindest words that he had said to his father in a long time. Steve hugged his son and just told him to call his mother when he got a chance. And of course he did he call his mother the next night, but there was another person in Ryan's life that he also had to tell because it was still too unbelievable to think about. While he would tell his girlfriend, Tara, he needed to tell his sister Amy so that he could prove it was possible for their father to do something nice for his children and that he wasn't the bastard he always seemed to be. But more importantly, he needed to tell Amy so he knew that none of this was a dream.

∞∞∞∞∞∞∞∞

Ryan was doing very well in his first game of the 2008 season. In fact, he pitched into the eighth inning allowing only two hits with no runs. But it was in the top of the eighth inning that he got into a little trouble. Ryan allowed two more hits and walked a batter to load the bases with only one out. The tying run was coming up to bat. The Cubs skipper had already gotten the closer and the set-up pitcher into the bullpen to warm up so they could replace Ryan. The Cubs skipper walked up to the mound to talk to Ryan along with the catcher and the first baseman. He looked at Ryan when he arrived and asked. "Are you getting sore? You're at 102 pitches."

"I'm fine, Skip." Ryan replied.

"Think you can get this guy to into a double play? Be honest, you've pitched a hell of a game today. There's no need to injure yourself trying to finish this game."

Ryan looked at the Skipper as well as the first baseman and the catcher and all he said was. "Three pitches Skip...give me three pitches and I will get out of the inning."

The Skipper smiled and said, "Let's see if you can pull it off like your old man used to do."
The Skipper went back to the dugout and Ryan stared down the batter. The first pitch he threw was an off-speed breaking ball and he made the batter pop it out to second base where it was caught for the second out. The next batter he faced he threw a 98 mile-an-hour fastball right down the pipeline. The batter tried to get a base hit too late and never caught up to the ball. And the next pitch was a curveball and the batter got just enough of it to hit a bouncer right to the pitcher. Ryan caught it and threw the ball to first base for the third and final out of the inning. After that pitch the fans at Wrigley Field gave Ryan Larson a standing ovation. Many of the fans had seen the entire performance before from a Larson...Jack Larson who was sitting in the stands that day. He just smiled at his grandson – he thought to himself "looks like I taught him well."

The skipper didn't let Ryan go out and finish the ninth inning, he had pitched enough that day, but he did get his first victory of the 2008 season. It was the beginning

of what would be a great year for him, albeit it would not be
an easy year; there were old demons that would come out
and show themselves once again. Ryan would have to go
through the same stuff that his father did when he became
a superstar in Chicago.

6

The Son of a Ballplayer

The TV was turned on to WGN as Amy was getting ready to leave for the ballpark. It was opening day at Wrigley Field, the first game of the season, and it was like a national holiday in the city of Chicago. Len and Bob, the two Cubs announcers, came on the television and started doing their pregame. Amy was listening intently as they started talking – it was one of her favorite parts of a Cubs Game, perhaps it was the journalist in her.

At the beginning of the pregame Len looked over at Bob and said. "Well today is opening day, it is the first game of the season for the Chicago Cubs and the first game on WGN for the baseball season. Today the Cubs host the Milwaukee Brewers. "

Bob said. "It looks like the Cubs have an exciting year ahead of them. They got everybody back with some added players to the roster including the left-handed bat of Milt Bradley, who was acquired from the Texas Rangers.

Getting a left-handed batter into the line-up was a major priority for the Cubs this year and it looks like they might have just found the right person."

"That's right, and despite all the problems he's had with other teams he wanted to come to Chicago, and he had a great year last year with the Rangers, and management thought he might be the perfect fit, so I guess as we start the season today we're gonna find out."

"Well, I have to say that we're glad for another baseball season and to see what the Cubs can do this year despite their devastating loss last year in the playoffs. Everybody was expecting them to go all the way and they just couldn't seem to do it."

"It should be noted, Bob, that one of the key moves for the Cubs this year was picking Ryan Larson for the fifth spot in the rotation. For those of you that may not remember he got called up in the middle of August last year and went 7-1 for the rest of the season. Now we didn't get to see what he could do in the postseason last year but this young man, who is the son of Steve Larson and the grandson of the great Jack Larson, who were both pitchers for the Chicago Cubs, has earned himself a spot in the rotation and we're looking forward to seeing what he can do this year."

"All through spring training he was being compared to his father and his grandfather, and what's been said of him is that he has a better arm than his father and is just as smart as his grandfather was on the mound. And for those of you who like a little trivia, Ryan Larson is a fifth-generational player for the Chicago Cubs. The first one in his family to play for this team was his great great-grandfather Paul Larson who played in the outfield during the last season the Cubs won a World Series."

"That would be 1908. Baseball and the Chicago Cubs have a lot of family history for Ryan Larson. I think some thought that he would never actually make the pros. He had been pitching in Double AA ball for the last four years until he was finally called up last year."

"Well I have to say that we're both excited to see this young man pitch for the Cubs, but today Big Z is the one taking the mound for the Cubs home opener against the Brewers and we are about 20 minutes away from the first pitch."

"So Cub fans, stay tuned: the 2008 baseball season is almost here."

Amy always had to listen to WGN before the game – it was one of her little rituals dating back to when Harry Caray would broadcast from the booth. She had to hear at least part of the broadcast before she left for the ballpark to cover the game. She was also meeting Chris, who had gotten a half a day off to see the game. He never realized how big of a deal Opening Day was at Wrigley Field – it was a like a state holiday and people could skip work for the game without the risk of being fired.

Opening day at Wrigley field is a celebration, the biggest celebration that you've ever seen as if it were Christmas in April. And if you've never been to opening day at Wrigley field it's hard to know what to expect — that's exactly how Chris felt when he arrived at the ballpark. He saw a huge crowd waiting to get in and people camping out in line. There were of course plenty of people skipping work knowing that they would not be fired because opening day at Wrigley Field is the same as a Federal holiday in the city of Chicago. Opening day also resembles the first day of spring when hope is in the air, when people are happy, and the only thing that you feel is eternal optimism. It's a day were grown men get to be kids again and it's allowed. It's understood that kids get to skip school, which is unheard of throughout the rest of the country. However it's OK here in Chicago because opening day Wrigley Field is that important and it might be the beginning of something great: the start of a winning baseball season for the Chicago Cubs. Who really wants to miss that? Because the excitement you feel on that day, can carry you all year long even if your heart is broken in October. The beginning of baseball season is faith renewed – the faith that all things are possible, and there aren't too many things that can do that.

2008 would be a special year for the Cubs and I don't think any Cubs fan knew what to expect even though it was the hundredth anniversary since their last World Series championship. All in all Chris was mesmerized and when he saw the people at Wrigley field, the only thing in his mind that he could compare this to was that of a Texas/OU game at the Cotton Bowl.

The other thing about opening day is the ballpark itself. There is no purer form of baseball than Wrigley Field on a warm Chicago day. The ballpark was built so that fans could have an intimate experience during a game and be close to the action, a concept very strange for ballparks built today. Wrigley field is the perfect complement to a summer afternoon and it sits as a great cathedral on the North Side of Chicago taking fans back to what the game used to be like before million dollar contracts and big league trades. The scoreboard is classic in nature and is still operated manually. The ivy that graces the outfield wall is an uncanny attraction to a baseball field, but it's almost like playing America's game in Monet's Garden and perhaps not even watercolor could capture the real beauty of the ballpark in a single image. However the true beauty of Wrigley Field can be experienced on a summer afternoon with a hotdog and a beer and most fans would tell you that it's the only way to see the ballpark in all of its glory. However the best way to understand how wonderful this place is to walk through the gate and watch the Cubs play, for by doing that a fan will come to know the way it should have always been.

Amy saw Chris outside the main gate and came rushing up to him outside of the ballpark. She kissed him and told him to enjoy the game as well as the festivities. Chris couldn't believe that he was here on opening day and that his boss actually gave him the afternoon off to come to this game — he had never had a boss that allowed people to go to a sporting event just for the fun of it. After all the last baseball game that Chris had been to was a company outing at the ballpark. On this opening day it was raining so there was a game delay and most of the fans just hung out in the rain drinking beer and eating hot dogs, still enjoying the fact that it was the beginning of a new baseball season for the Cubs. The Cubs that day were starting the season off against the Brewers and it would not be an easy game.

Finally the game started after an hour delay and it was pretty slow going in the first few innings. Both teams couldn't seem to get anything done but the Brewers would strike first scoring two runs off a prince fielder double in the top of the fourth inning. In the fifth they would get another run late in the inning and would lead the Cubs 3-0. The Cubs couldn't seem to do anything the rest of the game - they only had two hits and most of the long balls would never get out of the ballpark, eight of them were pop flies. By the eighth inning the fans were showing their displeasure with the Cubs and their performance. It was as if the Cubs had picked up right where they left off the year before - playing the same level of baseball that had gotten them swept in the first round of the playoffs. Not even their new right fielder they had acquired, Milt Bradley could do anything. He went 0-4. So it came upon the ninth inning and the Cubs were down three to zero. Up to that point the only happy moment at Wrigley field had been the seventh inning stretch when Eddie Vedder sang "Take Me Out To The Ballgame" to the crowd.

So there they were in the bottom of the ninth and the Cubs would get an unlikely hero. One of their off-season acquisitions had been a Japanese player. He had won the batting title in the Japanese league the last three years and the Cubs spent a lot of money to get him to come to the states. Although nobody could pronounce his first name everybody just called him Fukudome. He was known as a patient and a disciplined hitter. So far in his Chicago Cub debut he was 1-3. Cub fans didn't know what to make of him and it was too early to tell. Then with one out in the bottom of the ninth and two men on base Cub fans got their answer. He was at a full count and the Brewers' closer had already had eleven pitches trying to get him out. Throwing a slider down and away, Fukudome sent the ball into the left field bleachers and tied the ballgame with a three-run homer. For the first time throughout the game Cub fans roared throughout the ballpark and for Chris it was the first time that he got to see some real excitement from fans at Wrigley field. He was amazed to say the least. Although I'm sure there's a way to describe the excitement, the level of happiness that Cub fans can have after a three-run homer that ties the ball game in the bottom of the ninth, there really aren't any words to describe that. All one can do is sit back, listen, and see it for yourself - it's the only way to know.

The Cubs would go into extra innings, but unfortunately in the twelfth the Brewers would come back and win the game five to three. However this did not take away from the excitement that the fans felt from seeing the Chicago Cubs that day, and somehow I think every fan knew that it was going to a special year. Yes, the year would have its fair share of ups and downs, but somehow we all knew that it was going to be a great year. For Chris, it was a life changing experience and he was seeing the game of baseball in a whole new way — he was actually enjoying the game on the same level as football. Chris saw it as something poetic and perfect.

Amy caught up with Chris after the ball game and after she finished doing her interviews. Chris was standing outside of the ballpark hanging out in Wrigleyville with other fans. He was talking to them as if they were best friends and had known each other all their lives when in fact he only met them a few minutes ago. He quickly realized that's the way it can be with Cub fans. And that's not something that happens with any other sports team. Amy walked up to Chris and gave him a hug. She asked what he thought; he simply smiled and that told her everything and she knew the Cubs had a new fan. His life was forever changed. So of course she asked him if he wanted to come back again and as it turned out he already had the day off for when her brother Ryan would be pitching his first game of the year.

After the game was over, Amy and Chris went to go get a bite to eat. Of course they were talking about the game and Chris' first experience at Wrigley field, but Chris was curious about something else. He wanted to know the story of how Ryan had gotten called up as a starting pitcher for the Cubs the year before. He was at that game in Houston and remembered it vividly. It was one of Ryan's best performances and one of the greatest baseball games to watch. Amy looked at Chris with a weird look and laughed to herself because there was a part of that story that most people didn't know and it had to do with her father helping his son get to the majors. She told them that but she also said that it was a story for another time and then proceeded to tell the story of how Ryan got called up for that particular game.

While the Cubs were having a great year in 2007, by August, with their lead in the central division extending to ten games, they had suffered some injuries on the pitching staff and in the infield. That's when players tend to get called up from Triple AAA Ball. Also two other starting pitchers happen to be on the DL list for a month and that they were getting thin in the bullpen so the manager for the Cubs, "Sweet Lou" as everybody called him, did the best thing he could do: rest the starters, give them plenty of time to recover from their injuries, and give some young players a chance. It couldn't hurt considering the Cubs were beating the competition and there wasn't any close race for first place. It also didn't hurt that they were seven weeks from the start of the playoffs — plenty of time to rest some of his players.

Big Z and Teddy, the Cubs' left-handed pitcher in the rotation, went on the disabled list in the month of August. The Cubs happen to be playing a three games stand in

Houston when it happened. Now ever since Ryan Larson got to Triple AAA his numbers continued to improve and he was one of the leading pictures for the Triple AAA club. It just so happened that they were playing down in Round Rock Texas, a couple hours outside of Houston. For the Cubs it was the last game of the three games stand against the Astros.

Ryan was actually scheduled to pitch for the Iowa Cubs that night against Round Rock. He was going over notes a few hours before the game when the manager called him into his office within the visitors' clubhouse. He looked at Ryan and said that he had some news for him – there was a change of plans. All Ryan could think of was that he was being sent back down to Double AA ball.

The manager said to him. "Larson I got some news for you...you won't pitching here tonight.”

"Why not?"

"Because we are sending you somewhere else to pitch tonight.”

"Look skipper, my numbers are good and there's no reason to send me back to Double AA ball.”

"You're right about that, but we're not sending you back to Daytona and in fact you're being called up to the big club.”

"What?”

"If you haven't heard already, Big Z and Teddy are on the disabled list and will be there for about a month. With the bullpen being a little thin because of injuries the Cubs need a couple more pitchers from our squad. You're going to the show and you're being scheduled to pitch tonight at Minute Maid Park against the Astros."

"You're joking, right?”

"Son, we don't play those kinds of practical jokes here. When you get called up it's for real.”

"Are you sure they want me to pitch tonight?"

"They need a pitcher who's had five day's rest, and you're the only one from our squad and the big league club that's actually ready to pitch so they're scheduling you to pitch against the Astros. There's a car driving you down to Houston and it leaves in ten minutes. I'd get your stuff and if you don't have one I'd get a sports coat before you leave because there's a dress code in the major leagues."

Ryan did not know what to say, he was still in shock, but he was excited at the same time. Finally he was being called up to pitch for the Cubs. He didn't have time to ask more questions because he had to get his stuff together and get in the car that was taking him to the Houston. He would have to go over playbooks and notes on the Houston Astros while driving down there and hope that he would be prepared. Before he left, some of the teammates that knew what was happening congratulated him. It was one of the greatest moments in his life. The skipper walked him outside to the car and said one last thing.

"Congratulations Larson... looks like you're gonna be the fifth generation of Larson players for the Chicago Cubs."

There wasn't any time to call all of his family, but he would call the most important people to let them know, mainly his sister and his mother. They would make sure that everyone else knew the good news. It also happened to be a game that was being broadcasted on WGN TV and those that weren't going to be there would still see the game. The fact was no one would be able to get down to the game in time so there was no chance of anybody being there in person. It was just one of those things about being called up to the majors at the last minute.

About an hour later, Steve Larson, who was filling in as a pitching coach for the Texas Rangers, got called into the manager's office in Arlington, Texas. He was told that his son got called up to the Cubs and would be pitching in Houston that night. Steve was also told that he had the night off and was handed an envelope with a plane ticket and a ticket to Minute Maid Park for the ballgame along with a pass for the clubhouse. The organization thought that it was only right that Ryan Larson's father be there for

the game. Steve quickly gathered his things and got a ride
out to the DFW Airport to catch a flight to Houston.

On the way he made a few phone calls. The first call
he made was to Amy and Ryan's mother. While they had
not spoken very often over the last fifteen years since their
divorce he thought that Joyce should know that their son of
got called up to the Chicago Cubs and was going to pitch
his first game in the major leagues that night. She was
happy for their son and she told Steve that someone should
be there for his first game. Steve told her that he was on his
way and she was glad that somebody was going to be there
to see their boy pitch his first came in the majors. Joyce
still lived in Chicago and there was no way that her or Amy
could catch a flight to Houston in time and be there for the
game. In fact, Amy didn't even know yet. As Joyce was
crying on the phone because she was happy Steve said that
he would call their daughter and let her know. Then he also
reminded her that the game would be on WGN. Joyce gave
Steve a sarcastic laugh and replied. "I know and I still
watch the Cubs even though we're not married anymore."
He laughed at her and then hung up the phone so he could
call Amy.

As soon as Amy heard the news she tried to find a
flight out of Chicago to Houston so she could be at the
game, but of course there was no way that she could get
down there, not even with the paper — they already had
somebody covering the game. It was a stringer and Amy
argued with her editor that she should be the one to go
down there and cover the game because of who was
pitching but they wouldn't let her go and there were no
more flights getting down to Houston from Chicago anyway.
Amy did call her grandfather, Jack Larson, and asked him
if would be watching the Cubs that night on TV. He replied
to her. "Honey, what else would I be watching tonight."

"Good because Ryan got called up today and he's
actually pitching tonight in Houston." Jack began to smile
— he was the proudest grandfather on the face of the earth

and he didn't waste time talking to Amy anymore. He had to call friends and family and brag about his grandson.

As soon as Ryan arrived at the ballpark the other Cubs players were getting ready in the locker room. The first person he talked to was the skipper, Sweet Lou as everybody called him. The skipper brought Ryan into the office to give him some instructions for the game and go over strategy since it was his first game pitching in the major leagues.

Sweet Lou said to Ryan. "Don't worry about the game; it's not one that we have to win. Just letting you know that up front so you don't feel the pressure. There's only one thing I want you to do. You go out there and do what you know how to do on the mound."

"Is there any way you want me to handle this particular game?" Ryan asked the skipper.

"Don't try to strike everybody out. There's no need to try and break a record. Don't try and get everybody out with a fastball. If they keeping hitting off of you, just shake it off and continue to pitch your game. I know what you're capable of. I known what weapons you have and that you probably studied the Astros' lineup on the way down here so you should be just fine."

"You're not going to lecture me on how to pitch or give me any particular instruction?"

Sweet Lou smiled at Ryan and said. "You're the last pitcher that I need to tell how to pitch. You've been taught that since the day you were born by your grandfather and your dad and believe me they would know better than most pitchers on how to control the game from the mound."
That was all the instruction the skipper had for Ryan and believe it or not Ryan wasn't even nervous. He was getting ready at his locker when D-Lee, as everybody called him, the Cubs first baseman, walked over and introduced himself. He said to Ryan "So you're the new guy. I just wanted to tell you good luck tonight and if you get into a jam call a timeout and I will help you out of it. Sometimes stalling can be your best friend." Ryan smiled and shook

his hand — he was completely calm now because he knew that he had a good squad to back him up out there and that was all he needed know.

Most of the players had gone out to field for batting practice and Ryan was left alone in the clubhouse to gather his thoughts before he warmed up. That's when he looked up and saw a familiar face standing in the clubhouse. It was his dad, Steve Larson. Ryan was shocked because he didn't think anybody from his family would be there. Getting called up to the big club happened so fast that it was impossible for any of them to get to the game in time. He never counted on his dad being there and when he saw him, he asked him.
"What are you doing here, Dad?"
"I was told that you got called up by the skipper of the Rangers, they thought I should be here for your first big league game so I got on plane and here I am."
"I'm surprised you came."
"No matter what, I wouldn't miss your first big league game. My dad didn't miss mine and I'm not gonna miss yours."
Ryan smiled and said. "Thanks, Dad. Any advice?"
"Well, you know how to pitch so I don't need to give you any instruction. You should've learned enough of that by now. But I will say this...when you go out there tonight the last three pitches of your warm up on the mound should be hard fastballs just to let the Astros know what you're capable of. The first two pitches to the first batter should be wild, letting him know that he shouldn't crowd the plate and one of those pitches should nearly take his head off. Now you'll get a warning from the ump, but the Astros will think you're unpredictable and that will work in your favor because they'll take more chances with you since you're a rookie and won't be as conservative as they should be. After those first two pitches the game is yours and you can control it from there...that's how you'll win."

Ryan didn't know if it was good advice or bad advice, but he did know that his father was smart enough as a pitcher to give good advice especially when it came to controlling the game. He shook his dad's hand after receiving that advice and then walked out of the clubhouse to begin his warm-ups, and by the time the game started, Ryan still didn't know if he was going to take his father's advice or not. So there he was, all alone on the mound in front of 40,000 fans at the start of the game. He never pitched a game in front of those many fans before, and for whatever reason he wasn't nervous. He probably should have been, but he wasn't.

The game was starting and he was finishing his warm-up before the first batter was up and that's when he got down to the last three pitches of his warm up. He stood there with a long pause rubbed the ball a little bit, put his index finger in the middle finger of his right hand over the seams of the baseball and then reared back and let the ball go with everything that he had. Ryan threw three straight fastballs, all of them clocking at 98 miles an hour. He had decided at that moment that he was going to do what his father suggested.

The umpire motioned for the game to start and the Cubs began to bat. The first three batters were retired in a row. Ryan Larson strode to the pitching mound and threw a few pitches to get loose. The first batter in the Astros lineup came to the plate. Ryan thought it was now or never and his first pitch was a hard cut slider, making the batter jump over the plate to get out of the way of the pitch. Astros fans started booing. The announcers both spoke up and commented that Ryan Larson was nervous being that it was his first game in the Majors. The next pitch was a high and tight fastball that nearly took the batter's head off – the batter went straight to the ground to avoid being hit by the pitch. Steve was right; the home plate umpire gave him a warning about his wild pitches. The batter got up cursing at Ryan and shouting at him that he needed to go back down to the minors. Ryan didn't pay attention because now he knew...the game was his and he was in control of it. He could win it or lose it all by himself. The next pitch was another 98 mile an hour fastball straight down the pipeline at the knees and it was the perfect strike. Two pitches later Ryan got the first out of the game by striking out the first batter making him look silly swinging over a low and away curveball. That's when Cub fans erupted with excitement at Minute Maid Park. The fans at the ballpark that night and those watching WGN just got their first glimpse of Ryan Larson and for many fans it was like looking at a memory from long ago when they had watched Jack Larson and Steve Larson pitch for the Cubs.

Ron Santo who was on the radio for WGN broadcasting live at the game shouted into his microphone, "Holy cow, it looks like the Astros are in for a wild night. We've got another Larson on the mound and I have a feeling this is gonna be his night. You know I'm seeing something that his grandfather used to do when we played together." The other radio announcer, Pat, commented. "You may be right, Cubs fans, this rookie pitcher looks like he has the same stuff as father and grandfather and I think we're about to see an interesting performance tonight." That was the biggest understatement said by any broadcaster that night.

Ryan Larson would end up retiring the side in the first inning. The first batter was a strikeout, the second batter flied out to center field, and then the cleanup man in the lineup would strike out on three pitches. He was on a roll and what he didn't know yet was that it was definitely going to be his night.

The score remained zero to zero through the first three innings and the best part was Ryan was perfect. Not one Astro had been on base and he already had five strikeouts. At the top of the fourth the Cubs finally got on base and that's when Ryan got to help in his cause again. With one out and a man on second Ryan was able to lay down a bunt and get the man over to third. Soriano, the Cubs' leadoff man, sent a shot into the left field bleachers for a two-run homer after Ryan batted. The Cubs were on the scoreboard.

Ryan continued to pitch a perfect game for the next two innings and getting two more strikeouts along the way. His pitch count was only at 69 pitches and he was in complete control of the game. Not one Astro had been on base and he didn't even know it. All he was concerned with was pitching each inning and getting guys out. The Cubs held a two run lead and by the top of the seventh inning there wasn't any need for pitchers to start getting warmed up in the bullpen. With most rookies they might have gotten a reliever, but Ryan was doing great and nobody wanted to mess with destiny. He was pitching a perfect game so far and nobody in baseball ever "fucks" with a perfect game, not even the smartest managers.

This was Ryan's ballgame and there wasn't any jam that he couldn't get himself out of. He got to six full counts with the Astros' middle lineup and was able to pitch out of each one of them even getting the Astros to hit into two double plays to get the third out in the fifth inning. Ryan Larson was a rookie but there was no denying it he was pitching like an All-Star and not even his father or grandfather could have pitched a better game. The Cubs were able to tack on one more run in the seventh and it was at the bottom of the seventh inning that Ryan finally got into trouble. The Astros cleanup hitter who'd struck out once and flied out once with Ryan finally sent a crushing shot into center field. Everybody knew it was going to be a home run, but they didn't know that new Japanese player Fukudome who was playing in center field that night would make a leaping catch extending his arm over the center field wall and robbing the Astro hitter of a home run. It was a spectacular catch and would certainly make a highlight reel on ESPN. Ryan just pointed at Fukudome as his way of saying thank you. Fukudome tipped his hat to Ryan to let him know that he was behind Ryan 110% in this game and that nothing was going to get by him.

Ryan was able to get out of the seventh inning with another double play. He was pitching a perfect game with two innings to go. Up to this point it was history and with ten strikeouts. His numbers were beginning to be record breaking, but he still didn't know what was going on. He knew it was the eighth inning and that was it, but he also expected to be pulled. But there was no way that was going to happen.

The Cubs pitching coach did talk to Ryan before going to the mound letting him know that he could pitch a complete game if he wanted to. The only thing he asked the pitching coach was what his pitch count was. He was at 83 pitches. Normally at this point Sweet Lou would've taken out the rookie pitcher and put in the setup man for the closer, but he wasn't going to mess with a perfect game so Ryan was left in. The bottom of the eighth came without notice and Ryan took care of the first batter by making him fly out. Five outs away from a perfect game, but that's when it happened. The wheels came off and Ryan Larson was robbed of the perfect game by an umpire with bad vision. The number five hitter for the Astros came up and with two strikes on him he hit the ball straight down the third baseline but it rolled foul, or so everybody thought. It hit the outside edge of the white line, which would have made it a foul ball, and not even Ramirez, the Cubs third baseman, attempted to get the ball because it was clearly foul. But since it was right on the line the third base umpire ruled it a fair ball. The Astros batter was able to round first and make it into second for a double. The Cubs fan started to erupt in anger and boo the umpire. Ryan knew it was foul, but he did not lose his cool during his first game as to get ejected for arguing the call. That's what was the manager was supposed to do and Sweet Lou did just that. He charged out of the visitors' dugout and ran over to the third base umpire cursing and screaming at him for his bad call.

Lou shouted at the umpire. "What the hell, are you fucking blind?"

The umpire responded. "It was on the line and it was fair."

Lou continued to scream obscenities at the umpire and even kicked dirt on him — that's when he got ejected. Cubs' players and other coaches had to walk Lou back to the dugout so he didn't hit the umpire. But Lou shouted one more thing to the ump, "You're a bastard...you just robbed the kid of a perfect game. You should be ashamed of yourself. You're Bush League Ump!"

It was after that the Ryan realized what was going on in the game and although that he was mad that the perfect game and even the no hitter had been taken away he just continued to focus on his own game. Lou, before going back to the dugout walked up to Ryan and told him "They just took the perfect game away from you, if it were me I would shove it down their throat as you win this game. You did a hell of a job today and you should be proud. "

Steve, who was watching the game, was cursing because he knew what they did to his son and he couldn't do anything about it. Even Ron Santo the WGN broadcaster commented on the air. "Well this is a sad day in baseball — the Astros rob this young man of a perfect game over a blatant bad call. It seems that this kind of thing always happens here in Houston." He knew he should have never said that on the air and that he would probably be fined for what he said but it was true.

Lee, the first baseman, Soto, the catcher, and Ramirez all came to the mound to talk to Ryan and make sure that he was going to be okay and finish the game. He nodded yes and the truth was he wasn't nervous or mad at all. These things happen in baseball, but they still had a game to win. Then Lee, the Cubs' quiet captain, told Ryan to take a deep breath and do what he came here to do....to get the rest of those bastards out. And that's exactly what Ryan did. With the next batter he made him pop up the ball behind the plate and the catcher was able to catch it for the second out. The next batter he struck out on the fourth pitch swinging over his curveball. Ryan's curveball had been deadly all night and he embarrassed more than one Astro with it. It was at this point in the game that they were gonna put the closer in, but Rothschild, the Cubs pitching coach, said Ryan should finish what he had started. Ryan just smiled at him before walking out to the mound and said. "The next three batters are going down."

Ryan walked to the mound as the lonely warrior who had endured a hard-fought battle in the bottom of the ninth inning. He wasn't tired and he was focused. The first batter came up and he threw a sinking fastball: strike one. The he threw a breaking ball and the Astro hit a grounder to second base — the ball was thrown to Lee at first base for the first out. The next batter walked up to the plate and he had the intent look of hitting a home run. It didn't happen that way — Ryan threw an off-speed change up pitch and made the hitter hit a high and long straight away pitch into center field where it was caught for a fly out. He was down to one batter.

Ryan threw two straight fastballs making the batter foul them both off for two strikes. Then he tried to get the batter out by making him swing at the curveball. It didn't work this time and it was a ball. He tried to make the batter swing at a slider — it didn't work and it was ball two. He thought he could end the inning with a fastball, but the batter just fouled it away. Finally he stood still, moved fingers over the seams of the ball and loosened his thumb over the bottom of the ball. He was going throw the sinking pitch that his father and grandfather had taught him. It was a sinking fastball with a little break on it where the bottom just dropped out from underneath it as soon as it hit the plate. Batters would think they were swinging at a sinking fastball right at the knees, but the pitch was already below the knees when it got to the plate and batters would swing right over the top of it. Strike three. The Astro at bat swung right over the top of it and Ryan struck out the last batter to win the game.

He had pitched a one-hit shutout with thirteen strikeouts and it should have been a perfect game. It was for the most part and it proved to be Ryan's perfect game because he controlled every moment of it and proved that he belonged on the big league level just like his father and his grandfather before him. As soon as he got the last out Cub fans in the stadium jumped out of their seats with excitement. They had just witnessed a star emerge. Ron Santo was on the air shouting, "He did it....he did it...he pitched a perfect game just like his grandfather used to do when we played together. Pat, we just saw history tonight and a star being born."

The Cubs players on the field came running up to him and they picked him up in the celebration, right off the mound. Even though it should have been a perfect game they celebrated as if it were. He pitched like a champion in his first big league game and on that night to all the Cub fans an announcement was made, not out loud, but a silent victory where a new star was here for the Cubs and that another Larson had returned. He was being congratulated by all the players and coaches for the performance he had and the victory he achieved. But there was someone else in the clubhouse waiting for him, his dad. It was Ryan's day and he proudly hugged his son for the first time in almost twenty years. After that the Cub's skipper congratulated Ryan and said and that his way of breaking into the big leagues was a hell of a way to do it.

Of course Jack Larson was watching the game. He just smiled of the end of it and said to his wife, "I knew he could do it." Amy and her mother just cried over his performance that night. They wished they could have been there; but they also knew it was a good thing that Steve was there. Ryan needed his father. But with all the excitement that night and with everybody watching that game on WGN from Cub fans all across the country to the Larson family there was another special person who had been watching that night. It was Tara; the woman he had met the year before and said to him that she didn't like baseball because she never understood it. Well she understood the game that night and watched one of the greatest performances on the pitcher's mound in baseball. She understood the perfect art of baseball with all poetry in numbers – that's what appealed to her since she was a math person. However that night she saw something remarkable – she saw a man play the game with childlike innocence and he was completely happy when playing baseball. She saw the best of Ryan Larson.

7

So Close to Being Champs

It was a beautiful May afternoon in Chicago with great weather for a ballgame. The weather was warm with a light breeze, a perfect spring day in the city of Chicago. The Cubs were playing an afternoon baseball game. It was 30 minutes before the game and Len and Bob, the Cubs announcers, were getting ready to do their pregame. It was the beginning of May and the Cubs were on a winning streak holding a tight lead for first in the central division, but the injuries were starting to take their toll on the Cubs. Ramirez the third baseman had a pulled shoulder and would be out for four to six weeks. Zambrano had pulled a hamstring, he would be out for about the same amount of time. Even though the Cubs were still hitting and their offense was still strong there were a few weak spots, but the Cubs were 16 and 8 holding a 1-game lead for first place. Ryan Larson's won/lost record so far was 4 and 0, 3 of those games being won at Wrigley Field.

Amy was listening intently to the Cubs pregame when her editor walked to her desk humming "Take Me Out to the Ball Game." She smiled and asked him what he wanted as if it was an inconvenience for her to talk to her boss. It kind of was because the Cubs game was on. He said to her. "You know your piece about the last great championship team was good. We got a lot of letters because of it. "

"Glad everybody liked it." Amy replied.

"I think you should write another one. People identify with you writing about your family and you are the best person for it because after all they are your family."

"I thought this was going to be a one-time piece because it's the 100th anniversary since the Cubs' last championship."

"At first I thought it would be, but people liked it and they want more. And... we could use more sales."

"I don't want to exploit my family and what this year is."

"No one is asking you to, and I'm not even telling you to. Write about your favorite stories of your family and the Cubs. You know the ones that most people don't know about."

Amy smirked at her editor. "You do want me to keep writing about my family and it's not a little exploitation?"

"Well maybe it is, but I believe in giving our readers what they want because after all they buy our paper and advertise in it thus keeping us in business."

"What do you have in mind?"

"Talk about the Cubs' near misses in the World Series."

"That's not depressing or anything."

Her editor let out a small laugh and said. "You're still seeing that lawyer from Texas, right, write about what you've been telling him about your family. I'm sure there's a few interesting stories in there."

Amy smiled at him and then paused. She was thinking of a good story, one that most people probably didn't know about. It was the untold story of the 1938 World Series. She thought of the story about her great grandfather George Larson punching out two Yankee fans and the great Dizzy Dean. It was a story she hadn't even told Chris yet, but she would that night over dinner.

The 1938 season for the Cubs was another heartbreaker, but more so for George Larson, the son of the Paul Larson who had played on the 1907 and 1908 championship seasons. He was just like his father, same build, same athletic skill, and he could play every position. He had come up with the Cubs in 1936 and after two seasons had proven to be an all-star player. It was probably his batting skill that did it for him. He had never battered below 300 just like his father. If he had any downside as a player it was his temper. George had a passion for the game and he hated to lose – he never took losing well.

1938 was a year much like 1908. The Cubs started out slow and would compete for first all the way to the last day of the season with Pittsburg. The Cubs played the Pirates for the last games of the season and barely pulled out a victory to get to the World Series. George was stunning in that series, but it wasn't enough to get the Cubs over the top. In the last game against the Pirates while tied at five it took Gabby Hartnett's "Homer in the Gloamin'" in the bottom of the ninth to win the game for the Cubs and send them to the World Series. The reason it was called "Homer in the Gloamin'" was because Wrigley didn't have any lights back then and the sun was beginning to settle to the point that dusk was setting in when Gabby Hartnett stepped up to the plate and hit a home run into the bleachers, or at least that's what the players and umpires thought. Nobody could see the ball because of not having enough light at the end of the field nor could they find it so it was ruled a home run as Hartnett ran the bases to home plate. Because of that play George's performance in that series against the Pirates was overshadowed, but he was clearly the best offensive player of that series going 11 for 16 with two home runs and 9 RBIs. He would match that kind of play in the World Series, but it would be overlooked because they were playing the New York Yankees. The Yankees of 1938 were led by Joe DiMaggio and Lou Gehrig followed by other stars such as Gomez, Dickey and Ruffing. They were the best team in baseball and most people on the Cubs knew it. The Cubs played well, but they were no match for the Yankees and it only took four games for the Cubs to lose the World Series.

George Larson had similar numbers for the Cubs in the '38 series as he did at the end of the season against the Pirates; he was the only bright spot the Cubs had even though the Cubs had the great Dizzy Dean pitching for them, but that wasn't even enough for the Cubs to compete with the Yankees. Dizzy Dean had been acquired by the Cubs in 1937 after a long and all-star career with the St. Louis Browns, but by the time Cubs got him his arm was shot and his career pretty much over. Everybody knew it, but P.K. Wrigley, the Cubs owner, he didn't see it that way and paid nearly 100,000 dollars, big money at the time, to get him. The way he saw it, Dizzy could at least put fans in the seat because, well after all, he was Dizzy Dean. He was right, fans did come to see him, but that didn't help the Cubs in their quest for another World Series.

George honestly thought the Cubs could beat the Yankees and he was about the only one who thought that even on the Cubs team. Part of it was a sense of being young and naïve while being truly competitive. He wanted to win no matter what and always played the hardest in order to win. He hadn't been around long enough in the big leagues to understand that some teams are just plain better than yours and there's nothing you can do to win. None of that stopped him from playing hard in the series and giving the Cubs plenty of chances to win a game. Larson went 8 for 14 in the Series and he hit two home runs, but the thing that killed the Cubs and won it for the Yankees was pitching. The Cubs had some decent pitchers, but the

Yankees had better pitchers and the Cubs also relied on Dizzy Dean whose fastball had long since disappeared.

The first game that Dizzy pitched and couldn't produce got a violent reaction from Larson who was playing in the infield for the World Series. Even though he could play 7 or 8 positions he mostly played the outfield because of his throwing arm and speed, but for the series they needed him in the infield. Late in the game when Dizzy was getting lit up by Yankee batters George did something that he had never done before. He actually cursed at one of his players for lousy playing. He knew Dizzy could do better and after four runs had scored in the 6th inning George walked over to the mound to have words with Dizzy. It was unprofessional and caused a delay in the game. He even got a warning from the umpire that if he continued he would be thrown out of the game. George ignored all of that and yelled at Dizzy.

"What the hell Dizzy...where's the hard stuff?"

"Get back on second," Dizzy replied. "I don't need some rookie telling me how to play."

"I'm not a rookie, been with the team for two years."

"Then quit acting like one. Let me pitch."

"I'll let you pitch when you start pitching like 'Dizzy Dean' and not some woman who just picked up the ball for the first time."

Dizzy got into George's face and bumped him a little bit. Then he said to him. "If you don't get back to second, I'm gonna wallop you."

"Just try it Dean and see what happens."

By that time the manager came to mound to see what was going on. One of the radio announcers commented, "Well folks you don't see that every day, one of your own teammates threatening if you don't pitch better." The Cubs manager got in between George and Dizzy before they started fighting. He told Dizzy to focus on the game and he told George to get back to second and mind his own game or he would be out of this one. George responded back. "Well either he starts pitching better or you put me in because I know that I can do better." Dizzy tried to come after George and hit him when he said that, but he was stopped by the manager before anything could happen. Any normal manager especially in the modern game would have pulled the pitcher and gotten someone from the bullpen, but that didn't happen here. Dizzy was left in for another inning before he was pulled. After the last home run was hit off Dizzy Dean he solemnly walked backed to the dugout but yelled over to the Yankees dugout on his way and replied, "If I had had my fastball this would have never happened." Quite a few Yankees including DiMaggio and Gehrig nodded in agreement. Finally Dizzy Dean was pulled and the Cubs manager decided that since there was no way they were coming back to win this game in the last two innings he would put George Larson in as a relief pitcher. He had pitched before in semi pro ball and had fared pretty well. George was shocked to say the least. After a moment's pause, not believing what the manager had just said, he grabbed his glove and headed for the mound. The manager shouted to him as he ran out to the mound, "Let's see if your mouth can pitch any better." They were all in for a surprise.

George Larson had a unique talent for pitching that no one really knew about except for the boys back in Iowa. It must have been something that he inherited from his uncle. While the Cubs were a little surprised at his ability to throw strikes and get people out it was the Yankees who were even more baffled. In the eighth inning he faced the bottom of the lineup and they went three up and three down. The first two batters he struck out on 8 pitches. The third took a little longer because he kept fouling off pitches, but he finally got him out when the Yankee batter hit a line drive right over Larson's head and he somehow managed to catch it by sticking his glove up and ducking his head. It was a lucky catch for anybody else, but George Larson was one of the best defensemen to play the game and rarely let anything get by him.

[106]

As the Cubs were walking back to dugout the Yankee skipper shouted back to Gabby Hartnett the Cubs manager, "Gabby, you should have put this guy in instead of Dizzy...you might have actually won the game." Nobody on the Cubs team seemed to disagree. After the next three batters for the Cubs were went down at the beginning of the inning the last of the 9th inning was finally here. Larson was sent back out to pitch and he was going to face the heart of the Yankees lineup, DiMaggio and Gehrig. While he wouldn't strike everybody out and the Yankees would even get a hit off him, putting a man on base, he was still spectacular on the mound. The first two batters went down on strikes. Larson, who had never really learned to throw a curve, found out that he could throw the deadliest in the game. Nobody could hit it, not even DiMaggio. "Smokin Joe" would get on base after having swung over two of Larson's curveballs, but it was only because the Cubs shortstop bobbled the ball and committed an error to what should have been an easy out. Larson would face Gehrig next and it took only one pitch to make him pop up the ball for an out to the end the game. The Cubs may have lost, but they discovered a relief pitcher in Larson and another deadly weapon on the mound. He truly could play all positions.

They didn't use him the next game even though they should have because he was needed in the infield and it wouldn't make a difference anyway. The Yankees had the third game won by the fourth inning, although George Larson did get his second home run of the series to help the Cubs in their cause to win the game. The Cubs would lose by eight runs in game three. Game four should have been different for the Cubs, they should have had a different game plan, and it was like they had already lost. Dizzy Dean started the game and once upon a time that would have guaranteed a victory, but the Cubs were never that lucky in those days. Many wanted George Larson to start because at that point they really had nothing lose, but he was needed in the infield. Dizzy started out good for the first two innings holding the Yankees to four hits and only one run, but he couldn't hold it for any longer. The third inning was brutal. The Yankees scored five runs and when Dizzy should have been pulled he was left in the game.

The fourth inning was when the wheels came off for the Cubs, as if it could get any worse. They still kept Dizzy in the game when he should have been pulled. Many of the Cubs players wanted Larson to pitch the rest of the game so they might actually have a chance to win. Dizzy gave up two hits and allowed a man on first and third. He wasn't even trying to use trick pitches, things like the changeup or screwball. He kept trying the fast ball that had disappeared long ago. George Larson had finally had it. Dizzy may had given up on the game and the series on the mound, but George hadn't. He was too much of a competitor and giving up or losing wasn't something he could do especially if someone wasn't even trying anymore. After Dizzy gave up third hit allowing another run with no outs in the inning Larson threw down his glove and stomped off towards the pitcher's mound cursing at Dizzy. No one could believe it, a teammate marching off to hit one of his own teammates for not playing well and much less a second time in three days. Even the sports announcer commented, "Here we go again, George Larson is off to the mound to have words with the great Dizzy Dean." The announcer was a little excited and his calming voice seem to disappear – the same calming voice that sounded like a father who knew best when he address the United States on TV as the President fifty years later. The other announcer said. "Ronny, don't get too agitated, it will just be a small argument before they pull Larson for bad sportsmanship." The announcer was right about one thing, Larson would get ejected, but not for having words with Dizzy.

George Larson charged up to the mound cursing at Dizzy Dean for not playing hard and for throwing the same lousy pitches over and over. Everything in the game seemed to stop and players on both benches were on their feet waiting to see what would happen, but mainly waiting to see if both teams were going to end up fighting on the field. This was an unusual circumstance because usually a member of the opposing team would was the one that charged the pitcher's mound. As Larson was walking up to the mound Dizzy shouted at him.

"George, get your ass back to second, I'm the one pitching."

"Then start acting like a pitcher and not a tall pile of shit."

Dizzy pushed Larson back when he stepped on the mound and said. "Screw you rube, this is my game not yours. Quit acting like a whiny child."

Larson didn't even say anything he just charged Dizzy and pushed him down sitting on top of him and hitting him in the face. Dizzy got a few licks in before George was pulled off of him by Gabby Hartnett and some of the other players. They separated Dizzy and George, but George was hard to contain and kept trying to get at Dizzy. He was hard to hold because he was 6'3" and weighed a solid 225 lb. George kept shouting back at Dizzy, "Come back here you chicken shit."

Dizzy didn't do anything except try and keep away from George. Gabby kept saying to Larson, "He's not worth it and there are eight other guys out here who are losing this game as well."

Larson replied back. "But he's the only one deliberately giving the game to the Yankees."

After that enough was an enough, the umpire threw George Larson out of the game and Gabby told him to hit the showers. While walking away George picked up his glove and threw it at Dizzy hitting him in the side of the face with it – it was the best pitch of the entire game. As fans were yelling at George while he was walking off the Yankee players shouted insults to him as he walked into the visitor's club house, all except Gehrig, he was too nice for that. George Larson got cleaned up and walked out of Yankee Stadium. It was the last time the Cubs would play there in the post season and George Larson left a dark cloud over the house that Ruth built. While walking out he didn't turn around to look back at the stadium, he couldn't bring himself to. He did however find a tavern across the street and attempted to console himself with a bottle of Canadian whiskey, remnants of prohibition when good Canadian whiskey was smuggled over the border around Niagara Falls.

Dizzy was kept in the game for another inning before he was finally done and by that time the game was already over. The Cubs did try to spur on a comeback scoring four runs in the 7th and 8th innings, but it wasn't enough. The Cubs lost game four and were swept by the Yankees in four games. The city of New York seemed to erupt in a million strong celebrations including the patrons in the tavern that George Larson was hiding in while consoling himself with whiskey. Everybody in the bar stood up and cheered as the announcer over the radio said with great enthusiasm, "The Yankees have done, they are the World Champs." Everybody cheered except Larson. A couple of the patrons took notice of this as Larson was sitting in the corner with his bottle and small glass.

They walked over and asked George why he wasn't cheering and he told him that he just wanted to be left alone. They asked him if he was a Yankees fan or a Chicago fan. He replied again that he didn't want to talk to them, but that's when one of the gentlemen recognized him and shouted so that everybody in the tavern could hear, he was George Larson, the player that got thrown out of the game for hitting his own pitcher. Larson was in no mood and told them to shut up, but the two gentlemen started laughing and calling him names – that got everybody in the tavern making comments about Larson as well. Finally he had had enough, he leaped out of his chair and punched one of the guys standing before him and then he sucker punched the other one in the stomach when he wasn't paying attention. That's when three or four other patrons came after George for starting a fight in the tavern. Larson took all of them on and since he was big it wasn't that easy to get him down.

He got a few licks in and roughed up quite a few guys before someone hit him with a whiskey bottle breaking it over his head. It stopped George a little bit but he still kept throwing punches and nailing a few of the patrons in the process. The bartender and a few guys finally got him out of the tavern and roughed him up pretty good outside of the bar. All in all George had a couple of black eyes, a couple of broken ribs, and was bleeding from the nose — that was broken too.

Some of the other Cubs players found him across the street trying to stop the bleeding from his nose and they quickly gathered him up and got him to the train station where the Cubs were leaving to go home. News had already gotten around that George Larson after punching out Dizzy Dean during the game also tried to take out a few Yankee fans after he was tossed from the game. Some of the players thought it was funny because it just proved how much of a competitor he really was, but Gabby Hartnett, the Cubs manager was furious and didn't know if he wanted someone like Larson on the team for next year.

The truth was George Larson was a fiery competitor and he hated to lose. He was always the one guy on the team that would do anything to win. And that also meant hitting one of his own teammates if it meant he wasn't playing his best or was trying to give the game away as in the case of the great Dizzy Dean. But what was sadder than that was he was still young and didn't know who the better team was or when his was outclassed. Larson wouldn't even accept such a thing if his team wasn't that team and as far as he was concerned the team he played on was the best team around. Maybe that is just the sense of being young and an athlete, but sometimes a small few are blessed with such wonderful delusions.

As Amy was finishing the story Chris asked her. "What happened to your great-grandfather after that? Seems to me that's the kind of thing that teams do not look too favorably upon."

"No," she replied back. "P.K. Wrigley was mad as hell and during the offseason started to see who would be interested in George Larson. He didn't want a player like that no matter how good he was."

"Did they trade him?"

"A few months later they almost had a deal with the New York Giants, but one phone call convinced P.K. that the Cubs needed a player like that."

"Who made that call, some famous player like his father Paul Larson?"

"No, actually, it was Charlie Grimm, the Cubs former manager the year before. He told P.K. that he was ready to come back as the Cubs manager and if he did one of the conditions was George Larson remained on the team and that they retire Dizzy Dean. P.K. Wrigley had a lot of respect for Grimm and anything he wanted he pretty much got."

"Sounds like a hell of a manager."

"He was, he kept the Cubs winning which brought people to the ballpark and that's what really made P.K. happy. So of course he could pretty much get what he wanted. Besides he was right, my great-grandfather was exactly what the Cubs needed and the sad truth was Dizzy Dean was done in baseball. And that made him disappear."

Chris smiled as he poured Amy another glass of wine. He said to her. "My father always told me that the true champion was the one who had the right heart — he gave all that he had during the battle and if he was going to lose he would go down fighting. Those guys are rare because they only come along so often."

Amy paused for a moment taking in everything Chris had just said. He was right and so she thought about all the stories she had been told of George Larson trying to win the game all on his own. Then she remembered that he was one of the brighter moments for the Cubs during the 40's and early 50's.

Chris asked Amy what happened with the story after that. She chuckled to herself and said. "He became a legend — the man who hit Dizzy Dean and tried to take on Yankee fans. As a result he always had death threats when he went to New York, but then the Cubs played the Dodgers and the Giants, they never took him lightly, and nobody ever took a swing at him. "

Chris laughed and said. "Sounds like it was a legend that never died!"

Amy grabbed his hand from across the table to let Chris know that he had no idea what he was getting himself into with her family. The she said. "You have no idea, but that's the way it tends to be with my family. However, that's a story for another time."

8

The Curse of '45

As the 2008 baseball season was progressing there was a lot of talk about the Billy Goat Curse and why the Cubs had not been back to World Series since 1945. They had come close a few times. Both Steve and Jack Larson had shared in the disappointment of being so close to going to the World Series and not making it. All the baseball analysts were talking about the Cubs that year being that it was the 100th anniversary since their last championship and everyone of them had their own opinion on why the Cubs hadn't won it since. And of course every fan had their opinion as to why the Cubs were the loveable losers. But Amy knew better than anyone that there were a lot of factors to the Cubs not winning for so many years and why they had been so close only to have been defeated. She had lived the history ever since she was born. The Cubs history, in a way, was her own family history, and if there was one person who knew the real reason why the Cubs could come so close, but never win, it was her. True, the Cubs were like a Greek Tragedy or like a Tennyson poem that was wrapped up in tragedy, but no matter what there was always something that lost it for the Cubs and most often it was them.

As she was wrapping up some work before heading to Wrigley Field to watch her brother on a beautiful Friday afternoon, she was thinking back to five years earlier, the 2003 season. 2003 was the year that the Cubs were 5 outs away from the World Series and it was snatched away from them by a bad call and fan – truly poetic for the Cubs, one of their own was part of the cause. She and her brother were there watching with the Grounds crew. Both her grandfather and father had a great affection for the inner workings of a ballpark and how it was put together. Jack Larson was always fond of saying that baseball parks were like cathedrals and the field should be treated with the greatest reverence. Jack was the first to get to know the grounds crew at Wrigley and to learn what they do and so it came natural for Steve Larson while growing up at Wrigley Field that he would know the grounds crew as well. He grew up with them even working part time as a teenager with them to keep up Wrigley Field.

Both Jack and Steve Larson learned everything there was to know about how to keep a baseball field in great shape. Hanging out with the grounds crew and watching the ball games was a common thing and when Steve had his kids Amy and Ryan, well, they too got to know the grounds crew. When they were teenagers and in the beginning days of college for them, when they wanted to see a ball game all they had to do was call the head grounds keeper and he would let them in to watch the game with the crew. So in 2003, the famous game six of the National League Champion Series to see who would go to the World Series, Ryan and Amy were there watching as the Marlins' Louis Castillo hit that foul ball alongside the third base line and Moses Alou tried to catch it only to have the ball snatched away by the fan, that unfortunately everybody knew by name. 5 Outs away and that's when the wheels came off – many people saw it as a curse coming back to steal the wind out of the sail for the Cubs. Every Cubs fan knows the story of that fateful night – the fan interference and the bobbled ball by the shortstop for an error that would have been an easy double play to end the inning with the Cubs winning 3-0, but it didn't happen that way. An error and 8 runs later ended the Cubs flirtation with destiny. At the end of the inning Ryan leaned over to his sister and said.

"If there really is a curse on this on this team this has to be it."

"There can't be a curse, she said. " There's no such thing."

"To not believe it gives it its power."

"No, to believe in it gives power to the curse. This is just the unfortunate side of sports."

"You keep believing that if you want to, but I'm an athlete and I know better."

Some of the grounds crew who were standing around the siblings laughed because they knew Ryan was right to a point. Athletes believe in something entirely different and superstitions are just as important as religion or the right attitude in sports. After all, it's the power of belief. Amy didn't really understand why people believed in superstition but then again she couldn't believe why people believed in religion either. However she did know one thing with certainty – what gives a belief its power is our willingness to believe and in baseball that's why streaks are so important and powerful. To borrow a line from a great baseball movie – "if you believe that you're winning because you're wearing women's underwear then that's why you're winning, because winning streaks don't come along that often." "Never fuck with a winning streak!" And if you believe that you're losing because you're cursed then perhaps that's why you're losing – that's what Amy had learned after all these years.

2003 was a heartbreaker for the Cubs and even though they should have won game seven that one disastrous moment in game six killed any momentum the Cubs had and it seemed like the entire team had started to believe that they were cursed. It didn't help that all the baseball analysts were talking about the Curse of the Billy Goat. Maybe that's why they couldn't keep it together in game seven and win. Amy pondered another thought for a moment – all it took was one bad thing and it lead to a series of bad things for the Cubs and there was no coming back from that. If the team believed they could win it would change after that moment and it would be another year of loss and heartbreak. Amy couldn't help but think about that to herself in regards to the 2008 Cubs. She had watched too many Cubs' teams go down that same path and without them even knowing about it. It was just a thought and then she shook her head, smiled and put those thoughts away. Amy Larson didn't want to be one of those naysayers. After all, 2008 was the year to believe and she looked at the blue elastic bracelet on her wrist that said "We Believe" to remind herself of that as she got up from her desk at the Sun Times to leave for the ballpark.

It was a Friday afternoon and the weather around Wrigley was holding – it was a little overcast and the wind was a blowing just a bit, but it was still a great day to play baseball. Spring had finally come to Chicago in May and for Amy there was no better place to be than the baseball park. Ryan Larson was pitching that afternoon and his grandfather had made the trip to Chicago to see him pitch, Jack Larson was also to be the guest celebrity that day, getting to throw out the first pitch and sing during the 7th inning stretch. Amy wouldn't miss the game and it was a great opportunity to introduce Chris to everybody. By May, Chris was starting to get into Cubs baseball there were quite a few afternoons that he wouldn't schedule anything so he could go to the ballpark with Amy. And hey, it was Chicago, that kind of thing was allowed. Amy was coving the game, but she chose to sit with Chris and her Grandparents.

Ryan was a off to a good start so far. He hadn't allowed any hits or walks in the first 4 innings against the Astros. It seemed that his magic from the year before when he pitched his first game in the big leagues was starting to take form. By the end of the fourth inning he had 6 strikes out. His four deadliest pitches were working well: the curveball, the slide, the fastball, and the famous Larson sinking fastball that looked like a slider when coming towards the plate, but the bottom would just drop out from underneath it with about over 90 miles of speed behind it. The pitch would fool batters who were looking for a heater and then they would swing right over it. Sometimes it would get away from him and end up in the dirt before the ball had crossed the plate or take some bouncing action where if the catcher was paying attention, the ball would end up at the backstop. Ryan Larson hadn't been in the league long enough for opposing batters to figure out how to hit off of him and it had been 20 years since a Larson had used that pitch in a game.

In the fifth inning Ryan Larson walked his first batter and then he had another walk. The curveball was starting to get away from him. Jack Larson who was sitting up in the stands could tell what was wrong and commented to everybody, "it looks like his curveball might be done for the day; he's starting to get tired." Chris, who didn't know much about baseball, had to ask Jack what he meant. Jack replied to the young man. "He's coming over the top on it too much and is pushing the curve out too much where it's off the plate more than it should be. He's doing that because he's tired and is compensating for that by trying too hard and it's extending his body more than he needs to throw the curve and make it land where it's supposed to. He's probably throwing his curve too much because he doesn't want to rely on the fastball or the sinker too much while allowing the other team to figure out his pitches. He's trying to be smart about it, but now he will have to throw the other pitches even more and lay off the curve because it's not working. If he's really smart he'll slow down in between pitches, giving himself more time to rest and then start throwing some change-ups or off speed pitches. If he slows the game down a little more, then he will maintain his stamina to where he can pitch for a few more innings if needed. A good pitcher should always have more than two good pitches in his arsenal and know how to control the tempo of the game so he doesn't get tired. We used to have to do that in the old days when we knew that there wasn't any relief for us."

Chris smiled at Jack and replied, "That's probably the best answer I've ever heard about pitching."

"Would you expect anything less from a professional?" Jack said.

"I guess not."

Ruth Larson, Jack's wife leaned over and said to Chris. "You also won't get a short answer from a professional. Every answer they give is a teaching tool so the answer will always be long."

Jack smiled at his wife; he took great pleasure in her sarcasm. He did it because he loved her and as a pitcher's wife she understood all too well the trials of a baseball player. If you asked her whether she would want to be something else she would smile and simply say no. Her life with Jack had never been dull and Jack had never known a greater love except for his wife, children and the game of baseball itself.

Ryan Larson was able to work himself out of the fourth inning without giving up any runs. A pop fly gave him his first out and then he threw a slider and made the batter pull a grounder to Ramirez, the third basemen to force a 5-4-3 double play. He was playing smart knowing not to try to win the game all by himself especially knowing the curveball was fading away. Jack smiled at the end of the inning and said out loud. "I'm glad he listened to me about working smarter on the mound."

Chris, who was still curious about pitching in baseball, had to ask. "What do you mean, sir?"

"There are eight other guys on the field and each one is there to help you out of jam s when you're a pitcher. Some pitchers who are too prideful will try and do it all by themselves on the mound. They try to strike everybody out and won't rely on pop flies or grounders especially if they lead to double plays. When the pitch count is starting to get high for a pitcher they need to use everything they can to get guys out. Ryan's pitch count is at 59, which is high for only four innings. He needs to keep it down if he's going to last any more innings. What he did there was make the batter pull a slider around and keep it low so there was a good chance that it would be a grounder and with two men on it turned into a double play. Best of all he only wasted two pitches on the batter to get it done."

Chris just laughed and said. "I didn't realize that there was so much strategy in baseball?"

Jack looked at him with a serious look and replied. "You have no idea....just as a much as football, if not more." Chris had to chuckle at that.

Amy, who was making notes for her article looked over at her grandfather and said in a loving tone. "Okay Grandpa, you don't have to be the professor out here."

"Well, he asked." Jack said to his granddaughter jokingly.

Over the next couple of innings, Ryan played a little smarter and paid more attention to his pitch count. The Cubs had finally gotten onto the scoreboard with a pair of home runs from Derrek Lee and the rookie catcher, Soto. They led the game 4-0. In the fifth inning Ryan Larson did allow a solo home run for the Astros' first run of the game. The sinking fastball he thru hung in the air a little too much and the batter got a hold of it pushing the ball into the left field bleachers. It didn't matter though; Ryan was still doing good and working himself out of the innings using everything he had except the curveball. He had 8 strikeouts by then 7th inning and there was no reason to get anybody warned up in the bullpen. Ryan was only at 83 pitches and doing well. Jack Larson had already gone to up to the announcer's booth with Len and Bob to get ready to sing in the 7th inning stretch so he didn't even see what was about to happen.

Ryan was able to get the first batter out on a grounder to the shortstop. The next batter was Lance Berkman, one of the most feared Astros' batters and he was also one with a temper. On the second pitch with the count 0-1 Ryan tried to put a slider to the inside and get Berkman swinging over it. The pitch didn't break down, but went too far to the inside and hit Berkman. It was an honest mistake by the pitcher, but Lance Berkman didn't like Larson too much after he'd had four strike outs in Ryan's first big league the year before. In baseball, there's always long memories and when you dislike someone it usually never changes. Berkman took the pitch personally and charged the mound when Ryan wasn't looking. Soto, the Cubs catcher tried to get a hold of him before he could get to the mound to knock the hell out of Ryan.

When Ryan Larson did look up he saw Berkman standing close to him and trying to take a swing at him. Instincts kicked in – Ryan had, had batters charge the mound before and had to fight them off, but usually he saw them coming when they left home plate. This time it was different and he was caught off guard. He did the only thing he could think of, a half-assed karate move he had learned in college for flipping guys over your shoulder mixed with a Nolan Ryan where once you get a hold of the guy you just start hitting him in the face or the gut before he could hit you. Ryan was successful to a point, he did get Berkman flipped over his side and while he was hitting him he fell to ground with the guy and fell on his wrist. Ryan Larson made the mistake of hitting him with his pitching hand. Ryan didn't break his wrist, but he did pull something and he was hurt.

By this time both benches had cleared and a fight was underway on the field. It took about ten minutes to clear the field after the fight had started. Berkman was immediately ejected after everything was cleared up and then the home plate umpire decided to eject Ryan Larson as well. The ump got about 32,000 boos for that one, but Larson was another reason for the fight on the field and he did land the first punch. It was actually a good thing because he was hurt and he wouldn't have been able to pitch anyway. A pitcher from the Cubs bullpen took over and finished out the inning getting the next two guys out.

While Jack Larson was doing his 7th inning interview Len and Bob both commented that this was Ryan Larson's first fight in the majors and of course they had to ask Jack what he thought considering he was a veteran of a few fights in his day as a ballplayer for letting his curveball get away from him and hitting the batter. Jack laughed after their question and said.

"Well, I think Ryan did alright. The Bruce Lee move he pulled was pretty exciting, but he did a big no, no...never hit a guy with your pitching hand. "

"You never taught him to not do that." Bob asked him.

"Well of course I did, but I can't help it if he doesn't listen...has too much of his father in him I guess."

Len and Bob both laughed and commented on the fact that Steve Larson could be pretty wild and had a caused a few fights his playing days. They also reminded the listeners that one time when a batter was charging the mound towards Steve, he met the guy half way and sucker punched him with a left hook causing both benches to clear and of course he got ejected from the game plus was made to pay a hefty fine for the incident by Major League Baseball.

Jack laughed at the story that Len and Bob were telling and had to comment as well. He said. "Even though pitchers need to watch their tempers so they don't lose control of the game. I have to admit, if you're going to get hit by a guy charging the mound, might as well hit the guy first and not with your pitching hand."

[123]

All three of them laughed and joked around about fights, the "do's" and "don'ts" of the fight during the baseball game. Jack was known as being sarcastic when he gave an interview – he had a dark sense of humor and it could be mistaken for being serious. At the end of the interview he had to remind the listeners that the announcers like to have a lot fun and not to take it too seriously, he didn't want people to think that it was okay to fight in a game, especially young people.

The game ended about 30 minutes later and the Cubs were able to hold out and win giving Ryan another win at home. He was 4-0 at Wrigley Field, but it wouldn't last. Everybody caught up with him at the end of the game and it was actually Jack that figured out that Ryan was hurt when he shook his hand. He had a suspicion that he might he hurt and when they shook hands, both using their right hand, Jack placed his left hand on top of Ryan's and his hand right over the wrist applying a little pressure. Ryan winced and then Jack gave him a stern look. He said to Ryan

"I knew it, you did hurt yourself. How bad is it?"

Ryan gave his grandfather a smirk and replied. "It's not too bad...not anything that a little ice won't cure."

Jack was still looking at him with the same stern look and said. "Well, don't be stubborn, go get an X-Ray just to be sure that nothing is serious. Even a sprained wrist can affect your pitching game. You need to be sure."

"I'll do it tomorrow after putting some ice on it, besides, I'm hungry and would like to grab something to eat like we planned."

"Go do this first and then we'll eat."

"Really it's fine. It can wait."

"But it shouldn't have to wait. Do this first and then we'll eat. We'll wait for you."

Ryan wasn't very happy that his grandfather was giving orders like that, but he knew better to argue the point. It wasn't worth the fight and he didn't want to be the victim of an "I told you so." Ruth Larson looked over at her grandson and before he could say anything back said to him. "Don't argue with your grandfather, you know that he knows best when it comes to pitching."

Ryan leaned over and kissed her on her forehead and said. "Alright Grandma, I know that I'll never hear the end of it."

She smiled and said. "That's right."

Ryan and his girlfriend Tara whom he had met a year and half ago in Tennessee went to find the Cubs trainer so that he could get a X-Ray on his wrist and actually tell him and Lou, the Cubs skipper, that he was hurt. He didn't want to have to admit it and be out for part of the season. It was his first full season with the big club and the last thing he wanted to happen was to be sent back down to the minors. He still had that fear because it had taken so long to get to the big show.

Meanwhile Jack, Ruth, Chris and Amy decided to get something eat at Jack's favorite restaurant in Chicago, Berghoff's. They would just wait for Ryan to get done. Chris was still getting to know the Cubs and their history and he since he had more than one Larson at the table that night he decided to ask some questions. He did know that the Cubs had not won a championship since 1908 and he had also heard that the Cubs had not been back to the World Series since 1945. However he didn't know the full story – Amy hadn't gotten that far yet in telling him. But the thing that piqued his curiosity was the comments he had heard from other fans about the "Curse of the Billy Goat." Chris was an athlete and understood all too well the power of superstition, but he never understood how an entire team could be cursed and for a hundred years.

During the first round of drinks Chris asked Amy and Jack. "I keep hearing about this thing called the Billy Goat Curse on the Cubs, what is that?"

Amy got a disgruntled look on her face as if she didn't want to talk about it, and with good reason. Jack just looked at him, took a sip of his whiskey, and said to Chris. "I think if we're going to talk about that and 1945 it's going to be a long conversation. And if so then we will need a few more rounds." That's exactly what they did because it wasn't exactly a short story. Amy started to explain the history behind the 1945 Cubs team. They were known as the war team because most of the Cubs players were too old for military service during World War II and if hadn't been for the fact that Cubs got to keep most of their team and most baseball superstars were serving in the military the Cubs probably would have not been good enough to make the World Series that year.

Charlie Grimm finally came back to manage the Cubs – he would have been back a few years before after that phone call to PK Wrigley convincing to keep George Larson, but he didn't want to come back to manage the Cubs so quickly, and in fact it would be 6 years before he did. George Larson was released at the end of the 1941 season because of his temper, but it didn't take him long to find a job. The War came along and he served 3 years in the Navy. He came back for the 1944 season and the Cubs were so bad that they actually needed a superstar again, so his temper was overlooked by PK and Hack Wilson, the manager. It turned out to be one of the best decisions the Cubs could have made because with Larson back hitting in the lineup and a rookie outfielder by the name of Andy Pafko, the Cubs became competitive again, even against the St. Louis Cardinals, who dominated the early 40's in the National League.

By 1945, the Cubs had one of the best pitching staffs in the league with pitchers like Claude Passeau, Hank Wyse, Paul Derringer, and the midseason acquisition of Hank Borowy from the New York Yankees. Borowy was a superstar with the Yankees who helped them dominate the early 40's, he went 56-30 for the Yankees over the past 3 and half seasons. He was traded because he had developed blisters on his pitching hand and was considered done. The Cubs got him at a bargain, and although most people thought that is was another Dizzy Dean Episode, the gamble paid off. He was allowed to rest for a week and the blisters went away. He would get 11-2 for the Cubs the rest of the 1945 season.

While pitching and hitting made the Cubs winners that year there was another contributing factor and it was Charlie Grimm or "Jolly Cholly" as everybody called him. He was a veteran pitcher who never lost his patience and did something stupid. He was also a manager that encouraged his players to have fun and to play the game that way. The attitude was a lot different for the Cubs than it had been over the last five seasons and the players enjoyed the game as if they were kids again. That made a huge difference when it came to winning. And because of all these combining factors the Cubs would edge St. Louis to win the National League and play in the World Series. Their opponents would be the Detroit Tigers and for a small piece of irony the Cubs would win their last World Series against the Tigers and also play their last World Series against the Tigers. And for two Larson]s, Paul and George, their last World Series appearances would be against Detroit. Amy threw that in there just because it was fascinating and she remarked to Chris, "What were the odds?"

Chris and Jack both laughed at her comment. She continued the story and pointed out that it was a strange series from beginning to end and as most of the sports writers pointed out, the series was really a battle for who didn't have to be the worst team in baseball. If all of the professional ballplayers who were serving in the military had been back the Cubs and Tigers would not have been playing each other. Jack said that there was something unusual about the series, there were war-time restrictions that prevented the regular schedule for the series. The first three games would be played in Detroit and then the last four games would be played in Chicago. Traveling between Detroit and Chicago was not that far and should not have had any restrictions at all, but that never mattered to Major League Baseball.

The Cubs won game one in Detroit after Borowy shut down the Tigers, and the Cubs scored nine runs in the game. George Larson got the Cubs' first home run of the series and his post season magic had not disappeared. The Cubs lost game two 7-1, but shutout the Tigers in game three, winning 3-0. They were heading back to Chicago with a 2-1 lead in the series and home field advantage. However, whatever the Cubs had that was going right didn't seem to follow them back to Chicago. The Cubs would lose game 4 and 5. Borowy was shut down in Game 5 giving Detroit a 3-2 series lead in Chicago. But to this day that's not what Cub fans remember. Jack Larson pointed out that what fans should remember is that the pitching staff for the Cubs ran out of steam and it's what doomed them in the series, but baseball is filled with fascinating superstitions and urban legends – the Cubs would get theirs in Game four of the World Series. What fans remember now is "The Curse of the Billy Goat." And that's when Amy started to explain in her unhappy tone.

The Legend goes that On October 6, 1945, Game four of the World Series, William "Billy Goat" Sianis, a Greek immigrant who owned a nearby tavern, came to Wrigley Field with two box seat tickets for the fourth game of the 1945 World Series between the Chicago Cubs and the Detroit Tigers. One ticket was for himself and the other was for his pet goat Murphy. A squad of ushers at the stadium failed to keep Billy Goat Sianis and his pet Billy goat out of the ball park. Once inside the stadium, Billy Goat Sianis took the goat onto the playing field, causing uproar from the crowd before ushers intervened to end the stunt. After a heated argument, Billy Goat Sianis and the animal were allowed to occupy the box seat for which he had tickets. Billy Goat Sianis and his goat were ejected from the stadium, however, prior to the end of the game at the command of Cubs' owner PK Wrigley, reportedly because of the animal's objectionable odor. Sianis was outraged by the ejection, and in response, he placed a curse upon the Chicago Cubs that they would never win another National League Pennant or World Series. The Chicago Cubs eventually lost the 1945 World Series. After the loss,

[128]

Billy Goat Sianis sent a telegram to Wrigley that read, "Who Smells Now?"

The Cubs did win game six, but they didn't have any steam for game seven the next day. And as Jack pointed out about the pitching staff, the Cubs did not have a pitcher that was rested enough for game seven. While most of the team wanted George Larson to pitch game seven because he hadn't pitched at all during the series and was the most rested, Charlie Grimm felt like he needed him more in the outfield because the Tigers were on a hitting streak and he needed speed out there. Borowy volunteered to pitch and although nobody thought it was a good idea for him to do so he was selected to pitch Game 7. He had guts but it wasn't enough. He gave up five runs in the first inning and the game was pretty much over by then. The Cubs did try to come back, but they never got within 3 runs of the Tigers. George Larson did pitch a few innings and kept the Tigers from scoring again, but they did when George was relieved later in the game. The final score of game seven was 9-3.

Chris looked Amy and Jack and had to ask. "Do you really think it was a curse?"

Jack immediately answered. "No, they just didn't have enough steam to get through the series and they didn't have a deep enough pitching staff."

Amy said. "Honestly I don't know." Jack gave her a dirty look. She continued. "I can see evidence for both and let's face, in sports we like our superstitions and urban legends. You can make a good case for it, but maybe in the end the players curse themselves. "

And that was the truth as she explained. "Wrong Attitudes, players giving up, and not enough stamina are all things that happen in sports and they can lead to being cursed if you believe in that sort of thing. What it really comes down to is what we choose to believe and since it had been 100 years since the Cubs had won a World Series and 63 years since they had been to a World Series, one had to ask themselves is the curse for real or just an excuse because we can't explain anything else." No matter what the real answer was, it was something that Cub fans had to live with, and for the Larson family, it was a 100 years of hopes and failures. Jack didn't disagree with that assessment.

9

Mr. Cub and the Great Ones

The local news about the Chicago Cubs wasn't very good heading into the month of June. They were plagued by injuries and slipping below .500 in the win/loss column. That seemed to be all Amy was writing about these days with the Cubs and of course she had to write the article about her brother Ryan. He had injured his wrist from fighting with Lance Berkman of the Astros in his last pitching effort. The X-Ray that his grandfather Jack had insisted on getting revealed that he had a partial tear in the bone. Because of the injury he was going to be out for 6- 8 weeks – not exactly good news. But these things always happened to the Cubs, maybe they really were cursed she thought while sitting at her desk then again those were thoughts of frustration because the Cubs had too good of a team this year to be doing as bad as they were. Jack tried to tell her that it was the nature of baseball and what was happening with a team didn't necessarily mean that it would happen in August or September.

Amy let go of those thoughts and put on a happy face – she was going to interview one of her favorite people that day, Ernie Banks. He was known as Mr. Cub and embodied everything that a Cub should be. She usually got to interview him every year and get his perspective about that year's Cubs' team and he always had some great story about the teams that he and her grandfather played on. They were usually stories that she had never heard before so it was something new for her each time she got to interview Ernie Bank instead of the same old biographical information that every fan and sports journalist already knew about Mr. Cub.

She was going to interview him at Wrigley Field before the game. A few hours later she was sitting with him and about to start the interview. The big topic was the statue they had put up of Ernie Banks on opening day and talking a little more about his career. Her questions were a little different though; she wanted to know more about his most memorable moments as a Cub and not the usual highlights that most people knew already. She wanted to write about things that people didn't really know about. But before they got started he had to ask about Jack and how he was doing. Ernie was still humble and didn't want to say things about himself – that's part of what made him great. He was also wanted her to tell her brother that he wished him the best and that he hoped for a speedy recovery so that he would be on the mound again soon. Amy had to smile at that and that's one of the main reasons that she loved Ernie Banks, he was always thinking about other people instead of himself.

As they got started with the interview she asked Ernie about a defining moment in his career and one that people didn't know about. Ernie thought for a moment and said. "Probably how I came into the league and how I got to start at shortstop."

Amy smiled and asked. "You mean there's more to the story than what fans know?"

Ernie laughed and said. "Oh yes and the one I am about to tell you involves your great grandfather George. "

Amy was surprised because to her knowledge George and Ernie had only met once or twice. George Larson didn't even finish his last season in 1953 – he retired early before the season was officially over and went back to Iowa to help with the family farm. He played for the Cubs another eight and half seasons after the '45 season before retiring. He was once of the few superstars that played for the Cubs, but by 1953 age had finally caught up with him and all the great athletic feats he could do just seemed to hurt a little more. He had spent most of 1952 injured and while most didn't expect him to return for the '53 season he did because the Cubs needed a shortstop and he was still good enough to be competitive at the position. 1953 was also the year that the Cubs called up their first black player and as Ernie Banks explained, George Larson was instrumental in that. Amy had never heard of this story and she didn't think that her grandfather even knew it at the time because he was just a teenager when it happened.

Ernie went on to explain that even though Jackie Robinson had integrated baseball in 1947 the Cubs organization was still nervous about bring up a black player. It wasn't that PK Wrigley was a racist or thought that black players shouldn't be playing in the Major Leagues or in Chicago, he was worried about how the predominately white fan base of Chicago's Northside would react to a black player on the Cubs team. Even the north still had a Jim Crow attitude especially in sports. The southern weren't the only ones that could be racist.

It was finally decided that the Cubs were going to call up a black player to major leagues and they knew that they would have to replace George Larson at shortstop. The chances of him coming back in 1954 were slim and even if he did he was getting old and couldn't be the most effective player at that position. Ernie Banks was not the first black player that the Cubs brought up. They had a 27 year old shortstop by the name of Gene Baker who was playing in their minor league team in the Pacific Coast league, the Los Angeles Angels. He had been there the past four seasons and he was the perfect player to take over at shortstop at that time. They were happy with Baker, but Wid Matthews the Cubs General Manager realized something else, somebody had to room with Gene Baker and it had to be black player. The Cubs' scouts had, had their eye another player with the Kansas City Monarchs in the Negro Leagues for the past few years and that player was Ernie Banks who also played shortstop and second base. What impressed the Cubs was his ability to hit and his speed with a bat.

He was offered a contract with the Cubs with the idea that Baker could move to second and Banks could play shortstop. In addition Larson could be replaced at the end of the season and if they did well then George Larson would probably be released at the end of the season. He knew this too. All of this happened in September of 1953. Larson was doing well during the season, but he had, had a few errors at shortstop in the last month, which was unusual. He had not committed an error while playing in the infield in the past three years. Everybody knew that age was the factor for he was almost forty years old; he had celebrated his 37th birthday that year and was more than past his prime.

Ernie continued to tell the story of how he got his start. He explained that just because he and Baker got called up to the Cubs didn't mean that they were going to play. Within the first week of September and Banks being on the team George Larson had gotten hit during a home game against the Pirates by a line drive on his right hand and it swelled up to where he couldn't open or close it. He had to be taken out of the game. At first the Cubs skipper was going to put another older player in who was not very good at shortstop, but Larson spoke up and said that they might as well put Banks in and get it over with it. He also said that nobody knew how fans were going to react to him until he was actually in the game. The skipper agreed and Ernie Banks made his major league debut.

He was fabulous on the field and everybody there that day knew they were seeing something special. He never let a ball get out of the infield that day and went 2 for 3 at the plate. He hit two doubles and almost had one get out of the park, but one of the Pirates' outfielders robbed him of what would have been his first home run. He was clearly the best infielder the Cubs had and Larson knew it. What most people didn't know is that George Larson was considering retiring at the end of the season anyway and after watching Banks in that first game catching line drives that were zipping over his head and turning double plays he knew that was time to go. There was no way he could measure up to the new kid and while out of respect they would have let Larson finish out the season for his long and distinguished career with the Cubs even he knew that it was time to go and let the young kid start his career. George Larson played the next day after the swelling went down in his hand and he did pretty well going 2 for 4 at the plate and even hitting his last home run as a Cubs that day, but after the game was done and they had won he figured that it was time for him to be done too. So he asked for a meeting with PK Wrigley and Wid Matthews after the game.

The next day as the Cubs were getting ready to go on the road George Larson was in the clubhouse cleaning out his locker. His 14 year old son Jack was with him. The whole team pretty much knew the news; he had retired and wasn't going to finish the season. He told everybody that he had known for years on that team, it was time for him to go back to Iowa. The only one that didn't know yet was Ernie Banks. Banks came into the club house and saw Larson cleaning out his locker. He stopped and asked him what he was doing. Ernie wondered if George had been cut because of him and they weren't even going to let him finish the season. After all he was the type of guy that didn't want to put someone out of a job and he would have gone to the boss and argued on behalf of Larson to keep playing until the end of the season.

George Larson laughed to himself when he was asked by Banks if he had been cut. He replied to the young lanky kid. "No they didn't cut me, I retired as of today."

"Why, we still have a few more weeks left in the season?" Banks asked George.

"Because it's time Mr. Banks and it's your turn now."

"My turn, sir?'

"Yes, it's your turn. My time is over with this team and you are the future."

"You can at least play the next few weeks."

"True, but I want you to have the chance to play the rest of this season. You need to get all the playing time you can so that's why I am leaving early and asked that you start the rest of the season."

"I don't know what to say to that except thank you."

"That's all you need to say."

George extended his hand to shake Ernie's. Banks was kind of taken aback by this because every since he had been in the big leagues nobody rushed to extend that kind of respect to him. There were too many people still trying to figure out if he really belonged in the majors. Ernie shook George's hand and then he said.

"Maybe one day I will return the favor?"

"Maybe, but if you show the same act of kindness to someone else in the future then that will be alright with me and you can consider us even."

Ernie smiled and then George smiled back. Larson looked at his son and told him to shake Ernie Bank's hand and to remember his name because he would be hearing it for a long time. Ernie Banks was going to be a star. Jack did just that and Ernie told the young man that he hoped they would meet again sometime. The funny thing is they would in about seven years. George walked out of the Clubhouse and never looked back. He went back to Iowa to help run the family farm and he wouldn't return to Chicago until the day Jack pitched his first game at Wrigley Field.

George was right about Ernie Banks, he would become a star and play the position of shortstop for over ten years with the Cubs. He became one of the most dynamic defensemen in the infield for the Cubs as well as one of the greatest hitters the franchise had ever seen. The numbers he would put up at the plate would be unprecedented for a shortstop especially in that era. For most Cubs fans the event of Ernie Banks making his major league debut was the beginning of a new era in baseball while it also marked the end of one, the All –Star career of George Larson who could do it all, run, hit, and pitch.

As Banks was finishing his story he told Amy that he did have a chance to return the favor when Jack Larson was brought up to the Cubs in 1960. Three Chicago greats were brought up in the same year, Jack Larson, Ron Santo, and Billy Williams. And although Williams didn't play that long in 1960 a new era of Cubs baseball was born. Santo played in 95 games that year and Larson who at first was thought to be reliever proved to be a reliable starter and one of the Cubs regulars in the rotation. Unlike Santo and Williams who got their start in the minors Jack Larson had played for two years with the University of Iowa before going into the big leagues. He wanted to try college first and that proved too small for him as he dominated the college ranks – the only place for him after that was major league baseball.

Jack was a nasty pitcher with too many weapons in his arsenal, but he was also a student of the game having been taught by his grandfather and father. He could strike guys out just as well without throwing a 98 mile an hour fastball, which he could do effectively.

At first the Cubs skipper Lou Boudreau wanted to just use Jack Larson as a reliever, but the Cubs were so bad that year and didn't have enough starters who weren't past their prime that one day in July of that year the skipper decided to let Larson start as a rookie.

Ernie Banks remembered that day well because as the team leader it was his job to mentor the rookies and help them anyway he could. That's exactly what he had to do with Jack Larson during his first start at Wrigley Field. They were playing the Dodgers that day and Sandy Koufax was on the mound or the Dodgers, a very intimidating factor to say the least. And of course George Larson was there as well watching.

Jack Larson was nervous and it made him out of synch early on Banks remembered. Amy had heard part of this story, but she had never heard the part that Banks was about to tell her. Jack loaded the bases with two walks and a hit. The he walked in the first run for the Dodgers. The Cubs skipper was about to pull him when Ernie Banks called time and walked to the mound. Despite the bad situation and most of the players as well as the fans getting angry Ernie was jolly and talked with Jack in that playful excited way that he always had no matter what. He asked Jack. "Are you nervous?"

"Just a little, but I got this."

"I know you do...you just have to find your rhythm and it's taking a little while longer since it's your first start."

"I hope that's what it is."

"Don't worry we all get out of synch from time to time. You saw me strike out swinging yesterday ... that was ugly, but it was a beautiful day to play baseball yesterday wasn't it? So it wasn't a complete waste. "

Jack smiled at the comment and then asked Ernie. "Is that what you wanted to talk to me about?"

"Sure, I don't need to tell you you're in a pickle here; you're smart enough to know that."

"I guess, but what do you think I should do."

"Just throw the next pitch without thinking, throw it wild if you have to and get it out of your system. Then you pitch like you know how. "

That was all Ernie said and then he patted Larson on the shoulder and walked back to his position in the infield. Jack took a deep breath and threw the next pitch as hard as he could and with his eyes closed. The pitch ran inside too much and pushed the Dodger batter back off the plate. He didn't quite crowd the plate so much after that.

It didn't take anything else after that, Jack found his rhythm and ended up striking out the side to get out of the inning. He only gave up 4 more hits throughout the game and he went the full nine innings. Holding the Dodgers to 5 hits back then was not an easy feat. Koufax that day didn't fare much better and the Cubs were able to win 4-3 that day for Larson's first victory as a Cubs pitcher. At the end of the game Ernie saw George sitting behind the Cubs dugout about 5 rows up. He tipped his cap to him and George who was wearing his playing hat from the early 50's took his hat off as to say thank you for helping Jack that day and returning the favor.

Amy commented to Ernie Bank, "no one has ever told me before that it was you who gave my grandfather words of encouragement that day."

Ernie smiled and replied. "That's because most people don't remember that I did say something to your grandfather in the first inning, most people remember your grandfather outpitching Sandy Koufax that day, but I got to show a little kindness to Jack the same way George Larson did by stepping aside and giving me a chance to play."

Of course Amy and Ernie talked about other things during the rest of the interview, but they were not as fascinating. To Amy it was the small acts of kindness that veterans can show a rookie and help start their careers. Ernie pointed out it didn't stop there because there were plenty of times that Jack Larson would show him the same kindness throughout his career. It was those kinds of acts that really made a ball club a team and more importantly a family. Of course the Cubs' teams from the 60's have hundreds of those types of the stories this one was more meaningful to her. And when Amy wrote the article for the news paper the next day she included a supplement in her blog with the paper titled "A Family of Cubs and Random Acts of Kindness. It was something that every fan could appreciate because as a fan you're a part of the family with

even more stories of the kindness that go on and we never
know about. And as someone pointed out to her at the
paper, what's the best kind of an act of kindness, a ticket to
the ball game when you're needing an escape from the
everyday reality After all there's no better place to be than
the ballpark. Of course if you're Ernie Bank you would just
say, "let's play two."

10

Leo, Lou, and the Comeback Kids

It was the All-Star Break, and the first half of the season for the Cubs was not what everybody expected, especially coming off of the year before. They were plagued by injuries and bats went cold. Pitching was keeping them alive, but barely. The worst thing was all the sports writers and most of the fans had written the Cubs off for the year. They were sitting in fourth place 5 games below .500. About the only player that seemed to be having a good year was the young player from Japan that they brought over to give them a lefty in the line-up. The other lefty, Milt Bradley, that was supposed to be so good and resurrect the line-up turned out to be the biggest bust of all and he was proving to be confrontational with the fans. He was booed every time he came up to bat and his batting wasn't too spectacular, it was .215.

Things were not going so well for the Cubs, but they were about to get some rest. No one on the team was selected for the All-Star Game. As for Ryan Larson, he was getting ready to start throwing again in about two weeks. So while Amy didn't have many good things to write about, at least that was something. She was miserable watching the Cubs just like most fans and she didn't even have any good stories to tell Chris, but she was glad of one thing about him. While things were going well with him he at least was too busy with work to even pay attention to the Cubs and so he was spared the agony.

The Cubs would spend a couple of days during the break getting some much needed practice and it gave Amy a chance to see her brother at the ball park. Being injured didn't make him a very fun person to be around, and that was coming from his girlfriend Tara who had just been transferred back home to Chicago full time. Amy saw him at the ballpark over the weekend trying to be useful even though he couldn't do much. She walked up to him and gave him a hug. She had to ask

"So how is everything looking with the team?"

"Is that a journalist asking or my sister?" Ryan asked.

She gave him a dirty look and replied. "You should know better than that."

"I have to ask, we've been getting a lot of bad press these days and the last person I need it from is my sister."

"I write the facts, but I haven't lost my faith in you and this team."

Ryan laughed and said. "You must be the only one. It doesn't take long for this city to turn on us."

"And yet they still fill the stands. It's hard to get a ticket to a game."

"Maybe, and I guess I should be used to it considering we grew up with this."

Amy smiled and said. "I'm sure it's different when you're a player...Dad always said it was."

"So are you here to do an interview?"

[142]

"I have a couple to do, but I also wanted to see how everybody was doing and to see if we have anything to look forward to in the second half of the season."

Ryan smirked at the comment. He said. "Everybody is worn out and nobody can seem to figure out why they can't hit. It's getting so bad that I think Lou is going to have to get a witch doctor out here to tap all the bats with chicken bones and cut off a live rooster's head to take the curse off of the bats."

Amy laughed and replied. "Nice Bull Durham reference."

"Did you like that?"

Soto the catcher overheard the comment and said in a sarcastic tone. "Don't make fun of that, you don't want my mother up here taking care of business. It's not a pretty sight."

Ryan said to him. "No woman looks good trying to cut off a rooster's head."

Soto smiled and Amy laughed. At least part of the team seemed to be in good spirits. That's when Amy remembered a story their grandfather used to tell when they were kids about slumps in baseball. Amy reminded Ryan of the story and how Leo Durocher approached the subject. After 20 years of losing, PK Wrigley finally hired a manager with a winning record to turn the ballclub around and that manager was Leo Durocher. He had played with Babe Ruth and championship ball clubs with the Brooklyn Dodgers and the New York Giants. From the first day of his arrival he declared that the Cubs were no longer an 8th place team and he was right. He also declared that the days of slumps were over, the Cubs were going to be consistent and even though they would have some ups and downs they were going be to be a winning team. Both Ryan and Amy knew the story behind that – they had grown up with it. The moral of the story was that the attitude on the Cubs team from 1966 – 1971 was going to change. Ryan told Amy that was something she should write about because

not many people knew that story and every fan should
know it.

So Amy decided that she would tell the story through
the newspaper and her blog – at least it would be a more
uplifting story than writing about the Cubs' losing streak
and string of injuries. Fans needed a good inspirational
story about their Cubs for a change. But like all of her
stories there was a back story to it. Perhaps it was that way
because Chris, who she mostly told these stories to, didn't
know a lot about the Cubs, but then again every story a
journalist tells always has some background to it.

When Leo "The Lip" Durocher took over, he had what
managers for the Cubs had never had, a blank check book
to get the players he needed and total control of baseball
operations for the Cubs. He immediately started making
some serious changes, he got rid of the ball players on the
team that weren't cutting it and started making trades to
get the ones that were going to make the winning difference.
Jack Larson was almost traded in 1966, but he was kept
around because in Leo's mind at that time he was the only
consistent pitcher that the Cubs had. In 1966 the Cubs
traded for the All-Star catcher Randy Hundley, pitchers Bill
Hands and the great Fergie Jenkins. They also brought up
from the minors, Glenn Becket, Don Kessinger, and a
phenomenal lefty on the mound named Ken Holtzmen. He
was referred to as the Cubs' Sandy Koufax. While the Cubs
in 1966 finished in 10th place losing 103 games that year
the improvements that Leo made were about to take effect,
because by 1967 the Cubs had one of the best pitching
staffs in the Majors, and it was only a matter of time before
they all fell in sync and started winning ball games.

Leo always said that it didn't matter how many good
bats you had in the lineup, pitching is what wins games. He
was proved right because in 1967 the Cubs were not a last
place team anymore. They would finish in third place at
the end of the season but on one glorious day in July they
would get to first place, something that had not happened
since 1945. But of course it was the consistency that

always seemed to be the Cubs Achilles' Heel. Leo hated to lose and he always voiced his frustration. The attitude he brought to the Cubs was not always a pleasant one, but he was the smartest baseball man that the Cubs had, had in 30 years, at least to some people. He knew how to get the best out of his ball players and he could recognize talent. For example when they found Fergie, he was only a relief pitcher for the Phillies, but with the Cubs he would anchor the pitching staff and win 20 or more games 5 consecutive seasons for them.

To say that Leo was a son of a bitch was putting it mildly, but everybody respected him and he would find hidden talents in his ball players that would make them better on the field. When a man could do that, the son of a bitch part gets taken with a grain of salt. Of course if you ask most of the players back then they would tell you "he may be a son of a bitch, but he's our son of a bitch." And that was never clearer than in 1967 when the Cubs had hit upon a losing streak that nobody could figure out how to get out of. Leo would have to do something about it. Leo was frustrated and had one of his fiery inspiration speeches in the clubhouse before a game against the Pirates in June. The Cubs had started out strong that year and had a winning record after the first month of the season, but something happened and they started losing in May. Leo was not going to put up with it considering that he knew the level of talent that his team possessed. That's the way Jack Larson put it, according to Amy, when he told the story.

It was the beginning of June and Leo called the team into the clubhouse during one of their off days. He was mad and everybody knew it, but he didn't start cussing like a sailor as he did sometimes – he didn't even throw anything across the room like he did at times. He looked at everybody who was desperately waiting for some kind of answer from the wise old man that had been around the game of baseball longer than any of them had been alive. Leo finally said to all of them.

"Alright, playing childish games is over from this day on until the end of the season. If all you are going to do is act like a bunch a little whiny children, playing the game out there as if winning doesn't matter then I will give all of you some milk and cookies right now and you can be on your way because there is no place for you on this team." Leo looked over at the table of cookies and cartons of milk. The players looked over at them too and were surprised that there really was milk and cookies. Some of the players were actually thinking that the metaphor might be good, but it was sure was a waste of milk and cookies.

Leo spoke up again and said. "Now I know that this game is supposed to be fun and you're supposed to play it that way, but let's face it, nobody likes to lose and the game isn't very fun when you do. There's too much talent sitting in this clubhouse for you to not be winning. And I don't think this club is a sub .500 team. I can cuss at you, I can throw things at you, and be the biggest son of bitch you've ever encountered...a bigger son of a bitch than I usually am. But...I am not going to do that. You know how to win and you also know that you can't win without giving everything you have. Can any of you honestly tell me that you've done that? Well, can you?"

There was mumbling among the players and finally a few of them spoke up and said in unison, "No." Leo looked at everybody with a stern look and replied. "That's what I thought!"

He continued in his speech. "If that's the case then what are you going to do about it? If you are man enough then you will go out there from this day on and play the game I know you can. Don't be children, be men, and play this game with guts, with every part of your soul...with every ounce of strength you have. If you do that then I know that we will be winners and that the days of losing in this town will be over. But the choice is yours and I will tell this if you don't like it here...if you don't like what I just said then you can get the hell out of my clubhouse because I don't have any use for you. "

The players all looked at each other and it was as if they were all in agreement. They could play half ass and just get by, maybe they would win or maybe not. Or they could play like champions, playing hard on every play, diving for balls to get the out and they could swing like there was no tomorrow. If they failed at the plate then at least they would go down trying. Banks was the first to stand up and he said. "Let's do this…let's play like we know how to." The team agreed. They all started to walk out of the club, but Ron Santo walked over to the milk and cookies and grabbed some while pouring himself a glass of milk. Leo gave him a dirty look and asked him. "What the hell are you doing?"

Santo replied. "No use letting the milk and cookies go to waste. I can still play hard with the milk and cookies." Truth was he actually needed the sugar. Nobody in the Cubs knew that he was a diabetic. Even he didn't know much about the disease, but he had the heart of a lion and that's what made him play so well despite the disease. Leo just looked at Santo and said. "Get the fuck out of my clubhouse." Jack was the one that walked over to Santo and escorted him out before Leo actually did throw something at him for being a smart-ass. Santo just smiled at the comment.

Jack once told Amy and Ryan when telling this story that he couldn't say for sure whether it was the speech by Leo or the fact that they didn't want to be losers anymore that inspired all of them to play harder. Whatever the reason that's exactly what the 1967 team did and they started winning. The bats were on fire and the pitching staff was the best in baseball and for a few months it looked as if the Cubs were going to go all the way. But the day they actually got to first place, a bright beautiful July day, was a special one for Jack. He would throw his first no hitter in baseball. Jack had turned into a seasoned veteran and given the freedom to be the pitcher he could be made him very dominant on the mound. As it turned out they were playing the Pirates again.

Jack was solid that day and no one could hit off him. He was perfect through six innings and the pitch count wasn't even high. The Cubs managed to get 6 runs on the board from a Billy Williams three-run homer in the fourth and RBI doubles by both Banks and Santo. In the 7th Jack's curveball was gone and perfection was almost lost when a blast by Roberto Clemente into the left field bleachers turned out to be foul. He would end up walking Clemente for the only walk of the game. Leo almost pulled Jack because he had lost momentum, but Jack Larson was a smart pitcher and a breaking ball inside to the next batter made him pull for a grounder to the shortstop which was tuned into a 6-4-3 double play to end the inning.

The Cubs had been tied for first place with the St. Louis Cardinals for the past week, but couldn't seem to get past them because both teams had won six in a row. The eighth inning was trouble and Jack would get his second walk of the game. That's when Leo went out to mound to talk to Larson and of course Hundley followed too as well as Banks from first. He looked at Larson and asked one simple question.

"Are you done? You've had perfection up to this point, but now you're all over the plate." It was true his curve was completely gone and now going into the dirt. The slide was about a mile off the plate and his fastballs inside were nearly taking the batters kidneys out.

Larson looked at the skipper and replied. "I can get these guys out." Leo stared at him for a moment and then looked over at Hundley the catcher. He asked him.

"What do you think?"

Randy said. "He is battling."

"I said tell me what you think. You're my captain on the field. You should know if he's done."

Jack was already at point. He was five outs away from no-hitter and while most managers wouldn't take away the opportunity when he was so close he also knew that Leo was just the kind of son of bitch that would actually pull him at this point to try and win the game. Bank chimed in. "Skip I think he can get these guys out."

"I'm not really asking Banks, Hundley will know the right answer. "

Randy took a deep breath, looked up at the Majestic old fashioned green scoreboard in center field and said. "He's not done yet, he can do it."

"Alright then," Leo said. "But if he gets into trouble you call time and we'll get someone out here. " Looking at Jack he said. "Don't fuck this up, get these guys out."

After three balls in a row, Jack finally made the next batter hit into another 6-4-3 double play to end the inning. The Cubs went down three in a row at the top of the eighth so Jack didn't have much time to rest. As he was leaving the dugout Leo said to him. "Why don't you get the next three batters out so we can go home early." Larson smiled at him. Leo replied again. "I need outs…get me those three outs Jack. Year's later three outs would become synonymous when a Larson was on the mound for the Cubs.

Jack didn't waste time with the first batter, three fastballs that if they had been clocked would have been 97 or 98 mile an hour easy, and the batter was down on strikes. The second batter took a little longer. He actually got Larson to a full count before he sent a pop fly into left field for the second out. The last batter went down in a way that only a great pitcher could get him out. He pitched inside for the first two pitches backing him off the plate; it was a set up for the final pitch that would get him out. The batter had one strike and one ball on him. The next pitch by Larson got away from him and nearly took the batter's head off for another ball, but that pitch even helped setting the batter up for a strikeout. The fourth pitch was Jack Larson's famous sinking fastball – it was basically a slider with speed behind it that when you first saw it looked like a fastball right down the middle, but when it was at the plate the bottom would drop out from underneath it and curve to where it was almost in the dirt. The batter would swing right over it and that's what the Pirate batter did. The next was a thing of beauty and since the batter was already backed up off the plate more than he should have been because he was pitched inside on the first two pitches Jack could throw a hard slider off the outside of the plate and he wouldn't be able to reach enough to hit. That's what the batter did and he struck out by chasing a pitch off the plate – it was embarrassing to the batter to say the least.

Jack had pitched his first no-hitter and it was the game that finally put the Cubs into first place. The Cubs celebrated by carrying Jack Larson off the field, but it wasn't the most memorable moment of that day. The flags alongside the scoreboard in centerfield always signified the team's placing in the division, the flags were not usually changed until the next day, but the Cubs fans wouldn't leave the stadium until the flags were changed that day. They waited a half an hour before the scoreboard keeper finally came out and did it – that was the official moment that the Cubs were in first place and it had been 22 years since that had happened in Chicago. Steve Larson was there the day his father threw the no-hitter and he told his dad that he had never seen the Cubs in first place. Jack just told his son, now you have and it won't be the last time either.

It was great that day, not because of the record or that the Cubs had finally gotten into first place, but because the team had played the way the game was always meant to be played. They played the game with the hearts of children – they had fun playing the game. And as Randy Hundley commented one time, "we didn't play the game for the money, we played because we loved it and truth be told we would have paid to play the game of professional baseball." That kind of attitude is what made them winners in the late 60's even when they finished third in 1967 and again in 1968. The 1969 season would be different, though.

11

The Dream of 1969

It was the day before the Cubs were supposed to be playing again in the second half of the season. Lou, the Cubs manager, was in his office going over reports when he picked up a copy of the Chicago Sun-Times and saw the letter box in the top right corner of the front page with the title of Amy Larson's Column for this week – it was titled "The Fun of Baseball and Being a Cub." He put down what he was doing and started reading. The column was about Leo Durocher's speech in 1967, the Cubs getting to first place, and Jack Larson's no-hitter. He finished the article and smiled – he liked it and usually never liked anything that sports writers had to say in the papers, but the article was charming. That's when Larry, the pitching coach, walked in. Lou looked up and asked him. "Did you read Amy Larson's column in the times today?"

"Yeah, this morning…good article." Larry replied.

"I didn't know that about Durocher, did you?"

"The son of a bitch part I knew about, but never figured he was one to give inspirational speeches."

"That is surprising, but I think there is some truth in what she wrote."

"You think you've been too hard on the team and that's why they're closing?"

"I don't know about that, but you remember when this game was fun and we couldn't wait to play every day?"

Larry smiled and said. "Yeah I do…the game should always be fun, don't you think?"

"That's what I'm saying, maybe we don't have enough fun with this game and perhaps we worry too much about winning. I'm beginning to think that's what's missing these days and I don't want to see us treat this like a job we hate for the rest of the season."

"Well I guess it beats being mad and throwing bases at the umpires."

Lou smiled at the comment because he had been ejected from a game years ago for throwing first base into the home teams' dugout when a bad call had been made at first base. The incident became synonymous with his bad temper on the field even though he had mellowed out in the last few years, but the sports writers still like to call him the Bobby Knight of the baseball field. Lou looked at Larry and said. "I want us to have a new attitude for the rest of the season – win or lose this year I want us to have the right attitude. I want us to have fun this year. "

"Then tell the team that." Larry replied to Lou.

The next day the Cubs played their first game of the second half of the 2008 season. They had not been living up to their potential and certainly weren't playing like the championship team they were the year before. Before the game was to start Lou had the team gather around the middle of the clubhouse like he did when he would go over game plans with them. He needed to talk to them and it had nothing to do with that game's lineup or strategy. He looked around and saw a team that seemed to not care anymore or a team that was already worn down and wanted the season to be over. He paused for a moment and looked around the room and waited until the entire team was looking at him. The only player that seemed annoyed at what was going was Milt Bradley – the left handed bat they traded for who was supposed to be explosive in the lineup and turned out to be a dud. Everybody else was listening intently. Lou began to speak and he was speaking from his heart, not some everyday speech to get the team going for that game. This was personal because of the future as a team and whether they all had the chance to be winners again.

He said to them. "The first half of this season has not been what we wanted. Let's face it, it's been really bad, but I'm not here today to scold you as if you were children for playing bad. We all know in the game that you go through rough patches and hot streaks. But it has occurred to me that I never asked you at the beginning of the season one important question. We've been so busy thinking about winning and being just as good, if not better than last year and we've basically treated this year as a job that we have to do in order to survive or keep our jobs instead of something that we want to do. So let me ask you men, have you had fun this year...have you had fun playing baseball at all this year?"

Nobody knew how to respond to the question, Ryan looked around the room to see of the players who had been in the league a lot longer than him had an answer. He was looking for their answers because as a rookie he really didn't have one. Derrek Lee finally spoke up and said. "It's been fun at times, but there are a lot of times that we didn't have fun and we probably should have." Ryan Dempster, one of the Cubs starters and the team comedian replied. "We have fun winning, but who has fun losing...really, am I wrong?" The team laughed in unison and then Lou responded to the comment. "Thanks Dem, I think that goes without saying. You're a big help."

Dempster replied back. "Glad I could be."

Lou continued in his speech. " But you guys see what I am saying, there's one element that we've been missing...I don't think we've had enough fun and I would get out there with you and show you, but I'm too fucking old and fat." The team laughed again at the comment. "I don't care what the rest of this season turns out to be as long as we play the best we can and we have the same kind of fun as we did when we were kids playing this game in some sandlot. I know what this year is in Cubs history and I don't care. What matters is how you play the game, not whether we win or break any records. We're going to win some of these game and we are going to lose some. If you play this game with same level of fun and joy as you had when you were kids then the rest will take care of itself. Every one of you already know that you're a better team than the way you've been playing, but I think you've forgotten what it means to play this game the way it should be played. And I'm probably to blame for that. So as of today we are going to have a new attitude. For the rest of the season we're going to enjoy each day we play and be the best we can. Let that determine if we win or lose, but don't hold back and play with everything you have. And most importantly have fun doing it."

The team looked around at each other and there were smiles on each other's faces, something that had not been there in a while. They knew the rest of the season was not going to be easy and the Central Division in the National League was the most competitive division on baseball. It was not going to be easy, but each one of them knew that they would have fun no matter what the outcome was this season. They didn't have to say it for each of them to know it. And if there was any indication that it was going to be different it was the outcome of that day's game. They beat the first place Cardinals 11-3. The bats that seemed nonexistent in the first of the season came alive. Things were changing that season. Amy, who was at the ballpark that day, took note of it and it reminded her of how 1969 started for the Cubs and she also knew that it was a story Chris had not heard yet even though he was becoming a Cubs fan now. If he got the chance and the Cubs were playing in the afternoon he would watch the game in his office. Of course, working for a Chicago Law firm, it was allowed.

Later that evening, Amy, who was spending most of her nights at Chris' place, decided to tell him the story of the 1969 season and its ill-fated outcome. The 2007 season for the Cubs reminded her of that since they had won 97 games, were the best team in baseball, and would lose in the first three games of the playoffs. But just like the 1969 season, nothing could take away the feeling that fans had for the Cubs with how they had started the season. 1969, just like 2007, was one most disappointing seasons that the Cubs and their fans had to endure, but that's the way tragic stories tend to go.

Over dinner, Amy started telling Chris about the season. In 1968 the Cubs finished in third place for the second straight year, but they had improved again and had become a superstar team. The Cubs for the 1969 season had the best pitching rotation in the game –they had five pitchers that could easily be in the number one spot for any other team. Their rotation was anchored by Fergie Jenkins and had Ken Holtzman, Phil Reagan, Bill Hands, and Jack Larson. All of them were unstoppable and three of them would win 20 or more games that year. The Cubs started off that with the best record in baseball – they went 11-1. And that kind of success continued throughout the year. Amy explained to Chris how the Mets, who had only been in the league a few years up to that point got the name the Amazing Mets. They were in last place at the beginning of the season and stayed there for two-thirds of the season, but at the end of the season they were in first place. Amy told Chris in an angry tone that it does happen in baseball and unfortunately it happened to the Cubs in '69

1969 was a turbulent year in American history. We were at the height of the Vietnam War and Americans were growing angry with it. Richard Nixon was in the White House. Bobby Kennedy and Martin Luther King, Jr. were both assassinated the year before and of course, who could forget the riots and violence at the Democratic National Convention in Chicago in 68' But in the summer of 1969 Chicago was filled with excitement, and everything that was bad in the world was forgotten because the Cubs were playing Championship Baseball. As a journalist, Amy pointed out one of her favorite headlines from an old newspaper - it was from the Chicago Tribune on July 21, 1969. It was the day after Apollo 11 landed on the moon. The front page headline was for the moon landing, but right below was a headline for the Cubs, who had won a game that day and were still in first place.

The newspaper had similar headlines for the weekend of Woodstock. There were two great moments in history that year, and the Cubs were in first place. 1969 was a great year and, of course, who could forget the Bleacher Bums, which would come into existence that year as well, after a Life Magazine reporter took a photo of one with a sign that said "hit the Bleacher Bum." Amy was like a kid in a candy store when she told this story. But every Cubs fan smiles when they talk about the summer of 1969 because no matter what the outcome was anybody who was there could not deny the memories of that summer.

Even thought the season started out great and for five months it stayed that way it was in late August things changed – the Cubs stopped hitting and they ran out of steam. However, there were a few shining moments for the Cubs. On July 25th Jack Larson threw a perfect game against Houston. It is unarguably the best game he ever threw for the Cubs and he proved that day why he would be a hall of famer. A week later during a three-game series in Atlanta, Ken Holtzman threw a no-hitter against the Braves, who were in first place in the National League Western Division. Everybody seemed to know or at least they thought they knew that the Cubs were going all the way that year. They were simply the best team in baseball that year and their pitching staff proved it. How many teams have a pitcher throw a no-hitter and a perfect game in the same year? What made the series so remarkable was the fact the Cubs dominated the Braves on their home field and the Bleacher Bums with their yellow hardhats who traveled to Atlanta to be at the game. They filled the bleachers and brought a little bit of Wrigleyville with them. But Holtzman's no-hitter and Larson's perfect game would be the last great moments for the Cubs that year, for the bats went silent and the same team that started the year disappeared. After that game, the Cubs were in first leading by 7 1/2 games but the New York Mets somehow started playing real baseball during the summer and slowly started to climb in the standings. The Cubs would go 15 - 25 the rest of the season and the Mets would be almost perfect.

Of course, there are a lot of theories to why the Cubs collapsed that year, and the curse always top the list. That story gets talked about more because of Ron Santo and the Black Cat incident. During a crucial two-game series with the Mets at Shea Stadium, in the second game a black cat would jump from the stands and run towards Santo, who was on deck about to bat, and runs a complete circle around him before running into the Cubs dugout and disappearing forever into the night. What happened next in the series seemed like a dream – Santo would get hit in the hand by Mets Pitcher Jerry Koosman and the Cubs would end up losing both games to the Mets and their hold on first place.

The thing was as Amy explained; curses are always more fun to talk about than the actual facts. The Cubs lost steam; they were run down by August because Leo Durocher always had the same lineup and didn't rest his starters. Where most managers use their bench a lot more in today's game to give the starters a break from time to time, Leo kept the same guys in the lineup that he could depend on to win ballgames. At the beginning of spring training that year, Leo made out his everyday lineup with Randy Hundley playing catcher, Santo at third, Glen

Beckett at second, Don Kessinger at shortstop, Banks at first, with Billy Williams, Jim Hickman, and Don Young in the outfield. These guys played over a 150 games and were simply worn down by September. And as many of the players from that team have commented in later years if they had, had more days off or maybe played more night games. At the time the Cubs played only day games at Wrigley Field since the stadium did not have lights. No matter the real reason it became known as the greatest collapse in Baseball history and on the day the season ended the Cubs were 8 games behind the Mets in the East Division having to settle for second place. It was sad, but a way of life for the Cubs.

Amy had a sad tone as she told the end of the story, but she perked up and went on to say nobody could ever take away that year and the memories that fans had. Jack Larson had always said that it was the most fun he had playing baseball in Chicago and he never played with a better group of guys. Leo would take full blame for what happened that year and in later years apologize to fans. But it was Ron Santo who had the most profound thing to say about that year – "People were talking about war, politics, and economics that year all around the country, but not in Chicago...they were talking about the Cubs." Ron Santo pointed out in his autobiography that fans still come up to him and the other players thanking them for the memories they gave them in 1969.

Amy had a tear in her eye when mentioning the last part. Chris smiled at her and leaned in and kissed her. Then he told her. "Despite losses and the heartbreaks I would never trade the memories I have playing football and sharing them with my dad. I think that's the way it is with you and after hearing all of your stories so far this season I can see why."

She smiled and asked him, "Why is that, you think?"

"Because being a Cubs fan is a way of life and there is no greater faith than being a fan. It's a bond with fans, with the team, and the sport you love. That bond is greater with the Cubs and their fans than any other sports team. That's why you can automatically be friends with another fan. And even though the team may disappoint you at times and even though you may have your heart broken with them, they will never let you down. That's because of the joy the Cubs can give you whether you're watching them on TV or sitting in the stand – what other sports team can give you that feeling?"

Amy smiled again at him and asked. "You just figured that out?"

"I've been figuring it out this year and I have to admit I have become a fan and will be one for life."

"It sort of happens that way, but there are worse things that can happen to you."

"I don't mind it at all because I've never felt the kind of joy I have when I'm with you at a game. No other baseball team has made me baseball fan, but the Cubs did this year. Although I still would have hit on you that night in Texas if you didn't like baseball...because you are beautiful."

She leaned in and kissed him this time. The she said. "You know my father fell in love with baseball in 1969. He wasn't much if a fan up to that point and rarely went to the games. He wanted to be a police officer, but that year changed everything for him. He spent more time at the ballpark in '69 and found his love for baseball and the Cubs. After that year he started playing baseball and never wanted to do anything else. He also became a Cubs fan that year."

Chris laughed and replied. "You're right, it's contagious, but that's a good thing. "

The same day that Amy told Chris about the '69 season Ryan Larson was making his last rehab start at Double A Tennessee the place where he had gotten his start as a Cub. He was feeling a little bit of pain, but it wasn't enough to keep him from pitching and he was pitching well for the most part. He had completed all of his simulated starts and short outings, He had pitched 3 innings in one game as a reliever and everything was fine.

He was able to find his location, although a few pitches had gotten away from him. Most importantly, he was able to strike out batters, but he did not have the same velocity on his fastball – it was only traveling about 89 or 90 miles an hour. Ryan was having to rely on other pitches to get guys out, at least the curve was working good enough, but it was Double A ball, there was no way to tell yet if it would be good enough for the Majors. But while all of this was going on he was learning to pitch more inside and be more effective with it.

Ryan was solid for the first two innings of play and he had two strikeouts, but nothing over-powering. The third inning was when the batters got the better of him and he loaded the bases with no outs after giving up three straight singles. He walked the next batter while allowing the other team to score their first run. Still he didn't have an out and the score had been 0-0 up to that point. Finally Jody, the manager, went out to the mound to talk to him. He didn't get mad at Ryan, he just asked one question. "Is your wrist hurting because if you need to come out we can delay the game and get somebody warmed up?"

"I'm fine," Ryan replied. "I can get these guys out."

"Okay then, I need three outs and don't try to be cute."

"You mean like my dad?"

Jody smiled at the comment because that's exactly what he meant. He said. "You're doing good pitching inside, but the curve is working for you as well." Then he walked back to the dugout. Ryan took a deep breath and threw a breaking ball inside. The batter hit a one hopper to the pitcher's mound. Instead of going for the easy out Ryan picked it up and threw it to the catcher for the force out at home. He gotten the first out and saved a run. The next batter, it took him seven pitches before he struck him, but Ryan was still afraid to really throw a fastball -he mainly did changeups and other off-speed pitches. Two pitches later he forced the batter to pop it up for the third out. Ryan had gotten out of the inning by pitching smart and

confusing batters with different pitches just like Greg
Maddux used to do when he was with the Cubs, both times.
Ryan would pitch another two innings and he would only
allow one more run off a solo home run, but the
performance was good enough to get him back to the
Majors and be cleared to pitch. The thing was his wrist was
hurting and it hurt more every time he threw the curve. He
might have been ready to pitch again according to the
catchers, but not even Ryan was completely sure if he
should be back. He was about to find out in ten days when
he made his first start with the Cubs since early May.

12

When One Era Ends
Another One Begins

August had finally arrived for the Cubs and it came
with a winning streak. The Cubs were different ball team
than they were before the All-Star break and it was pitching
that was getting the job done. All the pitchers in the
starting rotation were doing well. Ryan Dempster had only
lost 3 games so far in the season and had a perfect record
at home. Lilly had only lost 5 games – he had won all of his
games after the All-Star Break and overcame a 1-5 record.
He was perfect on the road. And Big Z, well, he was
dominating everybody with his fastball. As the Cubs
pregame was getting underway on WGN with Len and Bob
this is what they were talking about. But they also
mentioned that the Cubs offense which had been in a
slumber the first half of the season had come alive. For the
month of July, the Cubs had the best record in baseball
and more importantly they were having fun, as Len and
Bob pointed out during their pre-game broadcast. But this
day in August when the Milwaukee Brewers were in town

marked a big day for the Cubs, at least it was for some people.

Ryan Larson was making his debut back from the DL list after almost three months. No one knew if Ryan was really ready to be back, but he was cleared to play and the best way to see if he was a hundred percent was to let him pitch in the majors. Ryan was a little nervous and he looked it like during warm-ups, he was having some control issues with the fastball and the sinker, but the true test would be on the mound during the game. He was facing a tough lineup for the Brewers. However, he had had some success against them before. Chris was at the game to see Ryan pitch as well as Tara, his girlfriend. She had been to quite a few games this year despite her work. Of course, this was a big one. And then there was Mary Larson, Ryan and Amy's mother, she had to be there to see if he really was ready to be back…you know how mothers can be.

Amy was sitting in the broadcasters' booth where media usually sat to cover the game. The reporter from the Chicago Tribune who usually covered the Cubs saw her and walked over. His name was Mike and he was a jackass. That's what most people thought about him and Amy hated him probably more than most — she could handle him being a jackass, but he thought he knew about baseball when in truth he didn't know a damn thing. That's what annoyed her more than anything and the fact that he really didn't know anything about the Cubs, which was just an insult to the team and the newspaper he worked for. Mike always said snide remarks to her and it was his way of flirting, which just came off creepy more than anything. He walked over to her and said "Well I guess we're going to see if your brother is like your grandfather or like your dad today…the perpetual screw up under pressure."

Amy gave him a dirty look and said. "I don't need to hear how women describe you in bed." The people around her heard what she said and started laughing including Ron Santo who was broadcasting for WGN radio. He was only about 10 feet from Amy and had to give her a smile and thumbs up for her clever retort. No one really liked this guy and he couldn't just keep his mouth shut, he had to respond. "I always new kitty liked to play."

Amy gave him another dirty look and replied. "And you wonder why no woman would marry you or go out with you, for that matter. Once a creep, always a creep!" As she finished her comment the game was about to get underway, the national anthem was finishing. Now it was time to see if Mike was right about her brother, but something else occurred to Amy. It was a beautiful day at Wrigley field and as Ernie Banks was fond of saying, "it's a great day to play too!" That's the way she felt every time she was at an afternoon game at Wrigley Field and the sun was shining...it always seemed to shine a little extra brighter over Wrigley Field, but then again that was just a fan's perspective.

The game started and it didn't take Ryan Larson long to get the first out. Two pitches and he made the batter pop it up behind the plate to where Soto, the catcher, could get the out. Ryan would walk the next batter, his fast ball was getting away from him and coming too much off the plate causing to him not to throw strikes. Ryan gave up his first hit of the game with the third batter; his slider didn't have enough movement on it because the batter hit a little blooper to shallow right field. But despite the rocky start Ryan was able to make the fourth batter hit into a double play. So far so good, Ryan thought, but his wrist did hurt a little bit.

Ryan was able to get through the next few innings without much trouble. He was pitching smart without having to use a fastball– he was pitching inside and making the batters chase his curveball for strikes, but even he knew that he couldn't keep that up before they figured out what he was doing and he wouldn't have a curveball left. It was working through the first four innings. Most fans would say that he was having a strong outing so far, but not many knew that he was compensating because his fastball was off the map and the sinker was ending up in the dirt. The Cubs were able to get a few runs in the bottom of the fourth to help Ryan. In the fifth inning was when the wheels started to come off for him. He was at 85 pitches after walking the first batter. The next batter hit a double putting a man on second and third. Ryan then walked the next batter loading the bases. Soto called for time and went to the mound to see if Ryan was okay and to give him a breather. He asked him. "You alright? The curve doesn't have much on it anymore."

Ryan replied. "I'm fine, just not getting the movement I want on the ball."

"Is your wrist hurting?"

"Not enough to make me go out of the game."

"Well you've been pitching inside good. Try and hit the corners and perhaps you can get the next guy out."

Before Ryan could say anything, Larry, the pitching coach, was already at the mound to check on his starter. He looked at Ryan and said. "Well Larson, you're making things interesting now. Are you feeling alright?"

"I wish everybody would quit asking me that."

"How long has the wrist been hurting?"

"Since May," Ryan replied.

"You want to come out or do you think you can get out of the inning? I'll give you a chance to get out of the inning, but you're coming out after that."

"I can get these guys out.

Larry smiled and said. "Alright we're going to see. Get some breaking balls inside and some changeups...trying making them pop it up so we can get them out."

Ryan nodded in agreement and Larry patted him on the fanny and walked back to the dugout. Ryan threw a change up and made the next batter pop it up around first base. D-Lee was there to get it for the first out. But he couldn't get the next batter to fall for it. He hit a blooper into centerfield and that allowed the men on second and third base to score. The Cubs only had a one run lead after that. Ryan lost his patience after that and slammed his glove down on the mound.

Amy was hanging her head in the press room at what happened. Len and Bob, the Cubs announcers, both commented that Ryan was mad and needed to regain his composure. Even Ron Santo commented on the air for WGN Radio. "Looks like Larson has let the fans see his frustration today, but that just shows how much of a competitor he is. Hopefully he will be able to get out of the inning."

Ryan was able to strike the next batter out. His sinker was finding its location now and it was a good pitch to fool batters with now that he didn't have a curveball left. However another hit scored another Brewer run. The game was tied. Pitchers were already up in the bullpen, but Lou, the manager wasn't going to pull Larson yet. He had one out to go and even though Ryan was approaching the 100-pitch mark they figured he could get the last out. He finally did after the last batter fouled off a number of pitches getting Ryan to the 107-pitch count, which was more than they wanted him to do that day. The last batter hit a ground ball to the second baseman for an easy out. The day had not gone according to plan for Ryan – he gave up three runs and let the Brewers tie the game. As he walked to the dugout he threw his glove inside against the back wall showing his frustration again as the TV cameras were on him. His was not completely ready to be back and he knew it and after that days performance it seemed like everybody at the ballpark that day knew it too.

His mother, who was at the game and sitting in the stands with Chris and Tara, commented after the inning ended, "I hope he's not too down on himself, it's only his first game back. Tara replied. "He's mad because he's hurting and he thinks if he tells anyone that he won't pitch the rest of the season. And he's also too stubborn to take himself out of the game."

"How do you know that?" May asked her.

"He's been hurting for a while — he always gets these certain looks. They're frustration looks for him and he's tries to hide them, but he's not that good at it."

"It seems that you're beginning to know my son more than me now. "

Tara smiled and said. "It's just because I see him a lot more than anyone now." It was true, they did spend most of their spare time together and had even moved in together, although only Amy and Chris really knew that. Ryan and Tara didn't want anyone to know how serious it was really getting between them, they didn't even want to admit it themselves, but they had been together for two years now and she got a transfer with her job when he made the big league club and wouldn't be in Tennessee anymore. She loved him and wanted to spend the rest of her life with him and he wanted that with her, he knew it the first moment he had a conversation with her and tried to convince her that baseball was the greatest sport in the world. But being a baseball wife is a tricky thing. Mary knew that all too well, being married to Steve Larson for ten years and being divorced from him for 15 years. Mary couldn't honestly say which was one worse because she still loved Ryan and Amy's father Steve Larson, but that's for another story.

The Cubs were able to regain the lead and win the game 5 to 3. The offense saved the game, but Ryan would not get the decision. D-Lee and Theriot, the second basemen for the Cubs, both came by Ryan's locker and told him that he pitched well that day and that they were glad he was back, but he didn't feel like a winner. He didn't have his old stuff and didn't even know if he could pitch well at all during the rest of the season. Although life is always up and down for a pitcher in the major leagues, a pitcher can't be up every day and they can't stay at the top forever. Both Steve Larson and Jack Larson knew that. The only difference between Steve and Jack was that Steve wasted his talent for the fast life and Jack had to deal with getting old in his 30's.

After the game ended Mike, the jerk from the Tribune that everybody hated, made a comment to Amy as she was packing up her things. "Your boy didn't look too good out there today, it would be a shame if he got washed up before he got to his prime, but all ball players get old before they're supposed to...ask your grandfather and dad." Then he walked away as Amy flipped him off for being a jerk. She would have hit him, but he was the kind of guy that would have filed assault chargers even though he got bitched slapped by a girl. The strange thing was Mike was right to a point. In the game of baseball, players tend to get old before they're supposed to and that's because of all the abuse they put their bodies through on the field, especially when they play for more than ten years. Players tend get old when still in their prime and that's never been truer than for pitchers.

Amy laughed to herself over the thought and she remembered how her grandfather Jack used to tell her and Ryan that the reason he didn't play as long as his dad or grandfather – he got old when it wasn't supposed to happen and it seemed to happen to him overnight. It seemed to happen to the entire '69 Cubs team except for a few players that went on to other teams and had great careers. The '69 team was the best team that the players of the era had ever played on and wouldn't ever be that way again when the season ended in tragedy. That was another story for Chris so he could understand fully how things can change from bad to worse in the blink of an eye. I'm sure that happens in other areas of life, but it seems to happen to all the time baseball.

Later that night over dinner Amy started to tell Chris about her '69 club and what happened to them. The same players returned in 1970, but they were never the same. I think everybody in Chicago expected them to be over the last season's late collapse and win it all, and judging by the talent they had they should have, but there were injuries on the Cubs and other teams had better ball clubs. Most thought that the Cubs had a better team that year, but they finished second to Roberto Clemente and the Pirates. The Pittsburg Pirates that year in the national league were too strong and would win it all. Ernie Banks spent most of the year on the DL list so that was a huge bat out of their lineup. The pitching staff was pretty average, they didn't have the same year as in '69 except for two players. Fergie Jenkins and Jack Larson would both win 20 games that year, but that was the only bright spot of 1970. The fact was some of the players were beginning to feel old after the season and that had to do with the constant play without some kind of rest from their manager Leo Durocher.

He still had the same philosophy that the best players should play all the time and that's how you win. The problem was the game had already changed too much from the 1940's when he was one of the greatest managers in the game. He also started to resent some of the best players on the team and one of them was Ernie Banks. As far as he was concerned Ernie should have retired a few years before 1970 and he let Ernie know it, but that was the son of a bitch attitude he could have at times. 1971 didn't fare any better than the '70 season; the Cubs finished 5th and losing became a way of life again. It had been nearly 25 years since the Cubs had had a winning season before 1969 and here they were right where they had been for so long. 1971 wasn't a very good year for Jack Larson. It was the first season that he was injured and he only played about two and half months during the season. After 1970 and 1971 somebody had to share the blame for the way the Cubs were playing and this time it wasn't going to be P.K. Wrigley, who didn't mind the "we don't have to win" attitude that had been with the Cubs for many years. This time the blame would get shifted to the manager, at least by the papers and the fans.

The 1972 season didn't start out that well for the Cubs. Fans were growing restless with a team who couldn't seem to get the job done anymore. Losing gripped the Cubs again and Leo Durocher was becoming frustrated, even more than usual. 1971 was a year filled with a lot of injuries and it seemed that the frustration for that was too much to bear for the manager, who was brought in to make a winning team. If it seemed that Leo was losing his patience, the Cubs' owner was even worse. But nobody could help 1971, it was Ernie Banks' last year and time for him to retire. Even Jack Larson spent half of the season injured. It was the only time in his career that he was injured. He had broken his hand during the all-star break while on vacation with his family since he was not playing in the game. Pretty much every member of the '69 club had spent some time on the DL list in 1971 except Billy Williams and Fergie Jenkins, who both had one of the best years in their career. But that didn't matter; the Cubs had another losing season and yet again could not reach the postseason.

Leo was growing restless in '72, and his attitude was affecting the team. The younger players who had not been around him since he had started with the Cubs were playing tight because they were afraid that Leo would release them if they didn't play well. And of course he was getting into it with the pitching staff. That part had already started with Fergie the year before. For some reason Leo didn't think Fergie was performing well, but it was one of his best years because he won 24 games. Leo also thought Jack Larson was washed up and that's why his hand got broken even though it was an off-field injury, but in 1972 he won 18 games. The situation was getting bad and it wasn't that nobody could take him being a son of a bitch, it was that he blamed losing on some of the most illogical reasons. Truth was he was part of the problem and nobody wanted to play for him anymore. Fergie Jenkins even quit at one point by taking off his uniform and walking out before a game in 1972. While it didn't cure the problem of losing for the Cubs, the Leo problem did get solved. He was fired in July of 1972 – the pressure from the press and the fans for the Cubs losing was too great for P.K. Wrigley so he had to do something and in his typical fashion the manager always got the blame and would later be fired.

Jack Larson always had a great respect for Leo because he was a winner and knew how to make winning ball clubs, but even in the end when the best manager that he had ever played for was fired, he wasn't sad to see him go. Before an incident in early 1972 with Leo Durocher he would have fought for Leo to stay, but that had changed. In May of that year Jack Larson was 3-3 for his record so far and Leo had decided that Jack Larson coming back to pitch for the Cubs wasn't a good idea, he thought the injury had ended his career, but Jack was fine and pitching well. He just didn't start out as strong because the Cubs were not the same offensive powerhouse that they once were. Leo had asked Jack into his office one morning before the game and told him that he was probably going to be let go or be traded – they had a young kid in the minors that they wanted to bring up in his place. Leo told Jack.

"I want you to know that you've had a great career, but all careers come to an end."

Jack looked at him with a weird look and said. "You think my career is over? I can still pitch."

"Maybe, but you're not what you used to be. You broke your hand last year and that affects pitching."

"Leo I'm fine and I can still pitch a complete game. I'm still young and can still do this for a while."

"You're not that young anymore and it's about time to start thinking about retirement."

"What if I want to stay and keep pitching for the Cubs, are you telling me that you're not going to let that happen?"

"I'm just saying that we will probably trade you in the mid season and if that's not what you want then you could always retire."

"Fuck you Leo, I'm still good enough to pitch for this team and better than some young inexperienced pitcher from the minors. Besides you need me more than ever since you traded Holtzman."

"I'm trying to give you options."

"No, you're trying to insult me just like you've done with Jenkins and Banks. I've been a Cub for my entire career just like my father and my grandfather. I'm not playing for anybody else nor will I give you the option to try

[172]

and trade me. You won't have me to get another player. I will retire before that happens."

Jack Larson walked out of the office angrily before Leo could say anything else. The subject of trading never came up again from Leo, but they never spoke to each other about anything else except when Leo had to go to the mound. Whatever good relationship they had before that was gone. Jack carried a grudge towards Leo ever since that day for insulting him like that. None of that mattered anymore after Leo was fired and took a job managing the Houston club. Jack made a point to really embarrass Houston when he had to pitch against them just to spite Leo. For the rest of his career Jack was undefeated against Houston and pitched some of his best games against them.

After Leo was fired the Cubs continued to get worse. In 1973 the Cubs didn't improve in the win/loss column at all despite another great year by Fergie Jenkins and Jack Larson. Jack would win 17 games that year, but the fact they were not winning caused P.K. Wrigley to make some changes. The rest of the members from the '69 clubs would all eventually be traded. Ron Santo and Randy Hundley were done in 1974. Fergie Jenkins would be traded after the 1974 season and Billy Williams would be gone in 1975. All the players that Jack had played with throughout the 60's and had the best years of his career with were gone because the owners didn't want then anymore. The sad thing was they all still had productive years left and were the best players for the Cubs to be in contention. At least that's the way Jack Larson saw it – he would also comment that they were the best group of guys anybody could play with.

In 1974 Jack Larson didn't start out that strong. He started out 1-4 through the middle of May, but it wasn't his fault when the Cubs didn't have the offense to back him up on the mound. By the All-Star Game he was 7-7. He was still pitching well and doing what he was supposed to in order to give the Cubs victories, but for whatever reason it wasn't good enough and they wanted to trade him. The day after the All-Star game that year he was called into the office of P.K. Wrigley along with the Cubs manager at the time and the general manager of the team.   P.K. told him that he had an offer to be traded to the Boston Red Sox and the team was going to take Boston's offer for a young left-handed hitter and some minor league prospects, but because of who Jack was and his family who had played for the Cubs since 1906 he had enough respect to tell him face to face and see what Jack thought about it.

Jack spoke up after hearing the news. "Mr. Wrigley. I don't want to go to Boston."

"But you want to keep playing...you're not ready to retire are you?" P.K. asked Jack.

"I do want to keep playing, but I'm a Cub. I always have been and won't play for any other team. If you don't want me to play for your team anymore then maybe it's time to retire."

"We need to start thinking about rebuilding and all of us in this room feel that there isn't much of a future for you with the Cubs. You've been with us 14 seasons and it's time to think about the future of this team."

"Well I guess I am the only in this room that still sees me as part of the future with this team and I can still play. I can still give you productivity even after 14 years."

P.K. Wrigley smiled and said. "Maybe, but we need to make a change and we still want you to have a chance to play so that's why we are trading you."

"Is that the same chance you gave Santo and Hundley."

"Of course, we don't forget around here your years of service."

"Then I guess mine are over and if it's all the same I would rather end my career in a Cubs uniform. If it's time to go then let it be that way."

"It's your choice Jack...we wanted to give you an option."

"It's not really an option in my book because once you become a Cub, you're always a Cub."

"Maybe so." P.K. smiled again. He respected his attitude and then he stood up and shook Jack's hand. But Jack had one request and he figured the Cubs owed it to him, if nothing else because his family was loyal to the organization. He asked P.K. Wrigley if he could pitch one more game at Wrigley Field...he wanted to win one more at home. P.K. Wrigley thought about it for a moment and said that it was fine. A week later when the Cubs were back home, Jack Larson pitched one more game at Wrigley Field, and it was against Tom Seaver and the New York Mets. Jack Larson pitched a 1-hit shutout against the Mets. Some fans believe it was the best game he had ever pitched even though he had a couple of no-hitters years before because it was an error made by the shortstop that caused the Mets to get at least one hit. If it would have not been for that Jack Larson would have pitched a perfect game, but he won and that was more important to the old warrior.

All Jack Larson ever wanted to do was to win and help the team to get victories. He never cared about the records, or the awards, or even being called an All-Star or a great pitcher. He was there to help his team win, and for fourteen and half seasons he did that. On his last day his family was there to see him walk off the mound one last time and tip his hat to the crowd. It was also at that moment that Steve Larson wanted to be just like his dad. Up to that point he just wanted to play baseball, but after seeing the respect and appreciation that the fans had for his dad he wanted to be a Chicago Cub. He also learned that day from his dad what it really meant to be a winner, despite the fact that he would forget it from time to time in his career. He learned that you play the best you can and you don't win it alone – you help your team any way you can and if you win as a pitcher it's because you have 8 other guys backing you up. That's the way it was done at Wrigley Field and it's the way the true warriors of baseball do it every day on the baseball diamond.

13

The Wild One

August was coming to an end for the Cubs and the 2008 season, Not only were they above .500; they were only 5 games out of first place in the central division behind the St. Louis Cardinals. The race for first place was getting tight and the Cubs had the momentum, but the Cardinals were still too good that year and could not be taken lightly. All the starting pitchers for the Cubs were good in the second half of the season except Ryan Larson. He was still struggling a little bit, but he was able to win a couple of games since his first start back. While his fastball wasn't overpowering and his curveball didn't always end up in the right location, he was finding a way to be successful, at least for five or six innings before the batters on the other team could figure out his pitches. He was 3-2 since being back and the two games that he lost, he gave away in later innings, and to top it all off he was still having control

issues, especially when he would throw his 3 big pitches:
the fastball, the sinker, and his curve. He could get a little
wild and the ball would get away from the catcher, but
when that happened it reminded fans of another Larson
that used to be the same way.

As the Cubs continued to hit and be an offensive
powerhouse in the National League fans started to talk
playoffs. In April at the beginning of the season when the
Cubs weren't doing so hot the playoffs didn't seem to be an
afterthought, but here they were in late August tied for
second with the Brewers and making a serious run for first
place. Everybody seemed to be excited, especially Amy.
Chris was also getting caught up in Cubs fever and
spending more time out at the ballpark. He was meeting
new fans every day and they welcomed him as one of their
own as if he had been a Cubs fan all of his life despite the
fact that he had only been one since the beginning of the
season. He would also tell fans that he was from Texas —
most fans would tell him that despite that fact, he got to the
Windy City as fast as he could and became a Cubs fan,
which was true in a way. Yes the Cubs were on a roll, but it
wasn't always wine and roses for them. There were a few
games they should have won and gave away because of bad
pitching. Kerry Wood, the rookie phenomenon from 1998
who had struck out 20 batters in one game his rookie year,
had been injured off and on the past ten years, but in 2008
he came back and had become the closer. He was doing
well, but even he had a few blown saves. However, through
it all they were serious contenders and they were having
fun.

The Cubs were on the road in Los Angeles playing
the Dodgers and Ryan was scheduled to pitch the first night
of the road series. He did fine through the first 6 innings,
keeping his pitch count down and only allowing 4 hits and
two runs, but the wheels came off in the 7th and he lost
control. He walked the first batter and then proceeded to hit
the next two and load the bases with no outs. The control
issues were now becoming a burden in the game. Larry, the

pitching coach, went out to see him and make sure that he
was okay and to see if he needed to take him. Larry was
always big on letting the pitcher get out of his own messes,
but sometimes he just had to take a pitcher out of the game
and put a fresh arm in to clean up the mess. There were
pitchers in the bullpen just in case. Larry talked it over
with Ryan and asked him if he could get out of the inning.
Of course he said yes, but every pitcher thinks they can
clean up their mess and aren't done when they really are.
Larry gave him a chance. Ryan did well at the beginning –
he pitched the batter to inside and got two strikes on him
by making him foul the pitches. The next pitch was in the
dirt, but Soto, the catcher, got in front of it and blocked the
ball from going behind the plate. With one ball and two
strikes, Ryan tried to go inside again with a breaking ball,
but it got away from him and he hit his third batter. It
walked in a run and loaded the bases again. The score had
been tied up to that point, but now the Dodgers were
leading by one run.

That was it for Ryan and he knew it. Anybody that
hit three batters in a row was done for the evening. He
wasn't mad that Lou had to come out and make a pitching
change – he understood that part, he was mad at himself
for losing control of his pitches and potentially losing the
game for the Cubs. When he got to the dugout he slammed
his glove down out of anger and muttered the word "fuck."
Big Z was the first to say something to him – he patted him
on the back and said "you'll get them next time, it's only
one game…but the next time we play these guys you'll have
them scared shitless…afraid that you're going to take their
heads off."
Ryan smiled at the comment. It did make him feel a little
better. After the inning was over, D-Lee, their quiet
captain, walked over and told him not to worry… the team
could get the lead back. He was right. The Cubs would
score two more runs and win the game 5-3 – Lee would hit
a double and knock in one run himself. That, too, made
him feel better.

The next day he got an email from his sister Amy who tried to cheer him up. It really didn't work, but it was nice of her to try. As he was surfing the internet on his laptop in the morning while eating breakfast in his room he caught a headline from someone's sports blog. It was from the LA news scene and it read, "Wild One: Younger Larson Seems to Be Just Like Dad." Normally he never read anything about himself, but the article intrigued him and it said exactly what he expected. The article compared him to his father, Steve Larson and his wild antics on the mound. Steve Larson had earned the nickname "The Wild One" in his first season with the Cubs for his brutal pitching style. At one point Steve could be eloquent and stylish getting guys out with a perfect 99 mile an hour fastball straight down the middle and steep curveball that made batters chase the wind, and that's all it would be, because Steve's curveball would be in a different place than where the batter expected it to be. The other times he would be wild and let pitches get away from him and those pitches would be in the dirt and at the batters head. But somewhere through it all, no matter how wild he was, Steve Larson always found a way to win and could dominate a game all by himself on the mound. That's also what made him great.

Ryan read the article and wasn't amused – there were some parts of it that were true, but just as Steve Larson with his own father, Ryan didn't want to be compared to him...especially the bad things his father was accused of doing. Amy had read the same posting and in another email to her brother told him not to worry about it...the writer was just a blogger. Then Ryan reminded her when he replied back that she had been one too. Even though she smiled at the email she knew that Ryan had a point and that the difference between good writers and hacks when it comes to blogs always had to do with the subject matter and whether the writer could make a good point. So she decided to tell her readers in her own words something about Steve Larson that fans may not have known...she would share something personal about the man they both loved and hated. Amy would tell the story of how a great pitcher could throw it all away, but still redeem himself.

∞∞∞∞∞∞∞∞∞∞∞

On September 11, 1982 Steve Larson would make his Major League debut as a starting pitcher. He was the fourth Larson to play for the Cubs and wasn't at all like those that had come before him. The other Larson's, including his father, would be considered average athletes compared to Steve; he could out pitch anybody and had multiple weapons on the pitcher's mound. He could hit and actually averaged about 7 to 10 home runs a year. And he could throw – throwing hard and long enough to get a guy out at home plate from the outfield. Steve Larson was a natural and players of his caliber only come around once every so often. But what made him a superstar was his confidence – he knew how good he was and never seemed to be nervous. Steve simply knew he was better than most ball players and would prove it on a daily basis. Even though he played for the Cubs and they were glad to have him, every other major league team wanted him as well and were probably willing to pay more for him. That didn't matter to Steve because there was only team he wanted to play for – he was a Cub just like his dad and when he became one most fans concluded that he was a better pitcher than Jack. In most ways they were right, but he never seemed to be smarter than Jack on the mound and would spend the rest of career struggling with that one fact.

He graduated high school in 1978 and didn't enter the draft so he could try out for the Cubs. He was sure they would take him because they needed pitching and he was the son of Jack Larson, but it wasn't that easy back then. P.K. Wrigley had died in 1977 and his son William was running the team – he wasn't as keen to look at another Larson for his club like P.K. Wrigley would have. And there were rumors that the team would be sold because the

[181]

Wrigley's didn't want to keep running them. That rumor would become true in 1981 when the Cubs were sold to the Tribune Company for 20.5 million. Jack Larson convinced his son to not be so hasty, college was the best thing for him at the time. Even though Steve didn't really want to go to college he knew he was right in a way and it was a good place to get some experience before going Pro. Steve Larson in 1978 accepted a full scholarship to the University of Iowa where his father was still coaching.

Steve Larson pitched three seasons at the University of Iowa and to say that he was an all-star was putting it lightly. He was a legend and broke nearly every pitching record at the school, including many of Jack Larson's records. When he left he had won 90% of his games and had career ERA of 1.21, which is still a college record at any school. He was a dominating pitcher who pitched 6 no-hitters, one of them being a perfect game while at the university, another record that still stands today. Jack Larson pitched 4 no-hitters and one of those was a perfect game. Steve Larson was one of most feared pitchers in college and one of the most sought after pitchers in the Majors and as luck would have it he was a first round draft pick for the Cubs in 1981 since they had the top pick and had a losing season the year before. But despite that, he didn't get called up right away. He would have to spend a little time in the Cubs minor league system, but he wasn't there long. In 1981 he spent the year at Double AA ball in Tennessee. After spring training in 1982 he didn't make the big club at the beginning of the season — he was still thought of as too young and unseasoned to be with the Cubs...no matter how bad they were doing and may have needed him. He spent most of the year in Iowa with the Triple A Cubs, which was a good thing because he had someone in Iowa waiting for him and she was pregnant in the summer of 1982.

Her name was Mary and she would eventually become Mary Larson, the love of Steve's life. She was smart and funny and best of all, she knew baseball, which just made her even more beautiful. She had grown up in Chicago and like her parents she would go to the University of Iowa and that is where she met Steve Larson. Mary wasn't the type of girl he would have gone out with on campus – she didn't think he was a "god" nor was she easy. Steve Larson was a big man on campus because he was the best pitcher on the team and the best pitcher the Hawkeyes had ever had since, well, Jack Larson pitched for them from 1955 -1958. Steve was already a legend on campus and more recognizable as an athlete in the baseball universe of the Midwest. So of course everybody knew who he was and that it was only a matter of time before he went to the majors. And Steve loved every moment of his life there and lived the life of a baseball legend.

Mary and Steve Larson met by accident when they were 20 years old– he was failing algebra and needed a tutor. She was the one assigned to him through the athletic office from the pool of student tutors working there part time. The first time they met she acted like she didn't know who he was and he was surprised, but she was trying to be serious and not give him a bigger ego than he already had by acting like she knew him. She didn't even let on that the she knew anything of baseball. During the tutoring session she was getting frustrated at him because it seemed like he didn't know anything and it was shocking because baseball is all about numbers. Mary couldn't figure out if he was lazy or really stupid. Truth be told, he was lazy and to him the only thing he needed to work hard at was baseball. She finally asked him after about 20 minutes of not getting anywhere with him. "How can you not get anything about math, you play baseball for god sake...you can calculate your ERA?"

He gave her a strange look because he was surprised that she knew what that was. He replied. "Of course, I'm a pitcher."

"Well then if you add the total number of runs that you've allowed and divide that by the number of games you pitched to get your ERA percentage then you should be able to figure out algebra."

He laughed and said to her. "I knew it, you know about baseball...I had a feeling that you were putting on an act."

"I know the math behind baseball."

"Yeah, but how many people really know about the ERA and reference it to a pitcher that they are talking to if they didn't know about baseball?"

"What's your point?"

"I just want you to acknowledge that you know the game and you probably know who I am."

"I think everybody knows who you are on campus or at least has heard of you."

Steve smiled again and replied. "I don't care about everybody else, just you."

"Why do you care about me...I'm not that important."

"You're pretty and you're probably the one person that doesn't give a damn about me and baseball."

"I don't care about you, but I do want you to help the team make it to the College World Series and if you do play for the Chicago Cubs one day like your dad, maybe you can help them win a World Series because we've been waiting a long time for another championship."

"Are you a Cubs fan?"

"I grew up there and my dad use to take me to Wrigley field to watch your dad pitch. We even sat in the bleachers during the '69 season."

Steve Larson was excited to say the least, she really did know who he was and didn't care, but she was also a Cubs fan. He asked her. "How long have you been a fan of the Cubs?"

"All my life...I grew up in a baseball family. My dad played baseball here in Iowa in the early 50's before your dad played here and before you ask, yes, I do know who your family is and the ties they have with the Cubs, but I don't care. You're failing algebra, and I am here to help you. "

Steve didn't want to talk about algebra, he was excited that an honestly beautiful woman knew about baseball, his family, and didn't want to be with him because he was famous – he even liked the fact that she didn't seem interested in him, but he could tell that she was. With Mary it would be a challenge and that made it worth it. She wasn't the usual dumb bimbo that he was used to on campus that could easily fall for him because of his smile or his athletic feats. He had to ask her. "Have you come to a game and seen me pitch?"

She gave him a dirty look and tried to bring the subject back to algebra, but he wouldn't talk about that. She finally answered him. "I've been to one or two games. Can we get back to studying?"

"Only if you come and see me pitch again…and let me take you out."

"What makes you think you're my type…you probably don't even know my name."

"It's Mary and if I'm not your type then why are you still here. Most people would have gotten up and quit trying to tutor me already. You're still here, which means I'm not that annoying."

"Fine, you're cute, but I have a boyfriend."

"Then bring him to watch me pitch too."

"What do you care if I am there?"

"I just want you to be there. I think it would be fun."

"Fine I will come to another game, now let's get back to studying."

It was true, she was dating someone, but she kept tutoring Steve even when he didn't need it anymore and so the attraction grew from there. Eventually she dumped the guy she was seeing and Steve quit sleeping around with women that he didn't care about on campus. Steve and Mary started dating and she never missed a game after that first day when she tutored him. Mary thought he was exciting and he could make her laugh. And as wild as he might have been his lust for life was an inspiration, but more importantly he was always there for her no matter

[185]

what. Steve fell in love with her during that first tutoring session – he knew there was something about her and there would be nobody like her. Jack had told him once that when you find that certain someone, something comes over you and you will never be the same. It only happens once in a lifetime, and when it does happen with a girl, she will be the one for you.

After a year and a half of dating Steve asked her to marry him and she didn't have to think about saying yes. Even though she never admitted it most people that knew her figured out that she fell in love with Steve about the same time he did with her. She also knew that it was a foregone conclusion she would end up a baseball wife, and that was okay with her. Mary loved the sport and she also loved that Steve could never completely walk away from it – it was a part of him and he was too good not to be a part of baseball. So they got married before both of them graduated college, and after three seasons in college Steve Larson didn't even wait to graduate before he moved on in the baseball world. He entered the draft in 1981 and was drafted by the Cubs. While Mary finished her teaching degree at the University of Iowa Steve went to the Minor League system, first to double A ball in Tennessee and then at the beginning of the season in '82 he was at the Triple A club for the Cubs in Iowa, not too far from Mary as she finished her last year at the University.

In that year Mary and Steve had another surprise she would end up pregnant – it wasn't something they were planning as young as they were, but they were excited. They couldn't help it, they both wanted to be parents. Most of the 1982 season Steve spent with the minor league club and he was a superstar that year. He had incredible numbers including the lowest ERA throughout the minor league system for the Cubs. The big club was languishing in last place in their division that year and so management decided it was time to start moving players up. The year before was the start of rebuilding for the Cubs as the Tribune Company hired Dallas Green, the general manager of the Phillies, to run the Cubs and make them a winner again. He had a great track record with other teams and as soon as he came in he fired most people that had had anything to do with the past including a lot of old players that were coaching like Billy Williams and Randy Hundley. There was a new attitude and it was that of winning – Green didn't want anybody that had to do with the losing teams for the Cubs.

Dallas Green's first priority was pitching and he started to trade for other players like Scott Sanderson and Steve Trout. He made a few trades with his old team the Phillies and got a few decent players, one of them being Hall of Fame second basemen Ryan Sandberg who would blossom into a star while with the Cubs. Part of the move for pitching was also finding young players that could "cut their teeth" in the minors and that's where Steve Larson came in. He was a top prospect and Dallas Green considered himself lucky to get him, but he also needed a little more experience in the minors and that's why he spent a year there, but he was too good for Triple A Iowa by September of 1982 and the Cubs needed more pitching, so on September 9, 1982 he was called up to the Cubs. He would have to leave his pregnant wife back home and she was very close to her due date. Two days after being called up he would get his first chance to pitch – it was a home game against the Houston Astros and the opposing pitcher for that game would be the great Nolan Ryan.

September 11, 1982 was a clear and gorgeous day at Wrigley Field and there were only about 25,000 fans there that day. The game wasn't that important and most fans thought that Nolan Ryan would be the one to dominate the game, but those who showed up were about to watch history and the birth of another Chicago star. At the beginning of the game when Steve Larson was announced as the Cubs pitcher, he didn't get much fanfare that day because nobody knew who he really was. Harry Caray, the Cubs announcer who was also new to the team in 1982, didn't have anything in front of him telling him that Steve

Larson was the son of Jack Larson. Harry, who would become a national icon as a baseball announcer through WGN, was in his first season with the Cubs after having replaced Jack Brickhouse who had been broadcasting Cubs game since 1948.

The game got underway and Steve was an immediate success, retiring the side in the first two innings and striking out 3 hitters in the process. He was working on all cylinders and his fastball and sinker were deadly that day. Even his curveball was devastating. However Nolan Ryan was having a great day as well. Both pitchers had a no-hitter through six innings and as Harry Caray pointed out on the air, "It's a pitching duel between the legend and the rookie…we're not even close to knowing who is going to win this game."

Finally in the 7th inning the gloves came off for Nolan Ryan and Steve Larson – they were both throwing their best stuff trying to continue the no-hitters and of course both teams were trying to break up the no-hitters. Finally Steve Larson with his competitive nature took matters into his own hands. The Cubs couldn't seem to get a hit off Nolan Ryan and when Steve Larson came to the plate in the 7th inning he was determined to get a hit any way he could, but the problem was he was facing Nolan Ryan who had the deadliest fastball in baseball back then. Nolan got two strikes on him; one of the pitches was a 100 mile an hour fastball and he knew because he was a pitcher that Nolan Ryan would throw it again just to keep the young kid from getting cocky and from showing him up. Steve leaned in and acted as if he was going to swing away, but at the last minute he twisted his body inside slightly and put the bat down for a bunt – because his body was turned to the inside he was able to pull the bunt toward the third baseman making the Astros catcher and pitcher have to go further to get the ball and giving him more time to get to first base. He barely made it as Nolan tried to throw him out – it was so close that nobody could tell for sure if Steve Larson was safe, but the first base umpire ruled him safe.

The Astros' manager protested the call and even got ejected, but Nolan wasn't. He respected the rookie pitcher for making such a gutsy move with his bunt and running it out. The next batter was a young rookie outfielder named Joe Carter who most don't even realize was with the Cubs. He hit a two run shot into the bleachers to put the Cubs up 2-0. Nolan Ryan didn't get his no-hitter, but those were the only two hits he allowed. Steve Larson would go into the ninth inning with his no-hitter. He even fanned three straight 99 mile an hour fastballs past Nolan in the 8th to strike him out and to prove that he had a deadly fastball too. Nolan just tipped his hat to Steve as he walked to the dugout. In the top of the ninth the fans were going crazy, this rookie pitcher was 3 outs away from a no-hitter. Harry Caray finally got the note that Steve Larson was Jack Larson's son. When he announced that to the crowd at Wrigley Field at the beginning of the 9th inning they erupted in joy – another Larson was playing for the team and they knew he was going to be a superstar. Unfortunately he didn't get the no-hitter. He gave up a solo home run that the wind carried out too much into the bleachers. If it had not been for the wind Joe Carter in the outfield would have caught the ball for an out, but things don't always work out the way you want them to in baseball.

Steve did strike out the next two batters to win the game and he ended with the 12 strikeouts and only one hit. There was a big celebration on the field with the Cubs as Harry Caray was shouting into the microphone in the broadcasters booth, "Cubs win, Cubs win…the rookie pitcher has announced to the baseball world that he is going to be a star just like his dad Jack Larson." The first pitcher to shake his hand was Fergie Jenkins who had come back to the Cubs in 1982 and would pitch the final two years of his career where it had all started for him. He was also the first pitcher to shake Jack Larson's hand when he threw his last no-hitter in 1969. As the Cubs were celebrating on the field over the great performance from the newest rookie sensation there was one more pitcher to come out and shake his hand…it was Nolan Ryan and he told Steve Larson that it looked like he was there to stay and would have a great career if he pitched like he did.

While the outcome of the game was great and Steve Larson's first game one of the most memorable since he had outpitched Nolan Ryan, there was something else about that day that would make it the most important of his career. During the 5th inning while watching the game on WGN back in Iowa Mary Larson went into labor. Steve didn't find out until right after the game had ended. He did a quick interview with the press, showered, and was rushed to the airport so he could get home to Iowa. The proudest moment of that day – the day he pitched his first game in the majors – was the birth of his son and daughter, Amy and Ryan Larson.

14

The Year We Were Close

Amy was sitting at her desk typing furiously trying to make her deadline. She had another great article about the Cubs. They were giving her plenty of stuff to write about. It was September and the Cubs continued to win; they continued to roll through their competition in the National League, but they still didn't have a claim on first place in the Central division and the race was getting really tight. But St. Louis was still too strong and continued to be the better team with the numbers. The Cubs would have to face them on 3 separate occasions in September and winning was even more crucial because they were behind the Cardinals in the playoff race. Amy already knew that it was going to be close, but she had faith in her Cubs. Sometimes that's all you can have.

As she was finishing up her story she was also thinking about her blog for that day. It was going to be based on a story about the Cubs in 1984 and her Dad and the rest of the team coming so close to the World Series. What was happening now with the Cubs and fans in Chicago getting caught up in the winning fever was a lot

[191]

like 1984 when the city was going crazy over the Cubs winning throughout the year – It was Cubs fever that year and it was happening again.

The Cubs were a completely different team coming back from the All-Star Break. They were playing up to their potential – they were playing championship baseball. It was exactly the same as it was in 1984. The Cubs that year didn't start well; they weren't even a .500 team after the first month in '84 but they got better and stopped playing mediocre baseball. But the big change that year came in June when they traded for Rick "The Red Baron" Sutcliff from Cleveland. Jim Frey, the Cubs skipper, and Dallas Green wanted another pitcher to make the Cubs have the best rotation in the majors and they got that with Rick.

For the Cubs in 2008 they were entering September with a winning record and having won two-thirds of their games in the second half of the season. Everyone on the pitching staff had a winning record or was at least even – Ryan Larson was 5-5 going into September. The Cubs were becoming the comeback kids, when they got behind in the game they found a way to come back and win. They even had one game in August where they were down 9-1 going into the 9th inning against the Colorado Rockies. The Cubs came back and tied the game to send it into extra innings and then won the game with a 2-run walk-off homer by Ramirez, the third baseman, in the 10th inning. The Cubs were definitely hot and had the momentum going into the last part of the season. And they demonstrated that by winning games against the top teams in the National League. They won two out of three against the Phillies on the road who had pretty much already won the East Division, the swept the Braves who were in contention for the Wild-Card spot at home, and most importantly, they swept the Brewers in Milwaukee. They won all four games against the team that was nipping at their heels in the central division pushing them 7 games behind the Cubs. The fever was back and it was getting interesting, but there was still a lot of baseball left.

Amy got the chance to write about the 1984 season and of course it was a great to be able to talk about it with Chris. He didn't know the full story, the only thing he had heard was that the Cubs were one game away from the World Series and blew it. It was another that they were so close and didn't make it. 1984 was also the year that players like Ryan Sandberg, Jody Davis, and Steve Larson really became superstars. The whole team was superb that year and a lot of the younger players really came into their own. Steve Larson would win 16 games that year and only lose 5. Jody Davis turned into one of the best catchers in the game and reminded Cub fans of Randy Hundley. And every Cubs fan remembers how Sandberg became the hall of fame player that warmed our hearts and it was because of the game that we have all come to know as "The Sandberg Game." By June the Cubs were starting to win and they had just gotten Rick Sutcliff, the all-star pitcher from the Cleveland Indians. Getting him had a tremendous impact on the Cubs – mainly because while he was 4-5 in Cleveland, he would go 16-1 for the Cubs in the second half of that season.

There is always one moment that fans can seem to remember when the Cubs truly became a championship team and it was "The Sandberg Game." The Cubs had a winning record going into that game against their long-time rival the St. Louis Cardinals. Steve Larson had pitched the day before and had won the game for the Cubs to put them into first place in the Eastern Division and now they were facing the Cardinals on June 26, 1984, which was a nationally televised game so everybody who was watching afternoon baseball in America got to see it. The Cubs were losing 7-1 going into the ninth and Bruce Sutter was on the mound – the best closer in the game at the time and who used to be a Cub. Everybody just assumed that the Cardinals were going to win, but the Cubs came back. They tied the game on a three-run homer by Ryan Sandberg to make the game go into extra innings. In the 12th inning the Cardinals were leading the game by two runs and it seemed that they were about to win the game when Ryan Sandberg stepped up to the plate and hit another home run off Bruce Sutter to tie the game again. Hitting one home run off Sutter was hard, but hitting two was almost impossible – he did it though, and the Cubs would win the game in the next inning. It was probably the greatest game of the season and the Cubs won, and more importantly nearly everybody in America got to see the game.

Because of that it seemed that America fell in love with them that year. The fanfare the Cubs have now all across the country really came to be because of 1984, "The Sandberg Game," and WGN becoming one of the first superstations. Everywhere the Cubs traveled that year there were thousands of fans and some of the stadiums they visited had more Cub fans than for the home team. For somebody like Sutcliff who was used to maybe 80 fans showing up to a game in Cleveland the fanfare was really something else and Cub fans sort of adopted him just like the rest of team and held a special place in their hearts for the Cubs. Rick pitched the next day after "The Sandberg Game" to 40,000 fans who cheered for him like he was one of the Beatles or Rolling Stones. The stands at Wrigley were filled everyday for the rest of the season and tickets were very hard to come by, but those who were treated to a game at Wrigley Field were never disappointed. The city of Chicago had pennant fever that year and for someone like Steve Larson it reminded him of the 1969 season and what it had been like for his dad when he pitched for the Cubs. Cub fans were really taken with Steve Larson by 1984 because he showed the same brilliance on the mound as Jack Larson did and he could win ballgames. When he struck someone out it was always an event because the pitch he usually threw was nasty and just embarrassed the hitter. Every time this happened fans would erupt in the stands.

It was an exciting year for Steve Larson. Ever since his first game in the majors everybody knew that he was going to be a star, but he did have some trouble during the

1983 season. The person who helped him the most and mentored him was Fergie Jenkins, who pitched his last year in the Majors that year. He taught Steve Larson the same things that Jack taught him, but Steve never really like to listen to Jack and it was easier to hear the things he needed to hear to be a better pitcher from somebody that he respected and had played with his dad. Fergie did a lot that season to help Steve Larson be a better pitcher in the Majors and it helped Steve become a superstar in 1984 instead of some pitcher who tried to get everybody out with fastballs and would eventually throw his arm out.

As the Cubs got through September some were worried the New York Mets would catch up and surprise the Cubs just like they did in '69, but it never happened. On a glorious September night in Pittsburg the Cubs clinched the National League Eastern Division and were headed to the post season for the first time in 39 years. The next day they played the Cardinals again at Wrigley Field and Steve Larson won his 16th game of the season. 40,000 fans refused to leave and wanted to celebrate so the Cubs went out into the stands and shook hands with the fans after the game. How many teams would have done that? It's part of the reason that there is such a love affair with Cubs and why the relationship they have with the fans is like a family. Is there really another team that can claim that? Amy and Ryan were there with their mother that day as the Cubs celebrated with fans. Mary Larson always said it was one of her happiest moments - she got to watch the man she loved hold his son and daughter among the team and fans that they all came to love so much.

While that day was about celebration it wouldn't necessarily end that way. And for Steve Larson his darker side would star to show. After that day in the stands Steve Larson went out with some of the other players and the party got a little wild. Since Cubs were superstars in the eyes of the fans especially the women; the women were throwing themselves at the players that night. Steve has a pretty good following of women and he did two things that

night that those who knew him thought he would ever do –
he tried cocaine for the first time and he slept with another
woman other than his wife. He was high that night and was
capable of anything – morality never played a part in his
actions that night. Steve loved Mary very much, but he
loved to have a good time. After all, he was "The Wild One"
and he got the nickname not just for what he could do on
the mound, but for the way he partied. It was shocking to
some of his teammates to say the least, but there has
always been an unwritten rule with the team you play on in
sports, you never tell other people of your deeds and to put
it more metaphorically, what happens in the locker room
stays in the locker room. Unfortunately it wouldn't be the
last time he did something like this – he lived life to fullest,
in good ways and bad throughout his career. And while it
should never be an excuse if everybody has a role then "The
Wild One" does not live by normal rules – he lives a life of
action and does things for one person only, good or bad.

The Cubs that year had to play the San Diego Padres
for the National League Pennant. They were nowhere in the
same league as the Cubs, everybody knew it and they
expected the Cubs to win the best of five series in three
straight games. Truth is they should have, but what should
happen never does with the Cubs. For a hundred years fans
and players have had to live with that truth. Rick Sutcliff
pitched the first game of the series and it was a blowout for
the Cubs – they won the game 13-0. The second game
wasn't as easy, but they won 4-2. Steve Trout pitched a
masterful game. The sweep looked very likely, but it wasn't.
The Padres won game three 7-1 in San Diego, but most fans
didn't seem to worry about it because Steve Larson was
going to pitch game four and most just assumed the game
was in the bag. It was a very tight game. As well as Steve
Larson pitched throughout the game the Padres would not
go quietly. The Cubs jumped out to an early lead and Steve
held the Padres scoreless through four innings, but he gave
up a three-run homer in the corner of left field that most
fans assumed would be a foul ball, but it was ruled fair.

While instant replay was not even a concern when it comes to blown calls like it is today one might wonder what would have been the ruling on that home run call in '84 if they had instant replay back then. And while it's fun to think about that play was not what sealed the loss in game four for the Cubs.

The game was tied in the 9th inning and by this time after the game had been going back and forth, the Cubs were just trying to get to extra inning so they could win the game there. Steve Larson was still on the mound — it wasn't time to get the closer since they were not in a position yet to win the game. Steve had two outs, and that's when Steve Garvey of the Padres came up to bat. Larson had already struck him out and figured he could get him again. On most occasions, Steve Larson could get most people out by striking them out. But he also had a dangerous side as a pitcher and it never served him well. He was cocky and would forget that there were eight other guys backing him up. Steve Larson was always the guy that wanted to do it all by himself.

Steve Larson had one ball and one strike on Garvey. That's when he started shaking off the signs from Jody the catcher – that irritated Jody because his job was to see things on the field and give pitching suggestions with the signs that might be the best pitch to get a guy out. Like for instance if the shortstop moved over a little towards second to shrink the area where a batter if he was pitched inside with a breaking ball might put the ball when he hit it for a grounder to the shortstop, who could get the easy out by throwing the guy out at first.

Steve Larson was the type of guy that liked to get guys out with a fastball or a curveball, even when the batters for the other team had already seen all of his pitches by the 9th inning. So Steve Larson shook off the sign and threw a fastball at 98 miles an hour when he should have thrown a breaking ball to cause a ground ball to the infield. He was lucky with the pitch because he put another strike on Garvey, but he shook off the sign again and threw a slider low and away when it should have been a sinker. They were one strike away from sending the game to extra innings and Steve threw the wrong pitch. Garvey got a hold of it and with one man on base sent the ball into the centerfield bleachers to win the game for the Padres.

Everybody was mad on the Cubs team and none more so than Steve Larson. As soon as the ball was hit he knew that he just gave up the game-winning home run. Steve slammed his glove and hat on the ground and then kicked them towards Sandberg at second base. Jody came to the mound and yelled at him for shaking off the signs and then cursed at him for being selfish. Jody never caught another game for Steve Larson after that day and although they had been pretty good friends, they hardly spoke to each other again while they played for the Cubs. As far as Jody was concerned, it was Steve Larson's fault that they lost the series and didn't go to the World Series. Even though Steve never acknowledged it out loud, he knew that he was to blame for the loss as well.

The next day they played game five of the series and even though Sutcliff was on the mound and the Cubs got an early lead, the Padres came back and won the game to go to the World Series. 1984 would be the year that they Cubs were so close to the World Series that they could almost touch it, just like in 1969 and 2003, but it wasn't to be. However, nobody could take away how wonderful the year was and the memories that fans had. And if you ask me, the Cubs became America's team in baseball that year – that's something that can never be taken away and the Padres will never be able to claim that fact. For the Cubs, I think every one of them went on a bender to get over the loss, and rumor had it that Harry Caray the so-called "Mayor of Rushtown" led the way in the bender.

It was a Sunday night when Amy was finishing her article about her the 1984 season and the year that the Cubs had come so close. It was a weird weekend because the Cubs were supposed to be in Houston for a weekend series with the Astros, but a hurricane had rolled in through the Gulf Coast and caused the games to be cancelled except for Sunday. Instead of it being played in Houston it would be played at a neutral site, despite the fact the Cubs were technically the home team. It was played in Milwaukee at Miller Park since the Brewers were on the road. Carlos "Big Z" Zambrano was pitching that night and it would be the best game of his career.

Amy didn't travel with the team, but actually stayed home in Chicago. Although she was watching it on WGN and while it was weird that she wouldn't be there, sometimes in certain cases when the travel expenses were too much the paper wouldn't send a writer. Having her fly to Houston then to Milwaukee and then back home was too much for the Sun-Times so she stayed home and watched the game on TV.

What made the game memorable was that Big Z threw a no-hitter and it was the first time a Chicago Cub had done that since Milt Pappas did it in 1972 – the longest drought for a team to go without throwing a no-hitter in baseball history. Amy and Chris were not really paying that much attention until the 8th inning rolled around and Len and Bob, the WGN announcers, finally said that Zambrano had a no-hitter through 7 innings. When they both realized what was going on they were glued to the TV. In the 9th and final inning with the Cubs winning 2-0 and after facing only 28 batters Big Z got his no-hitter. Amy was almost in tears at what she had just seen. No Cub had thrown one in her lifetime and although both her dad and brother had come close something had always happened to take them away...usually bad calls.

Chris and Amy both jumped out of their seats when it happened. Amy, with a few tears in her eyes, looked at Chris. He asked her what was wrong. She said to him. "This is it...we're going to do it. The Cubs are going to make the playoffs and I know that we say it every year, but this year we're going to the World Series...the Cubs can't be stopped."

15

The Pitch We Never See Coming

Amy had plenty more to write about now. Zambrano's no-hitter put them within one game of first place behind the Cardinals and they still had more games against them before the regular season was over in two weeks. The no-hitter was a great game and it basically put the Cubs into contention for the playoffs. If they didn't win the division they could still get the Wild Card spot, but it was going to be close because the San Francisco Giants, who were behind the Dodgers in the Western Division, were trying to catch up, and they could also get the wild card spot. The last two weeks of the season were going to be brutal and the Cubs knew it, but they had momentum and sometimes that makes all the difference.

After the no-hitter Ryan was scheduled to pitch; he would make at least 2 or 3 more appearances in the regular season. He was still having trouble with control and he would pitch good games and bad games. He was 6-5 on the

"

year with a few no-decisions, but he wasn't going to be benched. The Cubs manager needed every good arm he could get and Ryan could still win ballgames on the mound even if his sinker and curveball weren't working correctly. They had a series against the New York Mets at Shea Stadium and Ryan pitched the first game. When the Cubs were hot New York fans liked to bring in black cats and let them loose just to see if the superstition could get to the Cubs — it all started back '69 after the Ron Santo incident with the black cat. Ryan pitched well in through the first four innings, holding the Mets to two hits and no runs. The Mets were a long shot to win the Wild Card Spot, but anything could happen and there was always that small chance. When the fifth inning arrived that's when one of the New York fans let lose a black cat to run onto the field – it darted across the infield and across the pitcher's mound before he ran off only to be never seen again. Of course the baseball announcers had a field day with their comments about the cat. Ryan didn't even notice it during his warm-ups and truth be told, nobody on the Cubs really paid attention to it. Their heads were in the game.

However the fifth inning of that game is when the wheels started to come off for Ryan. The Cubs were winning 3-0 and Ryan gave up a 2-run homer to the Mets catcher. He loaded the bases with two walks and another hit, but with one out already he made the next batter hit into the double play. His pitch count was getting high – he was already at 89 pitches and Lou, the Cubs skipper, was just hoping he could get through another couple of innings. In the sixth inning back to back doubles caused the Met to tie the game. Ryan was getting frustrated and his pitches were getting away from him. He wasn't going to last much longer because his curveball was already gone – at this point he was trying to pitch batters to the inside and see if they would hit ground balls for easy outs. He struck the next batter out and made the next guy pop the ball up for the second out. He was working out of the inning like a pro, but he was also getting some bad calls because he was trying to nip the corners of home plate for strikes, and even though some of them were obvious he was getting the other calls. Three more hits put men on base and although one of them was not his fault because of an error from the shortstop that should have been an easy out at first base, here he was again faced with the bases loaded and giving up the lead to the Mets.

Two straight change-ups caused the next batter to foul the ball and have two strikes on him. Ryan threw the sinker and it was perfect – the batter went over the top of it even trying to lower his swing to get it. Ryan was on his way to the dugout when the home plate umpire ruled the ball foul. Soto, the catcher, protested with the umpire and asked him how he could make that stupid call. The ump said that even though the ball ended up in the dirt right between the catchers legs the batter got a piece of it and it was a foul ball. Ryan ran over to talk to the ump and after having all of this explained to him yelled at the ump and told him that it was impossible – if the batter had really gotten a pieced of the ball then it wouldn't have sunk into the dirt, the ball would have had a least a little bounce from the bat hitting it before ending up in the dirt. By this time Lou, the Cubs manager, had come out to calm his pitcher down. He was trying to talk to the umpire and get a clarification for the call. Ryan Larson didn't want to hear anything the ump had to say; as far as he was concerned, he made the wrong call and that was all. Ryan leaned over Lou's shoulder and said. "You must have blinders on because that was a cocksucking call." The ump got mad and asked Ryan if he was trying to call him a cocksucker, and Ryan simply replied. "Fine have it your way, you are a cocksucker."

That's all it took for the umpire to eject Ryan from the game. Ryan got into his face again and started calling him names and then Lou started yelling at the umpire, but was quickly moved away by Derrek Lee before he got ejected as well. It was a bad night for Ryan to say the least. He walked back to the dugout and then turned around to

throw his glove back at the umpire like he was an angry
child. Lou picked it up for him like he was the dad following
his kid to make sure he went to his room because he was in
trouble. It was a bad call, but that didn't excuse the
reaction from Ryan either, but at least he was passionate
about his performance...that's what Lou said to the Larry,
the pitching coach, when he walked back to the dugout.
The Cubs would take the lead again and eventually win the
game, but Ryan got a no-decision.

The next day there was plenty to write about with
sportswriters over the Ryan meltdown and all the articles
and blogs pretty much said the same thing – he had the
same anger problems as his father. It wasn't an easy thing
being a Larson in the Cubs organization because they
always got compared to their relatives. Steve Larson would
have himself compared to his father Jack all the time.
There was one blog that Amy caught the next day when she
was reading what other people had to say about her
brother... she mainly wanted to find the hacks that never
had anything good to say about a baseball player and
shouldn't even be writing to begin with, at least in her in
her eyes. The blog she found was from a local sports writer
in L.A. The first paragraph of the column asked the
question, "Could this be the end of the younger Larson's
career?" The rest of the article went on to talk about Steve
Larson's last two years with the Cubs before he was traded
to the Texas Rangers and all of his antics that would cause
him to lose baseball games. Then the article went on to talk
about why he was traded and compared what Ryan was
doing during the 2008 season to what Steve Larson did 20
years before to get traded and eventually kicked out of
baseball.

Chris had been asking Amy questions about her dad
because he kept hearing bad thing about him...things like
how he screwed up his career and burned his bridges with
the Cubs organization to where he couldn't ever get a job
with them. There were a lot of things that she still hadn't
told him about her dad. Amy never had a good reason for

it, but she always figured that it was because she didn't want Chris to think badly of her dad – what he did back then could happen to anyone.

Steve Larson had a pretty good career with the Cubs and it got better after the 1984 season. He would win 16 games again in 1985. He was a 20-game winner in 1986 and 1987, despite the Cubs having bad years, and in some ways was the only shining star in the pitching rotation. Even when Rick Sutcliff had bad years Steve Larson was still a superstar and sometimes carried the rotation on his shoulders. In '86 and '87 he was the ace. But despite all that he was wild and charismatic on the mound. Sometimes he would hit the batter intentionally just to get them out of their zone so he could out pitch them because they weren't thinking. He would yell and curse at umpires if they made a really bad call. He was the type of pitcher that likes to scare batters with his pitching and he was always the first to hit someone if they charged the mound.

Between 1985 to1989 he averaged four ejections a year for mouthing off at players or umpires and starting a fight with a batter. He still holds the record in Chicago Cubs history for being ejected the most times. Steve Larson lived up to the name "The Wild One." However he was a great pitcher and batters did fear him. There is also another record that he holds in major league baseball. In eleven and a half seasons Steve Larson 28 times went into the at least the 8th inning with a no-hitter or perfect game – no pitcher has come close that many times in a career without having one. But as good as he was on the mound there was another side to Steve Larson. He loved living life in the fast lane and he could party. That meant booze, drugs, and girls. Steve could out-drink anybody and his drug of choice was always cocaine. And no matter how much he loved his wife Mary he did play around and cheat on her with another woman quite a few times when the Cubs were on the road. For a few years the way he lived his life never seemed to effect his pitching, but in 1988 it was starting to take its toll.

Steve Larson never had a losing record playing for the Cubs, but in 1988 he went 13-12. It was the most losses he had ever had in his career. He was slipping and he never had a complete game in '88. The 1989 season was not any better for him. The Cubs were good again and would win the National League Eastern Division that year and would face the San Francisco Giants to see who would go to the playoffs. While the Cubs were good, Steve Larson was mediocre – the great god of a pitcher seemed like a mere mortal all year. His record was 12-12. Out of his 12 losses that year, 11 of those games were given away by him in the late innings, by allowing the other team to get hits and score runs.

By '89 he wasn't the ace pitcher he once was, Greg Maddux had become that for the Cubs and the Steve antics were causing his relationship with the organization to become strained. Managers in the past had put up with it because he could still win ball games, but Don Zimmer, the Cubs new manager since 1988, didn't have any stomach for it. He suspended Steve Larson more than once in 1989 for getting ejected and in his mind not being a professional ballplayer. Between the late night partying and confrontational attitude with players on the other teams it was becoming too much for Zimmer to bear. And despite all that, Steve still had great fans and was a favorite among them. He was also instrumental in their success that year. Steve Larson was still picked as one of the starting pitchers for the playoffs that year. He only pitched one game, losing it to the Giants, and the Cubs were out of the playoffs in five games. After pitching game three, Steve Larson tested positive for coke when major league baseball did some random drug testing during the playoffs that year and was suspended for the rest of the season. It didn't matter since the Cubs didn't go very far in the playoffs. He had been out partying and did a few lines at a party even though he knew that there was a chance that major league baseball would do drug testing during the playoffs, but it didn't seem to matter.

[206]

The drug incident was the last straw for the Cubs. The Cubs organization gave him a chance to redeem himself by going to a drug treatment center for a month. Steve Larson did and it seemed to work, but he was seen on the town partying in Chicago a month before spring training was to start for the 1990 season and even though it was not proven that he was doing anything wrong, the Cubs released him. Truth was they were looking for an excuse because they were tired of dealing with Steve Larson and his behavior. Also they felt like his best years were already gone and he was not that good of a pitcher anymore. That part was bogus because Steve Larson still had the tools to win and he could win the game all by himself on the mound. In his final appearance during the regular season of 1989 he struck out 15 batters and won the game all by himself. Steve Larson being released caused shockwaves throughout Chicago because he still was a fan favorite. He was also one of the best pitchers in the league during the 1980's. The incident caused even more turmoil within the family. His father Jack didn't want to have anything to do with him because of what happened. Their relationship had become strained during Steve's career because he never approved of how Steve handled himself on and off the field.

He wanted his son to be more like him and the ballplayers that he played with, but it was a new era and in the 80's ball players became more of the superstars that we know today – they became more like gods among men. Also Jack was ashamed of his son because never had a Larson ever been fired or traded from the Cubs – being a Cub was in their blood and to have them not want you was an insult. Of course when Steve reminded his dad before he moved Texas during the last time they spoke for a few years that the Cubs were going to trade him and he just decided to retire. That didn't seem to matter to Jack because he went out on his own terms and that's what mattered.

In February of 1990 Steve Larson was given a contract by the Texas Rangers and for more money than he had made with the Cubs. He was going to get 2 million a year. Part of what convinced him to come to Texas was a call by Nolan Ryan...Nolan had respect for Steve and saw him as one of the best pitchers in the game. Nolan Ryan had come to the Texas Rangers from the Astros in 1989 and having faced Steve a few times in the last few years knew how dominant he could be on the mound. It takes a great pitcher to know one!   So Steve Larson went to Texas, he knew that it was the only chance to continue playing because there were quite a few teams that didn't want him. Nolan Ryan was the type of guy who could look beyond the antics and know that Steve Larson had a winning attitude. The two of them together on the same team could make things interesting. Steve left Chicago and he didn't do it gracefully because it wasn't his style...he had a few choice words about the organization and the manager of the Cubs that sent some controversial shockwaves through the fan base in Chicago. There were mixed reactions to what he had to say.

Some fans hated him for it and some thought it was great because they agreed with everything he said in the interview, including that the best men he ever took the field with was his teammates on the Cubs. Steve told reporters that they were the only class act in the Cubs organization. And the sad truth 20 years later he still believes that...the real bad guys were the management and the Tribune Company who ran the Cubs organization. When he left it wasn't hard to leave Chicago because of all the animosity at the time, but the hard part was the strain on his marriage.

Mary and Steve's marriage wasn't great and his antics off the field certainly took their toll, but they still loved each other very much. She still thought he was exciting and he was a great father...always there for his kids and loved playing with them. Steve still romanced his wife, maybe part of that had to do with guilt over his infidelities, but most of it was because he still adored his wife. She never wanted to divorce him because she wanted the family to be together and she knew that he would never walk away from the marriage either despite his cheating.

She knew about it, she knew about what happened on road trips, but Mary convinced herself that he had two lives – one of them on the road to which she didn't want to know anything about and his other life with her. She was happy with that. However, Chicago was her home and she wasn't going to move to Texas. Her family was going to be in Chicago and somehow they would make it work during the rest of his career. Of course they would visit, but they were never going to be permanent residents in Texas. So that's what they agreed to and it worked for while, but the arrangement would not last. It would come to an end. And while Steve Larson would have an average career for the next three and half years in Texas, it would never match the career he had as a Chicago Cub, good and bad. Steve Larson would always be a Cub at heart and the way he played proved that because he was never the same in Texas.

The next day The Cubs came home from their road trip. It was a long one and they needed a day off even though there weren't too many as the 2008 season was coming to a close. It was a still a tight race in the Central Division and whether the Cubs were even going to make the playoffs was not out of the realm of certainty. Each day counted and each game was a big game – that's where they were now.

Ryan arrived home and Tara, his girlfriend, was just finishing dinner. They had been living together ever since they both moved to Chicago in 2007 when he got called up to the Majors. While he had not officially asked her to marry him they both pretty much knew they were going to be together the rest of their lives – for the both of them they were the one and didn't want anybody else. Ryan walked over to Tara in the kitchen and gave her a kiss on the cheek as she was stirring the sauce for their pasta. She smiled and made sarcastic remark. "I guess you had a tough day at the office?"

He laughed and said. "You can say that. Did you see the game?"

"I saw the highlights on ESPN; from the looks of it you must have called the umpire a cocksucker...the broadcaster said that you used a word that's a big no-no with the umpire."

"Well he deserved it."

"Hmm...If you say so."

"Well maybe, but he still got the call wrong."

"That part I noticed." She turned around and gave Ryan a hug. "Are you okay?"

"Yeah, just tired and worried."

"Worried about what"

"I'm worried that despite how well we've been playing we still won't make the playoffs. I'm worried that I am more of a liability now because I haven't been pitching great. "

Ryan was sitting on the couch and she walked over to sit next to him, putting her hands on his shoulders and giving him a backrub. She said to him. "I wouldn't go that far...your numbers are still pretty good — not great, but better than a lot of pitchers."

"Doesn't feel like it when you get ejected from the game and can't win it for your team."

"Dumpster, Lilly, Zambrano, and Harden all have no-decisions too, but it doesn't mean that they aren't winning ball games. All of you guys are doing good and the numbers reflect that. It's just that the Cardinals have a little bit better numbers."

Ryan still had a frown and said. "What if it still isn't enough?"

"Then it's not enough and while that sucks it doesn't take away from the fact that you are a better team than most in the second half of the season. Remember what you told me the first time we met...the numbers never lie in baseball and the numbers say that you are great team."

Ryan just sat back and pondered that for a moment, but then he also reminded himself that that may not be good enough for the Cub fans who have waited 100 years to see them win the World Series. Then Ryan also thought back to when he first met Tara. They met in 2006 in Tennessee. She was working for a branch of Chase bank as a mortgage analyst, which Ryan didn't really know what that was, but she as she explained it, it had to do with statistics. Ryan was grabbing a burger one day from a local hamburger joint and bumped into her as he was walking in and she was walking out, spilling her soft drink all over her blouse. She was a mess and pissed off at him because he had to get back to work. It was her lunch hour and she didn't have time to waste with a dirty blouse especially when she had a meeting that afternoon.

Ryan offered to pay for dry cleaning and buy her lunch. Lucky for them there was a one hour dry cleaning place around the corner that could get it done quickly. So Ryan stayed with her as she waited and they started talking. Turned out they enjoyed each other's company and he could make her laugh when most men couldn't. She tried to explain what she did at the bank and of course he was confused, but most people got confused when she explained what she did. That didn't bother Ryan, when he told her that he was a baseball player she confessed to him that didn't know anything about baseball even though her father and grandfather had both played college baseball for LSU. Ryan just couldn't understand how anybody could not know anything about baseball, it was America's pastime. She told him that she never got into it and it seemed boring.

When her dry cleaning was done and she was about to leave Ryan asked her out. She didn't know what to say at first because she wasn't sure about him, but she eventually said yes. He told her to meet him at the ball park for the Smokies on Saturday after the game – it was a day game and he was going to show her something that night at the ball park. Tara agreed to meet him even though she was meeting him at an unusual place. For their first date he planned a picnic at the ball park beneath the lights as the sun was setting behind the outfield. He was going to show her something of baseball that only a person who loved numbers could enjoy.

Tara showed up at the end of the game even thought she had thought about not showing up, but she also thought to herself, Ryan was cute and deserved a shot. He had dinner brought to them by one of the other players – sure it was hot dogs, but a little tradition at the ballpark never hurt anyone. They talked and ate, but then she had to ask him. "Why did you really bring me here to the ballpark?"

He answered her. "Because, I want you to see the numbers and science behind this game. It's not just about grown men playing a kids game although that part is good. Baseball is about numbers and I'm sure you can agree that numbers never lie."

"I can agree with that."

"Then let me show you the numbers behind what I do."

So they started talking about pitching and ERA. They talked about batting averages and on base percentages. Ryan basically went through the rules of the game and showed her how if the numbers are added up right it could lead to victory – one might say that there was a true science to the game and without that victory would be unattainable. Tara was a science person, she loved numbers and facts and what he told her made sense – she had never looked at the game of baseball in that way before. The way he explained the game made it seem perfect and beautiful and it was at that moment she actually fell in love with the game of baseball, but it also had something to do with another thing he said to her. Ryan told her. "Baseball is a game that you can't fake, you either love it or hate it and there is certainly no masquerading your way through it. But the science behind it is pure and it's the closest thing to perfection that we can get to, except maybe love. And the love that you can have for this game can make it that much better."

Tara kissed him after he said that and although she had had men try and impress her with poetry before what Ryan told her was one of the most honest pieces of truth she had ever been told. Tara became a baseball fan after that night and she would make it a point to be at as many home games as she could. But the most important thing for Ryan and Tara was they started dating and would be never be apart except for road games. When he got moved up to the Cubs she put in for a transfer and moved to Chicago with him. During the last part of their first date he taught her how to bat against the pitching machine that the team had, of course it could have just been an excuse to hold her.

Ryan and Tara continued to talk over dinner at their apartment that night. Ryan was still unsure about his future and even though Tara tried to remind him that he was not his father, the uncertainty was still there. But she did tell him one thing. "No matter what happens this year, no matter what happens with your career, or if the Cubs ever win the World Series, and it doesn't even matter whether you pitch like your dad....you still have a choice. You don't have to approach the game like he did."

"But what If I can't deliver?"

"Then so what, at least you tried and gave everything you had. At least you go down giving 100% with no regrets. That no one can take away from you. And if the fans get disappointed again and even if you're the cause of that they will get over it because true Cub fans are faithful and never leave their team. "

"I just don't want to have to live with the failure. I don't know if I can live with mine."

"It will be hard, sure, but you're not alone and that team won't be alone either...the fans will still be there. "

Ryan smiled at her and said. "How did you get so smart, in college?"

"I fell in love with a baseball player and the Chicago Cubs who taught me the purity of the game itself and he also taught me that there will be highs and lows in the game, but what really matters is how we climb out of the trenches. "

He smiled at her again and said. "I guess I just need to hear that."

"I know that and what will happen, will happen, but don't give up without a fight. "

That was all that needed to be said.

[215]

[216]

16

The Year Before

It came down to the last game of the season for the Chicago Cubs. The last game of the regular of the season would determine if they went to the playoffs or they would end the season in failure. This was supposed to be the year they won it all after 100 years. The Cubs were considered the best team in baseball based on their pitching staff and the strength of their bench, but they had not played like it until the second half the season and it seemed as if was too late for them — everything they had done in the last part of the season would be a waste of time because here they were one game away from being out of it all. They were playing the Giants the last game of the season and it they were fighting for the Wild Card Spot with them.

The Cubs were still one game out of first place in the central division in the National League and if they won while the Cardinals lost that day, then they would be tied for first place in the division and force a one-game playoff to

[217]

see who won the division and went to the playoffs. That was one scenario. If the cardinals won their last game and the Cubs won against the Giants that day then the Cardinals would take first place in the division and the Cubs would have the Wild Card Spot. That was the other scenario. But the final scenario was the one that no one wanted to talk about – if the Cubs lost and the Cardinals won then Giants would get the Wild Card spot and the Cubs' season would be over. It was a tense day for all three of these teams because two of them would be going to the playoff and the other would be going home. The Cubs had split the last 6 games they had with the Cardinals, winning three games and losing three games just to keep them alive in the playoff race.

It was hours before the game and Lou, the Cubs manager, still hadn't decided who he wanted to pitch. All of his rotation had pitched to get them to this point and none of them had had much rest. Besides, he needed them for the playoffs. His two choices to pitch were Big Z who he wanted to start game one of the playoffs and Ryan Larson who was probably more rested than anyone, but was not the most logical choice for such a big game because he had struggled all season long. However, he did have a good outing five days before against the Cardinals even though the Cubs lost the game. Everybody expected it to be Big Z because the Cubs needed to win and he was pitching great ever since his no-hitter. About an hour before game time Lou called them both into the office and announced to them his decision. He was going with Ryan even though Larry, the Cubs pitching coach, wanted Big Z, but as Lou pointed out he had faith in the kid. Although he did tell Zambrano to be ready just in case he needed to put him in for 4 or five innings.

Lou asked Ryan to stay as both pitchers were leaving the office. He asked him. "Are you feeling okay? And I want you to be honest with me because if you're not up to this we need to know now."

[218]

"I still have some pain in the wrist, but it's nothing that I can't handle, I can still pitch." Ryan said.

"Okay. But I don't want you trying to strike everybody out. Use your teammates... they're backing you up."

Ryan smiled and replied. "Are you telling me that because there's been a lot of stuff written about me lately comparing me to my dad?"

"If it were me I would be bothered by it."

"It's nothing I haven't heard before, but I have good things and bad things from it. However he did teach me how to pitch and he knows what he's talking about, just like my grandfather."

Lou smiled and said. "That he does. Just wanted to make sure you were okay, though. "
"I am...now let's go with this thing so we can get to the playoffs."

Ryan walked out of the visitor's clubhouse; in San Francisco. Ryan had never pitched at the Giant's stadium before and as that day it was the biggest game he ever pitched for the Cubs. He started his warm-ups and before Ryan threw the first warm-up pitch he smiled to himself for he was totally calm — he had a song playing in his head while he warmed up, Joe Cocker's "Feeling Good." Amy, who was up in the broadcasting booth with the other sports writers, saw her brother smiling as he warmed up – he was loose and that was something that he hadn't been in a long time. She leaned over to a friend of hers, Carrie Muskrat, who wrote for the Cubs and Major League Baseball. She commented to Carrie, "Better get your pen ready, this is going to be an interesting game, and I think my brother is going to give us something worth writing about today."

Carrie gave Amy a weird look and asked. "What makes you think so?"

"He's smiling, which means he loose and ready to have fun. He's just like my dad in that regard, when he gets like that he can be very dangerous and completely dominating on the mound."

"I hope you're right because I don't want to quite writing about the 2008 Cubs after today."

It was game time and Ryan Larson was ready. The game was on WGN and ESPN: Baseball Tonight, so everybody was watching including Steve Larson. The Rangers had an afternoon game and were done with their season now so he was already home watching the game to see if his son was going to pitch. He was in for a real treat. The Cubs coaches were also paying attention to the scoreboard at the Cardinals game, which had started an hour before. They were winning 3-0 in the fourth inning again the Pittsburg Pirates, the last place team in the central division.

As the game was underway now Ryan took a deep breath before his first pitches and then gave his catcher a mischievous smile. He was going to have a little fun. His first pitch was a fastball that got away from him and nearly took the batter's head off. The batter hit the ground diving out of the way and Ryan was met with boos from Giants fans. Soto, the catcher, chuckled and told the batter, "Don't stand too close — he'll kill you with his fastball." Soto knew what Ryan was doing, he was backing the batter off the plate a little bit to set him up with his curveball that would go outside, low and away. The next pitch was the curveball and the batter missed for the first strike. Ryan would strike him out on the next two pitches with a cut fastball and his sinker. Ryan was taking control of the game early. The next Giants batters were easy as well. He made then foul off pitched to get strikes and then he would throw a slide or curveball and make them miss it. After the first inning he had struck out the side and set the tone early.

Through the first four innings, Ryan had struck out the side twice and had nine strike outs. He was mowing the batters down and doing it with such dominance that it left Cubs thinking about two things: could he break Kerry Wood's strikeout record of 20 strikeouts in a game, which was done 10 years before, and could this be a Cuba perfect game? There was still a lot of baseball though. In the fifth inning Ryan did walk a batter to take the perfect game away, but he got out of the inning early after getting another two strikeouts and ending the inning on a double play. There had not been much action from the Cubs infield and the outfield had yet to make a play because the ball had never reached that far. This game was all Ryan, and the Giants, who were a pretty good team, seemed baffled by this pitcher. Ryan Larson had returned to true form and all of his pitches were working perfectly, especially the sinker. Not one Giant batter could get even a piece of it all night and it looked as if the second coming of Bruce Sutter had arrived. That was the comment Rick Sutcliff made to as he was announcing the game for ESPN.

By the sixth inning the Cubs had gotten a couple of runs from Alfonso Soriano's solo home run and a Derrek Lee double knocking a runner in. The sixth inning gave Ryan a little more trouble. He gave up a solo home run to the first batter to put the Giants within one run. Then he walked the next batter. Larry, the pitching coach, came out to see if he was okay and to stall a little bit so Ryan could catch his breath. The Cubs didn't get any of their relief pitchers up in the bullpen – there was no need, Ryan's pitch count was only at 69 pitches. He could throw a complete game at the rate he was going. After taking a break talking with the pitching coach and the Soto the catcher Ryan was ready. He proceeded to strike out the next two batters. It took about 17 pitches to do it because they kept fouling off pitches, but he got them. He was at 13 strikeouts after the sixth inning. The Cubs were able to tack on another couple of runs to help their cause. Ryan was out of contention for the perfect game and the no-hitter and even breaking the strikeout record would require striking out 8 more batters to break the record, which would be hard. Also, Lou had just gotten word that the Cardinals won their game so they won the central division. The Cubs had to win now just to get the Wild Card Spot. In the 7th inning, Ryan struck out the side and as the last pitch was thrown, which was his sinker, he started to walk back towards the dugout. Just like his father he knew that it was a strike and of course it was.

The ESPN announcers were commenting on the fact that it was pretty arrogant of a pitcher to start walking off the mound before the pitch reached the catcher and the pitch was called a strike for the out. But as Rick Sutcliff pointed out, it was also the mark of a great pitcher to be that confident and know where the pitch was going to be and what would happen next. Ryan was booed as he walked to the dugout. Ryan ignored it because he already knew that the Giants' season was going to be over.

When Ryan came out to the mound in the 8th inning he was booed again, but the Cub fans that were at the stadium were on their feet. The first pitch was a popup behind the plate for the first out. The next batter he struck out on four pitches he actually did with his curveball, which wasn't much use anymore at that point in the game. The final batter he made him foul off the first two pitches and then gave three balls for a full count. Soto called for the sinker, but the batter was looking for that because it was his "get out of a jam pitch." Instead he threw a change-up to the inside and nipped the corner for strike three. Ryan Larson had 18 strikeouts, but he was also at 101 pitches. Lou made a deal with him before the 9th inning. If he could strike out the first batter then he would leave him in and see if he could tie or break the record, but if not he was going to be pulled and the closer would be put in to finish the game.

Ryan had two strikes on the first batter, but he got a hold of it and went sailing into centerfield for a fly-out. Ryan wasn't mad at all; the Cubs were leading 4-1 and were about to win the game. He looked back at the Cubs dugout as Lou Pinella walked out to get the baseball from him. Ryan smiled and shrugged at Lou as if to say "Oh well." Kerry Wood came out to mound and congratulated Ryan on a well-pitched game. With Soto, the catcher, standing there, and in front of Lou, Ryan told Kerry, "I left your record well in tact tonight."

Kerry replied back. "Hey, you can stay in and tie it just as long as we get to the playoffs."

"I think if I did that Lou would have my head."

They all laughed and Lou told Ryan to go back to the dugout so they could get this game over with. As Ryan walked back to dugout he was given a standing ovation by Cub fans and his teammates, who were all standing in at the edge of the dugout waiting to greet him. Even Amy and Carrie Muskrat and the WGN guys were giving Ryan a standing ovation. Kerry Wood, their closer, took care of business early. On four pitches and two groundballs that never left the infield, the next two batters were thrown out at first baseball. The Cubs were in the playoffs by the skin of their teeth and on the shoulders of Ryan Larson.

The Cubs making the playoffs was the most exciting thing in Chicago all year and it seemed that fans would expect nothing less than a World Series title. Making the playoffs was destiny that a hundred years of suffering was about to end...those were the comments made by one sports blogger form the Chicago Tribune, but true baseball people knew better than to think that. It was far from being in the bag, so to speak, and the Cubs had a very tough road ahead of them. For the first round of the playoffs it would be a best of five series against the LA Dodgers and the first two games would be played in LA. The Cubs had a couple of days rest before they would be playing game one in LA. One of the important decisions for the manager was who would be the starting rotation because in the post season teams were only allowed a four man rotation. Ryan had a pitched a great game and he was a master on the mound, but still he had struggled all season and by the numbers wasn't choice for the starting rotation when the other four starters had better records than Ryan, he had finished 8-7 for the season.

Lou asked Ryan to come into his office during the one day the Cubs had to practice before heading to LA. He asked Ryan to take a seat just like he would if a guy was about to be cut. Before he could say anything Ryan spoke up first. "Skip...I know what this is about and I'm fine being in the bullpen for the playoffs."

Lou smiled and replied. "I guess it's that obvious why I needed to talk to you."

"Kind of is.'

"I want you to know that were doing this by the numbers and with you being injured you just don't have that much time in this season and besides you are a rookie. I need seasoned guys out there during the playoffs because it's not going to be easy. "

"I would do the same thing and already expected to be in the bullpen."

"At least you're prepared for it, but this doesn't take away from what you did Sunday night...that was one of the most incredible performances I have ever seen on the mound. You controlled that game from start to finish and won it for us."

"Thanks Skip."

"You are my first alternate to start if one of the guys gets hurt and I may need you to do a couple of innings throughout games just in case we go to extras. "

"I can do that for you."

Lou stood and reached out his hand to shake Ryan's. As the younger Larson shook his manager's hand Lou said to him. "Thank you for your support of this team."

"I've been a Cub my whole life...not going to stop now."

The two men just laughed and that was it. Two days later the team was in LA for game one.

As the playoffs started there was a lot of ink about the Cubs' post-season collapse the year before. The Cubs had won 97 games, had the best record in baseball, and were the heavy favorites to win it all that year. It wasn't to be...the Cubs were swept in the first round of the playoffs – they played three games again the Arizona Diamondbacks and were sent home for the season after those three games.

It was devastating and nobody could believe it. The Cubs had simply stopped hitting and couldn't get their offense going, but this year was going to be different. At least that's what everybody thought.

Game one against the LA Dodgers was not exactly picture perfect. Big Z was pitching that night and he ended up giving up five hits and three runs during the first inning for the Dodgers to take an early lead. Big Z was able to keep the Dodgers at bay over the next three innings even though they had a few more hits, but they didn't score any runs. The Cubs, on the other hand, still didn't have a hit through four innings and the great offenses that they had had during the second half of the season were non-existent. It seemed to be a repeat of last year. During the fifth inning the Dodgers ripped Zambrano for 6 more hits and 3 more runs to take a 6-0 lead over the Cubs. Big Z had loaded the bases with only one out before Lou decided to pull him. Sean Marshall, who came out of the bullpen, couldn't get the job done. One hit and the Dodgers scored two more runs to jump out 8-0. Marshall finally got the next batter to hit into a double play to end the inning, but the damage was already done.

There were a lot of Cub fans at Dodger stadium that night and their cheers were silent. The curse had silenced them...that's what one of the Dodger broadcasts said while calling the game. Things settled down with the Dodgers during the next three innings, but still no Cubs offense. They finally got a couple of hits in the 7th inning, but couldn't get the runners home. In the eighth a solo home run by Aramis Ramirez gave the cubs a run, but it wasn't good enough to catch up to the Dodgers, especially when they got another run in the eighth inning. The Cubs had one final try at the top of the ninth, but the Dodgers' closing pitcher struck out the side to end game one. The Cubs were already down in the Series and to say that Cub fans were dismayed would be an understatement.

Game 2 would be played the next day and the results would not be much better. Ryan Dempster was on the mound for game two and he had been nearly perfect all year long. 2008 was his first year back to the starting rotation in 5 years and he won 17 games that year while only losing 6 games. As good as he was all year he couldn't bring that magic in game two. Four hits in the 1st inning and two by the Dodgers got them to an early lead again. The Cubs offense tried to get started and despite the one or two hits they got during the first four inning of the game, they couldn't seem to score any runs. However, the Dodgers scored at least one run over the first four innings to jump out to a 6-0 lead early. Dempster just couldn't stop them, and it seemed every pitch he threw a Dodger batter would make contact, whether it was a foul ball or a hit into the outfield. Even a 96 mile an hour fastball couldn't slow the Dodgers down. After five innings and 6 runs Dempster was taken out of the game. It wasn't his night.

Ryan Larson came in to replace Dempster. He got the Cubs out of the 6th inning, but the 7th inning was more trouble for the Cubs. The Cubs just couldn't seem to get any runs and every inning they would strand runners. In the 7th inning, Ryan gave a couple of hits. He kept trying to pitch the guys inside but he couldn't locate his fastball where he wanted. He faced his third batter and on the second pitch his slider got away from him. He gave up a three-run homer to put the Dodgers up 9-0. Then it didn't stop there, he loaded the bases by walking two batters and giving up another hit. Lou decided he was done for the evening and his bad luck in LA continued. The Cubs were able to get out of the inning without any runs being scored by the Dodgers, who were too far ahead, and of course they won the game. They now lead the series 2-0 and it looked the Cubs' season was over – game three at Wrigley Field was just a foregone conclusion. Again, the cheers from Cub fans were silent.

In the post game press conference, Lou tried to offer some simple explanation that the Cubs always hard a hard time in LA, and that things would be better when they got home, but even he didn't sound convinced. Nobody had a good answer for why the Cubs had done a complete 180 since the last half of the season and nobody wanted to talk about it. The team was angry, but it was silent anger with no answers on what to do. The only vocal person was Zambrano, but he was an emotional guy and never could keep his mouth shut. He basically said what everybody felt on the Cubs team.

The Cubs flew back that night and when Ryan Larson arrived home he didn't even wake Tara to say hi. He just let her sleep and got a glass of scotch. He didn't want to remember and in his solemn boredom decided to surf the net and see what people were already saying about the Cubs so far in the playoffs. As a professional he knew he shouldn't read that stuff or even care what they sports writers and bloggers say, but he couldn't help it. He found a blog about him from some LA sports writer and it was titled. "A Line of Coke Can Stop Home runs: Ryan Larson gives up three-run homer to extend Dodger's lead." It was another reference to his dad, Steve Larson, and how he could be just like him.

17

The Cubs Come Alive

It was in the early in the morning when Ryan's cell phone started going off, he knew who it was by the sound of the ringtone because each of his contacts had their own special song. It was his dad and the song playing on his phone was the Darth Vader's theme from Star Wars. Ryan hadn't gotten much sleep the night before from drinking and surfing the web. Tara had already gone to work when he answered his phone. He said.

"Hello Dad, what do you need?"

"How are you feeling this morning?" his dad asked in a cheerful tone. He liked to call his son early in the morning and try and get him chipper because he knew his Ryan was not a morning person. It was a little joke he liked to play.

"I'm fine Dad; sore, but okay."

"Sorry about the game last night, it looked like it was brutal."

"Yeah, and it didn't help that I gave up a three-run homer last night either."

"I saw that...loosen your grip a little bit on the ball when you throw and you'll find better location. "

"I know, I was too tight last night. I think we all were."

Steve laughed at the comment. He had been in plenty of games like that before and paid the price for it. It usually happened when he lost. He said to his son. "I mainly wanted to find out how you were because I figured you might have seen that blog comparing you to me again, it hit the AP wires this morning."

"Yeah I saw it...you don't have some cocaine for me do you?"

"Funny! I would give you some it I thought it would help, but in the long run it never does you good...I should know."

"I guess the baseball bloggers have to have something to talk about when it comes to my pitching, but I wish they would find something original to talk about."

"Baseball bloggers are just pissed because they can't play the game."

"Did you just call to check up on me?"

"Yeah, wanted to make sure the article wasn't going to get you down."

"No, I'm fine...I've read that kind of stuff before."

"So did I with my dad, but we're not perfect, it can get to us if we let it."

Ryan smiled at his dad's concern. He said. "I appreciate your concern dad, but I will be all right. I just need to figure out how to help my team win before our season ends too early."

"Well good luck to you tomorrow, if you need anything I am only a phone call away."

It wasn't very often that Steve showed real concern for Ryan like that and the truth was, he was worried that his son would do something stupid like him. When Steve Larson arrived in Texas for the 1990 season he didn't exactly change his ways. He still liked to party and was still prone to doing lines of coke if he was at a party where they had it. He might have been a great family man when he was home with his wife and kids, but he was a different kind of animal when he was out on the town enjoying the night life. Steve had a pretty decent season in with the Texas Rangers in 1990. He was 12-11 for the year and he also knew that he was not the star pitcher of the team. That title went to Nolan Ryan. Nolan had a lot of respect for Steve Larson because he knew how great of a pitcher he really was, but he didn't agree with Steve's lifestyle. The two pitchers became good friends during Steve's tenure with the Rangers, and Nolan Ryan showed Steve a different side of the game. He was a like a father figure to Steve and one that he was more willing to listen to because Steve didn't get along with his own dad – there were too many years of being compared to Jack Larson that pissed him off and made him resent his father. In a lot of ways Jack was a better pitcher, but when it came to raw natural talent Steve was much better and what angered Jack was that his son would squander that talent.

Steve Larson's stay with the Rangers wasn't totally unpleasant. He had some mild success with them. In 1991 he went 12-10 and in 1992 he went 9-9 dues to a few injuries, but his ability had diminished and his fastball was in the low 90's now. While the steroid error had begun in the early 90's, that was mostly for hitters trying to get an extra boost in their swing, but some pitchers tried them as well. Steve Larson was not one of those pitchers; his problem was the booze and the coke. He drank like Mickey Mantle and used coke like a rock star. It never affected his family life, but it did ruin his ability to play. In 1993 Major League Baseball started doing heavy random drug testing again. Midway through the season Steve Larson tested positive for coke and it was the second time in 4 years. This time it was an automatic suspension for the rest of the season, but the commission of Major League Baseball wanted to take it a step further – they needed to set an example of what would and would not be tolerated. Steve Larson in June of 1993 was kicked out of professional baseball for good and he was scrutinized just as "black sox" of 1919 were. The decision was controversial, but nobody denied that he needed to be punished and even his own father, Jack, voiced that opinion to the media by agreeing with the decision.

A few harsh statements by his father to the press and the lack of support for what Steve Larson was going through started a fallout between the two. Steve felt that at the time he needed his family the most they abandoned him, even Mary, his wife. Steve went to rehab again while his lawyer and agent were trying to appeal the decision – he figured rehab would show Major League baseball that he was serious about getting better and that they might reverse their decision and let him play again. While he was there Mary had had enough and filed for divorce. She could handle him being away and only being there during the offseason or when the Rangers came to Chicago to play the White Sox, but she couldn't handle a drunk and an addict and affairs. She figured he was playing around after the 1984 season, but she stayed because she loved him and she knew that despite all that he loved her more than anything – his activities were just being a part of professional ballplayer on the road. But finally she had enough and left him – she had their kids to think about. Mary still loved him, but they couldn't be together while he couldn't get his life together, and she hoped that being out of baseball would help with that. The funny thing was, Mary never got remarried and hardly ever dated. It was the same thing for Steve as well as the years went by.

Ryan was reminded of that after speaking with his dad and no matter how scared he was that he might end up like his father, Steve Larson was more scared of that happening than his own son was. Perhaps that's why he decided to finally help him down at Tennessee. But for the rest of the day Ryan had a smile on his face because of his dad calling to check on him. He called his sister Amy to tell her that…she would get a kick out of that.

Later that day when Ryan arrived at the ballpark, Lou, the manager, was standing around talking to reporters. He was trying to get his interviews out the way early so he didn't have to waste time doing it later. He had other things on his mind and the reports kept asking the same questions. Like anybody in the press that wrote stories for the fans they all wanted answers – answers to how the Cubs were going to come back and keep their season alive. Another reporter standing near asked Lou. "What do you think is the problem with the team to why they haven't played as well as they should have?

Sweet Lou replied in a sarcastic tone. "For the umpteenth time as I have said before… hitting has been our problem. You should already know that answer since I've already said it before."

"What are you going to do about it?"

"We are going try to get our offense started…it should be obvious."

"Do you have an secrets that you can share with us on how you're going to do that?"

"So you can write about it and give it away to the opposing team? No sir, we don't have any secrets for you."

The other reporters started laughing. Finally someone said to Lou. "Come on Lou give us something to write about."

"I think the Cubs have given you plenty to write about."

"I meant in strategy, Lou."

"I am going to tell you all of this and then I'm done. Not going to answer the same questions over and over. We've played bad over the last two games… no doubt about it and if we play that way tomorrow then our season is over, but start paying attention because I think this team is just about to get started and you can make all the comparisons that this year is going to be the same as last year. We've got to start hitting plain and simple. And our pitchers have got to settle down and do what they're best at. As far as I am concerned, we have the best pitching staff in the league, and they are about to show you that. We didn't start out like we should have, but hey, we have to give you guys something to write about. If we would had swept the Dodgers then all of your news stories would have been boring, wouldn't they?"

Amy Larson was among the reporters and she asked Lou. "What are you saying, skipper, you just wanted to give the fans their money's worth this year in the playoffs?"

Lou smiled at Amy. He had always liked her because she had been fair about the Cubs in her writing and she was probably the most objective reporter in Chicago on the Cubs when it would be assumed that she wouldn't. He replied to her.

"Amy Larson, the last thing I want to do is disappoint you and Cub fans so you better be out here tonight because you're not going to want to miss it."

That was all Lou said to reporters until the end of game three and it was all that needed to be said. As he walking back towards batting practice he passed Ryan Dempster. Dempster replied. "Need me to say anything to the reporters or did you confuse them enough?" Lou smiled and said. "I think I did a good enough job, but be my guest if you want to tell them one of your fantastic stories so they will have something else to write about and quit asking the same damn questions." Dempster could always get people loose with his sense of humor and get their minds off of the stress in their lives, and he knew that Lou was aggravated at the reporter's questions. All they seemed to want to talk about was how the Cubs were on the verge of a total collapse and they couldn't win the big games. They were about to proved wrong.

Game three was a lot different. For one they were at home and that was always a good advantage. Ted Lilly was on the mound for the Cubs – he was the gritty lefthander that just wore down batters inning by inning. That's exactly what he did the first two innings of the game, retiring the side both times. The Cubs even started out with an early lead in the second inning, getting two runs. For the most part it was a pitcher's duel between Lilly and the Dodger pitcher through the first six innings. Ted Lilly had not allowed a hit through six innings and it was a breath a fresh air for the Cubs who had gotten beat badly in the first two games by runaway scores.

The seventh inning would prove to be a little more difficult. Ted Lilly walked the first two Dodger batters in the inning. After striking out the next batter Lilly had a fastball that hung a little much with much sinking action. The Dodger batter hit the shit out of ball and sent it into the centerfield bleacher. Just like that the Dodgers were up 3-2. It was the only hit he allowed in the game and it gave the other team the lead. The Cubs tried to threaten in the 7th by getting a man on second and third base, but the other Cub batters could not get them home. Lilly remained in the game through the 8th inning and retired the side for the fifth time of the game. The Cubs opted to bring out their setup man Carlos Marmol to pitch the top of the ninth inning just in case they needed to use their closer Kerry Wood in extra innings. Marmol pitched great and faced only four batters before shutting the Dodgers down.

It was the bottom of the ninth inning and the Cubs' last chance to either tie the game or win it. The Dodgers closer came out to the mound and he was ferocious as a pitcher – he had won his last 14 save attempts including the game one and two of this playoff series. The first Cubs batter went down with a pop fly into center field. The second batter went down on strikes. Alfonso Soriano of the Cubs managed to draw a walk and get the tying run on base. It was down to one batter, their rookie catcher Geovanni Soto who had been magnificent all year. His batter average was .302 and he ended the year with 27 home runs.

The Dodger pitcher tried to get him out early and make him pop the ball up for an easy out, but the first two pitches were fouled off into the stands. Every Cubs fan at

Wrigley Field that night was on their feet as one strike could end their season. A hush went over the crown as the pitcher went into his windup. Joe Morgan up in the ESPN booth said over the airwaves, " The Cubs are down to their last strike, will their season be over on this next pitch or will the Cubs still be alive? " The pitch was a slider, trying to get Soto to swing and miss it since it was outside the plate, but it didn't get enough movement on it. Crack! Soto got just enough of it and sent it high into left field." Rick Sutcliff the other ESPN announcer started shouting, "It's a high ball deep into left field…it's got a chance…way back…way back… it is out of here. A two-run homer by Geovanni Soto…Cubs win, Cubs win!"

Soto hit a two-run walk-off homer to win the game and keep the Cubs alive in the series. The Dodger pitcher slammed his glove on the ground in anger. He was greeted by his entire team at home plate. At the post game press conference Lou, the manager, didn't spend too much time talking with reporters. He only had one comment for all of them. He said. "I told you all that you didn't want to miss the game. My Cubs have come alive and this series is far from over." That was it, he was done and didn't answer questions. All he did was go back into the clubhouse and talk to the team. He had one thing to say to them as well. "You guys played great tonight, but if you want your season to be over tomorrow night then you better play that well again, and I know you can. "

The message was heard loud and clear. Because the Cubs team that took the field in game four was the same team that had played the second half of the season. Rick Harden was on the mound that night for game four. He set the tone early by striking out the side. The Cubs jumped out to an early lead in the first and didn't stop there. The entire offense belonged to the Cubs and the Dodgers on only three hits never got past first base. Rick Harden pitched a complete game that night and never reached a hundred pitches. The Cubs had a hit in every inning. They won game four 9-0. They had forced a game five leaving the

Dodgers mystified on how this could have happen, but as Joe Torre said to the media, they would just have to win it in LA, but it would not be that easy. However, t he Chicago Cubs had all the momentum.

Game five would be played in a couple of days. Big Z was on the mound for game five and he was certainly better than he did in game one. He gave up only one hit in three innings. It was a two-run homer to give the Dodgers the lead, but it was the only runs allowed for the Dodgers the whole game. The Cubs came back and had the 7-2 lead going into the bottom of the ninth inning. By that time only Cub fans were cheering at Dodger Stadium in LA. After a three-run homer in the third inning by Derrek Lee and two unearned runs in the fifth and sixth inning the Cubs had put the Dodgers away. The Dodgers tried to come back by loading the bases in the seventh inning, but Big Z in his last inning made them hit into a double play to end the innings and not allow a run to score.

Kerry Wood walked to the mound to close out the game and get the Cubs win. Cub fans were on their feet. Three batters came up and three batters down by Kerry Wood. He struck the first two out with such precision it reminded Cub fans of the 20 strikeout in 1998. He made the last batter pop the ball up over to first base. Derrek Lee, the quiet captain, got the last out and celebrated with his team. They had come back and won the last three games to beat the Dodgers and advance to the National League Championship Series. While Lou knew that his team could do it, what had happened was stunning to most sports writers and fans.

Amy was at the game covering it for the paper. As the gamed ended she saw Mike Stanley from the Tribune, the reporter she despised, leaning back in his chair. She said to him. "I told you the Cubs could win this series."

"Who cares if you're right. The Cubs are going to get killed in the next round. The Cardinals are too good."

Amy replied. "We'll see." But the thing is she wasn't so sure he might be right. The St. Louis Cardinals were a

very good team, but were they the better team. On paper
the Cardinals were, but the way the Cubs had been playing
made them seem like champions.

18

63 Years in the Waiting

The Cubs had been here before, one playoff series and four wins away from the World Series. They had been here three times before in the last 25 years and every time had the same result – close but no victory. Amy Larson stared at the word document on her laptop with the first two lines of her article. The National League Championship Series was one day away and she was trying to make sense of the Chicago Cubs being in it. It was miracle some had said, others including most of the fame were still in disbelief. The Cubs should not have been there, but realty has cruel sense of humor sometimes. Even Amy could not believe what was happening.

Chris had finally woken up and poured himself a cup of coffee then he walked over to Amy's desk and refilled her cup. She was in her own little word and didn't really pay attention to the nice thing that he just did. He asked as she finally looked up and smiled at him. "Stuck on what to say?"

[239]

"You can say that."

He read what she had written so far and replied. "It's good so far."

" All I did was state the facts...hard to screw that up. What I am trying to do is figure out how to be objective and excited, but to also not show that I have doubts."

"You don't think that the Cubs can win?"

" Anything is possible, but we've been here before and if you look at the numbers then the Cardinals are a better a team."

" I don't think anyone is saying that it's going to be easy for the Cubs and it's very possible that it could go to seven games in the series."

"Then again we can also be swept in four games."

Chris gave her a hug and said to her. "No what happens, it's been a remarkable year and I'm glad that I got to be a part of it with you."

"Me too."

Chris went to get ready for work and Amy went back to writing her article. She pointed out some of the history of the Cubs over the last 25 years and the near misses. The last time the Cubs had been here in the playoffs they were 5 outs away from the World Series – they were so close and their self-destruction began with a controversial play with one of their own, a Cubs fan. Of course it wasn't his fault in the least for what happened to the Cubs in 2003 because the Cubs had plenty of chances to win after that play or in game seven of that series. In 1984 Steve Larson had caused one of the games they should have won to go to the World Series to be lost because of his own selfish acts. He has lived with that blame by fans and one of his best friends for 24 years. In 1989 the Giants that year were too strong and the Cubs didn't play like the team they really were causing them to lose and only get close to the World Series again. Here they were and no one could say for sure whether they good enough to get to the World Series or much less win it. After 100 years of futility there was more uncertainty about the Cubs chances than absolute guarantees and perhaps that would work in their favor. But there was one thing that Amy could say for sure in her article – the Cubs had been full of surprises all year and predicting what they would seem to be a waste of time.

Game one against the Cardinals would be played in St. Louis at Busch Stadium. As it usually goes with this rivalry the there would be just as many Cub fans and Cardinal fans at the game dividing right down the middles the number of die-hard fans. Ryan Dempster would be the starting pitcher for the Cubs. Amy was there covering the game as was her grandfather, Jack Larson, with her grandmother, mother, and Chris. Ryan was sure to get some action because every game had a real chance of going to extra innings. Game one got underway and it was what most people expected, a close battle through every inning. It was a pitcher's duel as well. Dempster was doing well and after three innings the score was tied 1-1. Both offenses sparked a little bit after the third, but the score remained tied at 3-3 at the end of the sixth. The Cardinals pitcher lasted through the middle of the eighth inning as he allowed two Cubs on base. Dempster had already been taken out in the seventh inning. The Cubs were able to get one run to take the lead 4-3 in the eighth. Cubs pitching held the Cardinals in the eighth inning. Ryan Larson was sent in as the setup man for the closer and he retired the side with great poise and ease. He struck out two batters including the Cardinals' best hitter, Albert Pujos. With the Cubs leading in the bottom of the ninth inning Kerry Wood came up to close the game, but it wasn't his night. He got the first batter out with a fly ball to right field, but he allowed hits from the next two Cardinal batters.

Wood didn't try and strike everybody out to end the game and be the hero, but he did try to get the next batter to hit into a double play. However, it didn't work out that way, a slider hung too much over the plate and the Cardinal batter smacked it deep into centerfield for 3-run homer. The Cardinals had won game one in the bottom of the ninth. Kerry Wood was frustrated and voiced it in the form of many curse words for all to hear. It was a hard fought game, but the Cubs could not close the game out. As soon the home run was hit and before the Cardinal batter could reach home plate, the naysayers and sports writers all seem to be writing the same thing – that one hit proved that the Cubs did not belong and were not in the same league at the St. Louis Cardinals. It was disappointing for sure, but Lou, the Cubs manager, reminded his team in the Clubhouse that it was only one game and they had been here before with their backs against the wall. They had six more games to play and what happened in the end could happen to any team, but most fans would probably agree, it usually happens to the Cubs more often than not.

Ted Lilly was on the mound for game two of the series and it would be played again at in St. Louis. The Cubs started out early with a couple of runs in first inning and they never lost the lead to win the game. Ted Lilly pitched beautifully, allowing only two hits the entire game. The Cubs won the game 7-1. Kerry Wood was given the night off and Carlos Marmol pitched the last two innings retiring the side both times with three strikeouts. As Amy wrote in her article the next day game two, the Cubs silenced the naysayers and the Cubs proved that they did belong in the series.

The Series was now heading back to Chicago for three games and most fans expected the Cardinals to dominate the Cubs at home because they had done it all year long. The Cubs had only two victories again the Cardinals at Wrigley Field during the season. Rick Harden was on the mound for the Cubs in game three and he pitched great, keeping the Cardinals to only three runs through 7 and a half innings of work. Ryan Larson came in the top of the eighth inning to get the final two outs of that inning. The game was tied at 3 runs through the ninth. The Cubs couldn't win it the bottom of the ninth even though they got two men on base. So the game went to extra innings. In the 11th inning the Cubs won the game with a 2-

run homer by Alfonso Soriano. The Cubs now had a 2-1 lead in the series, but most of the sports writers who were covering the game wondered how long this would last. The Cubs had barely won game three.

But the next day Big Z, the Cubs 6'5" 240lb ace pitcher, silenced critics again by pitching a 4-0, 2 hit shutout against the Cardinals. Great pitching had stopped St. Louis, the great offensive powerhouse of the National League. The Cubs were leading the series 3-1 and were one game away from the World Series. But the Cubs had been here before and no matter how close they were to destiny they could never seem to touch it. The Cubs season always had the same outcome – they got close, but it ended with disappointment.

Game 5 would be played in two days and during those two days the papers in Chicago had a lot of ink dedicated to the Cubs. Sports bloggers wrote a lot stuff about Cubs and opinions were mixed on whether the Cubs could win or if they were destined to fail as usual. Lou Pinella didn't have much to say to reporters and he wasn't going to answer the same questions over and over. He usually had one phrase for reporters, "In game five we are going to see what happens, and this is baseball, anything can happen." Ryan Dempster was scheduled to pitch the game, but the day before it seemed that bad luck for the Cubs once again reared its ugly head. Dempster had a pulled a hamstring, it seemed to have started in his past pitching performance. He was not any condition to pitch and would have to sit out for a week to ten days.

Lou and Larry talked about it in the manager's office after receiving the news from the team doctor. Larry asked his friend. "What do you want to do?"

"Ted Lilly has the most rest, we can put him in."

"But we will need him in two days if we lose this game. We can't survive on three starting pitchers. I think we only have one option."

"Ryan Larson."

"Yeah, and I know what you're going to say."

"Oh you do, Larry?"

"Of course I do, you think he's the right choice because he's been hot and cold this season since coming back from his injury?"

"Okay maybe you do know what I was going to say and I don't care about the last game of the season, this game is a lot bigger than that."

"I know, but he's a seasoned starter and we have used him the last two games. He's rested too."

Lou sighed for a moment and said. "I don't know for sure if this is the best choice, but I guess we have to do something."

" I guess we are about to find out, though."

Ryan Larson was called into the office. Lou told him what happened told him with Dempster and then told him that he would be starting game five. Ryan asked him. " Are you sure you want me?"

"We're not sure about anything these days, but I know what you can do and I think you're the best choice for tomorrow. I also know that this will be the biggest game of your career and know the legacy that comes with your family, but I need to know one thing."

"What's that, skipper?"

"Will you be the pitching the game for you and your family or for the Cubs."

Ryan smiled at Lou and he knew that it was logical to think that the younger Larson had something to prove and wanted to avenge his father's action from '84. He replied. "I'm a Chicago Cub, they're the ones that I am here win for. I want to win for this team because it's my team."

"Okay then," Lou said to Ryan. "Then just remember that they all of them will be there on the field backing you up...don't forget that."

"I won't." After that Ryan walked out of the office full of joy and scared all at the same time because he knew that this was the biggest game of his life and he could easily give the game away as his father did back in '84. He called his family and told them what was going on and then tried to secure enough tickets for all of them including his father who he wanted there. He couldn't say because most players in his place wouldn't want the person that could be deemed as bad luck there at the game. But Ryan had always been one to face his deepest fears and one of them was turning out just like his dad.

Ryan couldn't sleep that night, he was nervous and he kept thinking about what the game meant. Tara tried to calm him, everything from talking to having sex with him. Nothing seemed to work, but Ryan was also a smart enough ballplayer to know that he couldn't do anything about it except take a deep breath and play the game like he knew how. He had been playing baseball so long that it was automatic and he could do it in his sleep.

The next day came fast as did the evening when the game was supposed to be played. There was a lot written in the sports media about Ryan Larson pitching this game and of course it seemed as if everyone of the writers wanted to talk about the Garvey game in 1984 when Steve

Larson had given up that home run. And then everybody had to compare Ryan to his dad expecting the same kind of performance – it wasn't very original and naysayers always get more attention. Ryan didn't read any of it for he had other things to think about. The Larson family was at the game including his father and they were all sitting together around the player's wives section.

The Cubs clubhouse was quiet and for the most part Ryan was left alone in peace. The only real conversation he had was with Derrek Lee. D-Lee said to him as they were getting dressed for the game. "Hey I read your sister's article from the other day... I liked what she had to say."

"My sister was optimistic and being a fan all at the same time."

"Maybe, but I think she's right...doesn't matter what happens this year. It can't take away what we've done and how we improved. Besides it's been a fun year, one of funnest I've ever had anyway. Just remember that no matter what happens. "

In his own quiet way, he was trying to tell Ryan that it was okay to relax, one game wasn't going to determine his career or the end result of the Cubs 2008 season. Ryan smiled at Lee and finished getting ready. He was the last one still in the clubhouse, trying to take his time before he had to go onto the field and start his warm-up. Suddenly he looked around the corner of his locker and standing there was his father. Ryan had a funny look on his face while looking at his dad, he was mainly surprised to see him. He asked him. "What are you doing here Dad...I though you weren't allowed in the Clubhouse anymore?"

Steve Laughed and replied. "I'm not, but Yosh still likes me and he let me in." Yosh Kawano had been the Club House manager for 40 years and had been working there since 1943. He had seen four Larson's play for the Cubs. He liked them all and had a great respect, but Steve was always his favorite because he made Yosh laugh anytime he saw him.

"I guess management is not going to argue with a man that's been here 65 years."

"Probably not...How are you holding up?"

"I'm a little nervous."

"It'd be foolish not to be...you've never pitched a game like this before."

Ryan smiled and said. "I don't think that's what everybody is worried about."

"They think you're going to be me."

"Yeah."

Steve grabbed a chair and sat down next to Ryan at his locker. Then he began to tell his son something that he had never had the courage to tell him. "Let me tell you something kid. You're not me anymore that I was my own father. You know that deep down, but it might make it easier to hear it from me. You have the have the best and worst of us both when it comes to pitching, but not how you might act or the decisions you make. You know how to pitch each game brilliantly in order to win because me and your grandfather taught you how, but that doesn't mean

[246]

you will automatically make the same mistakes we did...you are your own man and I don't care what the sports writers and critics want to say. They've never stood on the mound and faced what we have."

Ryan with a serious look asked him. "In '84 why did you do it?"

"Why did I shake off the signs and give up that home run to Garvey?"

"Yeah."

"Because I was foolish and wanted to be the hero. I wanted to win the game all by myself and prove that I was better than my dad."

"That's it."

"It's the simple truth. I made a mistake and didn't listen a teammate and my foolish pride cost us the game and the series. There isn't a day that doesn't go by I don't think about that game and what I did. I wonder what might have been if things had been different, I wonder would have happened. If I hadn't screwed up my career and ended it early. I wonder what would have happened if I had retired as a Cub and been revered by fans just as much as my dad is."

"All that over one game," Ryan asked his father.

"If people try and tell you that one game can't make all the difference and that you won't live with your failure every day. They're full of shit. We do take it to our grave."

"Yosh spoke up and said. "Your great grandfather George never got over hitting Dizzy Dean in the 1938 World Series...he had to live with that mistake all of his career."

Both Ryan and Steve smiled at what he said for they both knew the story of George Larson in the 38' Series. Steve said. "See even Yosh knows I'm right."

Ryan stood up and grabbed his glove. Then he asked his father. "So what does someone like me do?"

"The only thing you can do, play with no regrets. Play the best you can and leave it all on the field. And whether you win or lose tonight, walk away knowing that you gave everything you had."

Ryan shook his dad's hand and said. "Thanks dad...for everything."

Steve hugged his son and wished him luck. Ryan walked out of the clubhouse to a sellout crowd and glimmering lights. It was a big day not only for him, but for the Cubs and the media couldn't see to stop talking about the younger Larson and the biggest game of career. Ryan was doing his warm-ups when Steve returned to his seats with the Larson family. He sat down next to Mary and smiled at her. She asked him. "Did you go and talk to him?"

"Yes I did, Yosh let me in the clubhouse."

"Good Lord Steve...our son is probably nervous enough without you making it worse."

"Calm down Mary, he's fine and I didn't mess anything up."

"Better not have."

"Geez, Mary, you always did worry too much, but I still love you anyway."

She smiled at him and squeezed his hand because she knew that no matter what happened between them they would still love each other and know exactly what to say to make each other feel better. Jack leaned over and asked his son. "What did you say to him?"

"I told him the truth dad." Jack smiled an approval at his son.

Game time had finally arrived and both the Cubs and the Cardinals knew that it was going to be a fight right down to the end. The Cardinals would not go quietly into the night and the pressure had never been greater for Ryan Larson. When the first Cardinal batter took the plate Ryan Larson decided to be a little unpredictable just like he did in his first game in the majors. First pitch nearly took the batter's head off as he ducked quickly and fell to the ground to avoid the pitch. The second pitch was low and at his feet, making the batter jump and lose his balance to where he hit the ground again. The Cardinal fans started booing and the home plate umpire gave Ryan a warning – if he threw a wild pitch again he would be tossed from the game. Soto, the catcher, went out to the mound to see if Larson was okay. Steve Larson was laughing at what his son was doing because he used to do the same thing. His father Jack gave him a dirty look because he never liked that move even though it worked most of the time.

Soto got to mound and asked Ryan if he was okay. Ryan just told him he knew what he was doing and that he was trying to get into the Cardinals heads during the game. Soto smiled and told him that if it backfired and he got into trouble to let him know so he could help him. The next three pitches were perfect strikes, two fastballs inside and a curveball to get the first out. The next batter hit a fly ball to right field for the second out. The third batter hit a breaking ball and popped it up behind home plate so Soto could get to it easily and make the third out. Ryan had retired the side and set the tone for the game, and as he walked back to the dugout he was greeted by cheers for the fans for taking the first shot against the Cardinals in the game. As he walked into the dugout Lou, the manager, smiled at him and asked. "Are you trying to scare the Cardinals by being unpredictable with your pitches like you did in your first game in Major League Baseball?"

Ryan gave him a mischievous smile and replied. "Just setting the tone, skipper…letting the Cards know that this game is not going to be easy."

Amy was covering the game in the press box at Wrigley Field and couldn't help but laugh at what her brother did. Carrie, the Cubs reporter with Major League Baseball, commented to Amy that it looked like her brother was toying with the Cardinals. All Amy could to say that was that it was going to be an interesting game.

Ryan only allowed one hit through three innings, he was nearly perfect. The Cubs were able to get on the board early in the third inning with a two run homer by Derrek Lee. In the fourth inning Ryan Larson loaded the bases with a pair of walks and a couple of hits that resulted in a run for St. Louis. The inning had moved him up to the 50 pitch count, but he held his own through the next two innings even though he gave up a solo home run to Albert Pujos of the Cardinals to tie the game. However it didn't take long for the Cubs to come back and score another couple of runs in the bottom of the sixth inning to regain the lead.

In the 7th inning the wheels started to come off for Ryan Larson, he loaded the bases with another pair of walks and then three hits that scored two runs to the tie again and with only one out. Larry the pitching coach came out to talk to him because he was approaching 90 pitches. Most thought that Ryan would be done and the bull pen would take over since a couple of pitchers were getting warmed up, but they left Ryan to see if he could get out of the inning. He did by making the next batter hit into a double play.

The score remained tied through the top of the eighth inning after Ryan was able to retire the side. They didn't want to get Kerry Wood, the Cubs closer, up yet just in case the game went to extra innings. It looked like Ryan Larson was done for the game since he was at the 100 pitch mark. The Cubs were able to get men on base and score another run to regain the lead off a Ryan Theiot double. Larry asked Lou if he wanted the closer to go in the 9th inning and he said no, but to let him start warming up. They were going to let Ryan Larson start the 9th inning. Lou told him Larry. "Let's see what he can do, he might be able to complete this game."

Cub fans were on their feet in the 9th and he FOX Sports broadcasters said over the airwaves as if they were in disbelief. "The Cubs are three outs away from the World Series." It was hard to hear at Wrigley Field because the fans were on their feet and cheering loudly. Ryan took the mound and again was greeted with cheers. He said to himself. "3 outs, all I need are 3 outs!" He pitched the first batter to the inside for one ball and one strike. A 97 mile an hour fastball that batter swung right over because he never caught up with it gave Ryan a second strike. He slider in the dirt put the count and 2 and 2. While he didn't have much of a curveball left he reared back and gave everything he had to try and make it dip on the outside corner. The batter didn't swing, but the umpire called a strike to give the Cubs their first out. The batter threw his bat down and started to argue with the umpire. He was ejected from the game and that's when Tony LaRussa, the Cardinals manager came out of the dugout to argue the call and his player being thrown out. Lou came out to home plate too after the Cardinals started calling Ryan names and trying to start a fight, which Ryan was happy to be a part of.

Lou was trying to keep his players calm as this whole thing got sorted out, fans started to boo the umpire and the Cardinals manager, feeling like the game was going to be stolen from them. As Lou got to the mound, LaRussa said to Lou. "You don't need to be here... the ump can admit on his own that he made the wrong call."

Lou replied. "I'm not here to argue the call, but to keep my players safe since you can't control yours. Besides you had a lot calls go your way tonight, be a man and deal with the fact that one didn't go your way."

"Hey you guys are going to cheat your way to the World Series."

"If we wanted to cheat we'd be winning by ten...we're beating you fair and square."

LaRussa and Lou continued to argue until finally the umpire ejected LaRussa and told Lou to get back to the dugout before he got tossed as well. Everybody returned to their respective place and the game continued.

Ryan might have gotten the first out, but he couldn't continue the success. He allowed two singles and put a man on first and second base. The winning run was on first base now. Lou went back out to the mound along with Soto and Lee to check on Ryan Larson. He was tired even though he would not admit it. Before Lou could say anything Ryan told him."Skipper, I'm okay, just setting up the double play."

Lou replied. "I know you would like to think that you can do it and end the game, but they just got two hits on you."

"I can get two more outs without giving up any runs."

"You probably could, but I need a fresh arm. This game is bigger than you and I need 9 heroes out here instead of one."

"Skipper, let me do this."

Lou looked over at Soto and asked him what he thought. Soto replied. "He's got the talent, but he's done."

Ryan said out loud. "Fucking hell!"

Derrek Lee put his hand on Ryan's shoulder like the great captain of this team he said to him. "Hey man no one is denying that you didn't get us here tonight, but don't try and win it by yourself. We can do this."

Ryan was still mad, but he knew that Lee was right. He had to swallow his pride and let his team win the game. There was not room one for hero – the Cubs would have to win with a team of heroes. Lou took the ball from Ryan and signaled Kerry Wood, the closer, to come in. As Kerry was passing Ryan Larson on his way to the mound he stopped the younger Larson and said. "You did great tonight, we all owe you, but don't worry about this game. I've got in the bag. Cheer up, we're about to go to the World Series." Ryan smiled and shook Wood's hand.

Ryan walked back to the dugout and he was met with a standing ovation by the fans and his teams. He had pitched a hard fight and won the battle, but the warrior needed his comrades that night, for the battle on the baseball diamond is never fought alone. Ryan looked up and saw his family. His father Steve tipped his Chicago Cubs hat to his son, he was proud of Ryan, the proudest he had ever been during Ryan's career.

Cub fans were still on their feet and the cheers were louder than ever. You could hear them shouting, "2 outs away...2 outs away!" Kerry Wood pitched his best stuff to next batter – two 96 mile an hour fastballs to the inside and got two strikes on the batter. A breaking ball was pitched next and Wood was hoping that the batter would pop it up for an easy out, but it was fouled off behind home plate back into the stands. Wood reared back and threw a hard cut slider making the batter chase it by swinging over the top of the pitch for strike three. The fans went wild and now they were shouting, "1 out away…1 out away!"

Kerry Wood took a deep breath and paused for a moment. Then he had a smile on his face as he faced the next batter. One little hit could send the runner on second home and tie the game, but Wood wasn't going to let that happen. The Cubs were too close now. The FOX Broadcasters were commenting on the fans and what they were shouting. Joe Buck, one of the announcers said. "I don't think anything could quell this crowd tonight…the Cubs are one out away from the World Series as if anybody couldn't hear the crowd shouting right now."

Kerry Wood, the Cubs long time pitcher, who had battled injury after injury for years only to return to the Cubs and become their closer, wrapped his fingers around the ball. Like a bird in slow motion he started his wind up and released a breaking ball towards the inside of the plate. The Cardinal trying to be the hero and keep his team's hopes alive tried to hit and send it into the outfield for a base hit. He got a hold of it, but it was popped up around first base. A silence came over the crowd as Derrek Lee waved his arms for everybody to get out of the way. The runners went as fast as they could, hoping the inevitable would not happen. The ball seemed to take its time coming down and then all of sudden it dropped into Lee's glove. Fans started going crazy and cheering. The Cubs players rushed out of their dugout onto the field in celebration. Joe Buck, the FOX broadcaster had only one thing to say and it was all that needed to be said. "Cub fans you've waited 63 years to hear this…you are going to the World Series."

19

It Was Never Going To Be That Easy

The World Series is a different place and sits on a higher plane filled with glitz and glamour where the pressure to win is almost unbearable. Good teams usually fold under that pressure and great teams come out victorious. Despite the winning records, ERA's and batting averages the numbers on paper can never truly judge who will win the World Series because it is anybody's ball game while upsets are just as common as magnificent plays by the ball players. And that is what's make the pressure unbearable. That has never been more so than for the Cubs after a 63 year wait, Amy wrote. She was writing her article for her blog about the Cubs' historical event, trying to be objective and excited all at the same time. It was hard because she was a fan and had been all of her life. It was even more exciting because her brother Ryan was the first Larson in 63 years to play in the World Series while wearing a Cubs uniform.

The city of Chicago was filled with excitement because of the Cubs getting to the World Series. It was all that people were talking about and it seemed that just because the Cubs were there now they were going to win – it was the will of the baseball gods and 100 years of futility was long enough. However things are never that easy especially in Chicago – a city where joy and disappointment run parallel with one another. And to make matters worse the Cubs would be playing the New York Yankees, a team that had been to the World Series many times before and won it. The Yankees once again were considered the best team in baseball and were expected to walk all over the Cubs in the series just like in 1938. It seemed that every sports writer in America came to the same conclusion about the World Series – the Cubs did not have a chance and it would all be over in four games. But no matter what was written about the Cubs, being the underdogs and having no chance of winning, none of that bothered Lou Pinella, their manager, and the rest of the team. The Cubs knew in the grand scheme of things that they shouldn't be there, but here they were, in the World Series and they were a team that was full of surprises.

The Cubs knew that it would not easy and the Yankees would be a lot tougher than the St. Louis Cardinals, but they were not scared and were surprisingly excited to be playing the Yankees. The first two games would be played at Yankee Stadium in the Bronx, the house that Ruth built and then the next three games would be played at Wrigley Field while the last two games of the seven game series would be played at Yankee stadium if the series even got that far. And so a few days after the Cubs beat St. Louis and the Yankees had beaten the LA Angels, Chicago was heading to New York for the final games in Yankee Stadium since it was being torn down. The 2008 World Series would be the last for old Yankee Stadium and the Yankees did not want to disappoint their fans, they planned on winning it one more time in the house that Ruth built.

The Cubs were heavy underdogs before game one of the World Series. After the game was played they were still underdogs and game one proved to be what everybody expected. Ryan Dempster pitched game one for the Cubs and it was the best performance that he had had during the playoffs. He gave up only 2 hits during six innings of work and by the time he was taken out of the game the Cubs had a 2-1 lead, but the Cubs bullpen could not hold them. Ryan Larson and Carlos Marmol both pitched 1 inning and held the Yankees, but a 2-run walk-off homer by Kerry Wood gave the Yankees the win in the bottom of the ninth inning. The Cubs played tough, but it wasn't good enough and the Yankees led the series 1-0. The only surprise to most fans and sports writers was that the Yankees didn't run away with game one.

Game two in New York was another tough battle. Ted Lilly pitched 7 great innings and gave up only 4 hits, but the Yankees led the game 3-0 by the end of the 7th inning. The Cubs were able to come back and tie the game in the bottom in the ninth inning sending the game into extra innings. Ryan Larson would pitch the last half of the ninth inning and pitch the tenth inning as well. The Cubs were able to scratch out a run in the tenth to take the lead 4-3 and instead of the putting in the closer Lou, their manager, decided to keep Larson in the game and see if he could get the three outs they needed. Ryan was brilliant. He struck out the first batter and then walked the second. But it didn't matter because Ryan was able to get Derrek Jeter to hit into a double play and the end the game. The Cubs knew that they had to win at least one game in New York if they were going to have a chance at winning the series and so they did. Cub fans were excited and most sports writers would comment in their articles that the Cubs might have a chance with the next three games at Wrigley Field. The odds on the Cubs shrunk just a little bit with a game two win, but Amy pointed out in her article, things are never that simple.

Chris even asked one night over dinner what chances the Cubs really had. Amy answered trying to be objective and not sound too depressed with her answer. "I figure that the Cubs have a 1 in 3 chance of pulling this out."

Chris replied. "So you think the Yankees are really the better team?"

"Of course I do…it would be foolish to not think so, but that doesn't mean the Cubs can't beat them. "

"At least you're being honest about it."

Amy smiled at him and said. "I don't want to be, but I'm a journalist. I'm supposed to be."

Game three of the World Series would be a disaster for the Cubs. The Yankees pretty much had it won by the second inning. It would not be Rick Harden's night. He would give up 5 hits and four runs in the first inning and then give up 4 hits and two runs in the second. He was finally pulled after four innings of work. With the Cubs down 6-0 in the fifth inning they tried to stage a comeback and scored two runs, but it wasn't enough. Yankees pitching stopped them cold for the rest of the game silence fell over the fans at Wrigley Field. The Cubs lost 6-2. Game four would be another hard fought game as well as Big Z pitched six fantastic innings giving the Cubs a 3-0 lead, but the Yankees came roaring back. They tied the game in the 8th inning and scored the go ahead run in the 9th inning. Cubs pitching could not hold the Yankees in the later innings and the Cubs bats went quiet in the bottom of the ninth inning as the Cubs side was retired to end the game. The Yankees now lead the Series 3-1.

There was no explanation for the Cubs dismantling. Some fans would state the obvious that the Cubs had gotten cold and the heart that they brought into the playoffs was now gone. Other fans said it was the curse of the Billy Goat. Sports writers talked of reality and the Cubs were not in the same class as the Yankees. Even Lou Pinella didn't seem to have any good answers as to why the Cubs were playing poorly. He told reporters the same usual bullshit that managers always tell reporters when they don't want to be mean about their team's bad play. Lou told reporters that the Cubs were not playing at their best level and that if they were going to survive they needed better pitching and offense. It was the obvious answer, but Lou didn't want to say that he didn't know what to do. The Cubs had their backs against the wall, but they had been here before. The Cubs had come from behind many times before and it seemed to define their year.

Game five was a day away and no one knew what to expect. Steve Larson was in Chicago for the Series and to watch his son pitch. The night before the game he asked his father, Jack Larson, if he wanted to grab a beer. They had not spoken very much over the last 15 years since Steve was kicked out of baseball and his divorce from Mary. There wasn't much to talk to about. Jack was very disappointed in Steve and had voiced that many times over the years. He still loved his son though, but it was hard when his son had thrown away his career and never applied anything he had learn from his father about pitching and being a professional ballplayer.

Steve figured it was time to have a beer and hopefully get past all the bad stuff between them. Steve Larson had come a long way over the last couple of years and had been made to face a lot of his demons. He took a big step towards that when he went down to the Double A ball club in Tennessee to help out his son Ryan, but that doesn't mean everything was automatically fixed between him and his own father. But Steve knew all too well that eventually we all have to face the fire and see if we have the strength to walk with it.

There was a neighborhood bar around Wrigley Field that Jack and Steve had been going to for over 20 years. Jack had always lived downtown near the stadium when he was in Chicago the same as Steve and Mary when they were married. In fact Mary had never really left the area, it was home and the neighborhoods around Wrigley Field had a certain appeal to them that had never left her. Jack and

Steve talked about the one thing that would not start a fight, baseball, but not even that conversation could stop the tension completely. The talked about the Series and of course Ryan. Steve asked his father. "Do you think the team actually has a chance to win it?"

"So, anybody has a chance even in a 3-1 series, but do I think it's probable...not really."

"You're absolutely sure?"

"I wouldn't say that, but the Yankees are too strong...they have a great team, no denying that."

"Yeah, but I don't think they have much class."

"Won't disagree with that." Jack and Steve clanked the bottles of beer they were drinking together as if it were a toast of agreement.

Jack said again. "No matter what happens, we can't deny what happened with the Cubs this year...they had a hell of a year and nobody expected them to be in the World Series after the first half of the season."

"What good is it though if they don't win it all? That's the way we felt about it in '84 and isn't that the way you felt in '69?"

"Sure we did, but if they don't succeed then there is always next year for them."

"Aren't you just a little tired of having to say that?"

"I would like to see a Cubs team win it all, but I'm not going to lose any sleep over it. I played my years and now I'm done. I don't get to share in the glory if they did and neither do you."

"Dad I don't want their glory, I just don't want Ryan to come as close as we did and not feel victory."

"He is playing in the World Series, son!"

"And that's all well and good, but it doesn't mean anything if you don't win it."

Jack gave Steve a disappointed look and replied. "Is that why you tell him to try and psych out the batters by trying to take their heads off with pitches."

"You never liked me doing that."

"It's juvenile and good pitcher shouldn't have to do that."

"It's just another way, Dad, even if it's not your way to win. Besides I remember you drilling Pete Rose in the ribs with your fast ball one time for talking back at you on the mound."

"That was different. He deserved it and I intentionally hit him."

"You did it to show him who was boss and to get a psychological advantage. That's all I tried to teach Ryan and believe it or not, it works."

"So does being a smart pitcher!"

"And being smart on the mound comes in different forms...you never could understand that."

Jack in an angry tone replied to Steve. "You might think it was fun to be called the 'Wild One' but you could have been better."

"Fine Dad, let's just admit it...you were the better pitcher and I was the screw up."

"Well, you were a screw up, but being the better pitcher, I don't know about that. You had better stuff than I did, but you just weren't smart about it."

Steve Larson stood up and faced his father. "You know Dad, I did things different than you and that pisses you off. It worked for me, but I know that I made mistakes and threw my career away. And I've had to live with it every day...that's what you want to hear, right?"

"No, I don't, but I don't want you teaching Ryan all your bad habits when he could be a great pitcher."

"And the sad thing for you is you won't think he's a good pitcher unless he does it just like you. Ryan is smart enough to figure out the good things we've taught him. He's smart enough to figure out his own way and it might not be just like you or like me, but it will be his way and it will serve him well throughout his career. And just in case you're wondering, I think he's smart enough not to fall into the same traps I did that caused me to kicked out of baseball...he had to watch his father leave him and his parents separate after all that happened. It would make an impression on anyone. The best thing we can do is give him a little advice and let him figure out his own way."

Steve threw some cash on the bar to pay for the drinks then walked out of the bar before his father could say anything. He knew that the best thing he could do for the situation was walk away before he made things worse between him and his father. The next day before the game none of the Larson's spoke to each to each other. Jack and Steve were mad at each other. Ryan was left alone so he could concentrate on the game. With the Cubs one loss of away from the season being over no one wanted to bother anybody on the Cubs team so they could focus on what they had do.

It was quiet in the Clubhouse for the Cubs. No one really spoke to each other. They were in a place that most people don't often go, a place inside of themselves where they find the will and the courage to walk through fire. It is a place reserved only for warriors and those willing to sacrifice everything for one goal. It is in that place that most people are afraid to go because it is dark, rough, and filled with more truth about ourselves than we will see in the everyday lives that we live. Lou gathered the team together. He had only a few words to say. "Men, I don't have to tell you what this game means and I don't have to tell you what you have to do in order to win. We're beyond that point now, but this season won't be over if you don't want it to be. You can win this if you really want to."

That was all Lou needed to say. The Cubs that night were unstoppable from the first inning to the last. They would not go quietly into the night. They scored the first runs in the first inning and they never gave up the lead. Ryan Dempster, the pitcher who had won 17 games but had struggled all through the playoffs came through on the biggest night of his career. He pitched 7 scoreless innings and held the Yankees to two hits and two walks. The Cubs would win game five with a score of 8-1. If was a great way to end the season at Wrigley Field for they all knew that the

Series, no matter what, would end in New York...of course that's what everybody thought.

Two days later the Cubs were back in New York for game six. Most people thought that this was going to be the last game – whatever magic the Cubs might have had in Chicago couldn't possible continue in New York, but as they had been all year the   Cubs were full of surprises. Big Z would pitch Game 6 and the Cubs ace showed the same form he did a month earlier when he pitched his no-hitter. He held the Yankees to 1 hit through 6 innings as the Cubs jumped to an early lead. They were leading 3-0 in the 7th inning when the Yankees tied the ball game with a three-run homer. Yankee fans were ecstatic and saw it as a sign that they were going to win, but the Cubs proved again that it wasn't that simple. Ryan Larson pitched the 8th inning and held the Yankees to zero hits. The Cubs would take the lead again with an Alfonso Soriano two-run homer in the top of the 9th inning. The Yankee's closer could not hold the Cubs. But the Cubs could hold the Yankees. Carlos Marmol pitched the bottom of the 9th inning and after giving up a walk struck out the next three batters to claim the win for the Cubs.

It was unbelievable, one sports writer in New York wrote the next day, the Billy Goat cursed team from the Windy City proved yet again that they shouldn't be doubted. The Cubs had forced a game 7 and had all the momentum going into the game. It seemed that if history was going to be made in the house that Ruth built it would be revenge from '32 and '38. But the Cubs coaching staff knew better, especially Lou, their manager. He had seen the Red Sox upset the Yankees time and time again in New York when it seemed that the Yankees had it won. In 2004 the Red Sox gave the Yankees the most devastating defeat in their history when they were down 3-0 in the American League Championship Series and came back to win the next four games and go to the World Series. The Cubs' chances could just as easily be squashed in Game 7.

The team knew that as well and again when it came to the last game of the season the clubhouse was silent so the Cubs team could find what had made them win the last few months and stay alive in the playoffs. The odds were still against them to win Game 7, but even the most cynical of fans could not deny that they Cubs had defied the possibilities. So here they were again, one loss away from the end of the season, Lou didn't have much to say again. He just told his team, "There isn't much to say about a game 7. One of us will go home with the trophy and one of us will just go home. But no matter what there's no denying what you have accomplished this season and what you did to get here and I am proud to be a part it Win or Lose, you should be too. I have always said and tonight is no different; you can win this game if you want to. It's up to you."

Ted Lilly was on the mound for the Cubs that night. The lefthander had been nearly perfect all through the playoffs and game 7 would not be any different. He held the Yankees to zero hits through five innings while the Cubs jumped out on top 2-0. The only hit Lilly would give up was a two-run homer in the 6th inning to tie the game. The Cubs regained the lead 4-2 in the 7th inning, but it would not be kept for long. Lilly was replaced in the game after 7 innings and the Yankees came roaring back in the 8th inning – they tied the game at 4 runs apiece. In the 9th inning the Cubs could not score and they did not put in their closer in the bottom of the 9th knowing that this game would have to be won in extra innings. Ryan pitched the last of the 8th inning after the Yankees had tied it up and he started the 9th. He walked the first two batters before being replaced. Both times ball four had been questionable and Lou even went out to talk to the umpire the second time it happened. It was a miracle that he had not been thrown out of the game. Larson was replaced with the Cubs lefty Sean Marshall who quickly got the first out with 3 strikes. The next Yankee batter hit a line drive towards third base and the Cubs got the second out at third base, but could not get the other two batters so again men were on second and first. One hit could probably do it, but then again a pop fly in the outfield could get the third out.

What happened next was the most bizarre play in baseball and would later be called the most controversial. For years it had been argued that instant replay should come to professional baseball so that umpires could have an easier time making the right calls. There had been too many blown calls when it came to home runs and pitches that could have caused an out at the plate. On this particular night there would be one call that goes in favor for the argument of instant replay in baseball. On the next pitch, Marshall threw a slider to the inside that didn't get enough movement on it and Alex Rodriguez, the Yankee batter sent the ball deep into left field. It was right at the wall in the deep corner of Left Field and Soriano for the Cubs went back. He had a play for the ball and was about to grab the ball even though it was at the wall and looked as if it was about to go over the wall for a home run, but as just the ball was about to go over Soriano reached up and grabbed it. But as he was heading down from jumping up and as fans were reaching for the ball in that split second a Yankee fan grabbed the ball out of the glove and Soriano came down with nothing. He was furious and screaming at the Yankee fans in Spanish. Some saw what happened and saw the so-called home run.

Most Yankee fans thought it was a home run and that the game was over. The Yankee players rushed onto the field to start celebrating, but Lou and the rest of the Cubs coaching staff rushed to the field to protest what had happened. The home plate umpire ruled it a home run, but there was also a disagreement among the other umpires about what the call should be. Lou argued with the umpires as the Yankee players were celebrating their supposed win that it was fan interference and should be ruled an automatic out or at least the pitch and the hit didn't count. Even the Fox baseball announcers were commenting as they watched the play over and over that the ball was snatched from Soriano's glove and that it would have been an out. But the umpires had a made a ruling and the game had ended with a three-run homer giving the Yankees the win. Lou argued the call and even bumped the home plate umpire which caused him to be escorted off the field by security.

It was chaos on the field and the rest of the Cubs coaches tried to get the umpires to reverse the call, but there was no instant replay. The only thing the Cubs could do was file an appeal with major league baseball, which they did immediately with their lawyers since the baseball commissioner was at the game. Within 30 minutes the appeal was filed and the award ceremony was postponed. Yankee fans never left and a riot almost happened outside the stadium. The Cubs players were told to quickly shower and dress and get on their bus. They would need a police escort to get out of the stadium and get back to their hotel. While Amy was covering the game she made the comment in the press booth that the Yankees were going to steal this away from the Cubs. She was met with hostility from some of the New York writers...not very objective, but hey, it's New York. Game seven ended in a nightmare and it reminded Amy of hearing about the Merkel Game a hundred years before.

The commissioner ruled that evening before anybody went home that there would be a formal hearing the next day to decide what happened. It didn't sit well with the Yankees and their manager who commented to reporters that the Cubs were cry-babies and after a hundred years still couldn't lose graciously. Lou made his comments to reporters as well. He was the only one in the Cubs organization that was allowed to. He told reporters. "In my day with the Yankees we didn't have to cheat to win, but I guess things have changed in 20 years." That was all he said and the war of words for the media began. What should have been a magnificent game seven ended in controversy, but most Cub fans didn't expect anything less. It would never be that easy for the Cubs and that's what

Amy wrote in her blog that night sharing her thoughts with fans. The 2008 World Series would now have to be decided by the court of baseball and if the universe can make things right or even then that should never happen.

20

Game 8

Game seven was supposed to be it, the defining game and a champion was supposed to be crowned. That's how it usually goes, but as usual the Cubs hardly ever fall in the same sentence. Baseball is filled with controversies, but never had it happened in Game seven of the World Series and never had a World Series victory been called into question until now. The grievance filed with Major League Baseball on behalf of the Chicago Cubs left the Series with no clear winner and the Commissioner had to make a decision. Never had he been faced with this kind of decision and he was in the steroid era where cheating ran rampant and records and games were considered controversial. But it was an unruly New York Yankee fan that had caused all the trouble and would it be nice it say that it was the first time for both teams, but the Cubs could not claim that. At the game with the Cubs fan, it wasn't intentional.

Major League Baseball would decide the fate of the Series at noon the next day and nobody from Chicago left New York until a decision was made including reporters. The Cubs manger and General Manger along with the Yankees manager and General Manager would meet with the commissioner that morning to decide what to do. In baseball there is a first time for everything and this was certainly one of those times. The commissioner reviewed the tapes of the incident. It was clear that the Yankee fan reached into Soriano's glove and stole the ball for what would have been a clear out to end the inning and send the game into extra innings. But there wasn't precedence for this when it would be a third out and the game was ruled over by the umpires – baseball didn't have instant replay. And this was the World Series, game seven. Rule books were researched and along with records of others where a similar incident might have occurred. The commissioner and his assistants were like a judge and his law clerks sifting through case law in order to make a decision based on the best interpretation. Finally a decision was made and the commissioner convened with managers and general managers for both teams as well as the umpires. No press was allowed during this meeting. Amy was outside the commissioner's chambers along with a hundred other reporters trying to get the first scoop.

The baseball commissioner said to the men in the room. "Okay, we have finally reached a decision and since this has never happened before we will be making a decision based on old rules and similar incidents. Fan interference will be ruled here and therefore it is an automatic out thus ending the inning."

Both teams figured that would be that call, but the next thing he said was shocking.

The commissioner continued. "Now because the game was ruled by the umpires as being over the game officially ends in a tie and a new game has to be played."

George Steinbrenner, the Yankees owner and somewhat acting general manager piped up in a combative tone. "This is crazy...the game shouldn't be completely ended, we just start the tenth inning."

The commissioner looked at George and replied. "On the contrary, according to the rules when the game is called by the umpire if it is past the 7th inning then the game is completely ended and cannot be replayed and the game can be called on account of weather or security issues, or a threat to the ball players, which I know is very general. But this could fit into the category since fans rushed the field and players were fighting after this happened. And let's not forget security had to be called onto the field."

The Yankees manager asked. "So what now we play a game eight?"

"Yes we play a game 8," the commissioner said. "We have to play a game eight because the series cannot be tied and if the series was 3-2-1 then it might be a different story, but as it stands the record is 3-3-1. We need a clear champion so one more game has to be played."

Finally Lou Pinella asked a question. "If we play a game eight then where do we play it?"

"Well with how we do the schedule two more games were played in New York. The next game will be played in Chicago."

Steinbrenner stood and yelled at the commissioner. "Oh come on this is bullshit! You end the game that we were playing in favor of the Cubs and now you want to give them home field advantage. Why don't you just give them the trophy since you're being so fair?"

"Does that mean you're forfeiting?" Lou responded back to Steinbrenner.

Before Steinbrenner could say anything the commissioner spoke up and said to all the men in the room. "Enough...A game eight will be played and it will be in Chicago. And before you say anything George here's how it works. Both teams get a fair shot at this game and winning the World Series. Both teams have to get on a plane and travel. Both teams have won on the road and if the Yankees are really that good then they'll win. Besides you're outspent everybody in the league for your team and if you have the best team that money can buy you should have no problem winning."

Steinbrenner shouted. "Fuck You!"

"That will be a $100,000 fine George!"

"I'll write you a check!"

The Commissioner announced that the game would be played two days later in Chicago on Friday night. When the news was finally announced the baseball world was stunned. The thing that wasn't a surprise is what the New York papers said about the decision. It was stated in more than one paper and sports blogs from New York, that a 100 years later Chicago was still trying to steal a Championship from New York by cheating. The irony about that statement is that both times the Chicago Cubs were the ones following the rules. But history does tend to repeat itself. For two days until game eight the papers in New York and Chicago had a war of words through the media about the decision. Sports bloggers, writers, and commentators were split down the middle about the decision that was made. Amy tried to be objective as possible in what she wrote about it. She basically said that the best thing a baseball commissioner can do is try to be as fair as possible when making a controversial decision, especially when it was made on something that had no precedence of any kind. New York fans thought that they were being screwed and Chicago fans thought it was a fair ruling...those opinions were to be expected. However, both the Yankees and the Cubs had just as much of a chance to win game eight.

The night before the game the Larson family had dinner together. Of course Steve and Jack didn't say anything to each other, but for the most part it was a pleasant evening. The family told old baseball stories and laughed with one another trying to keep their minds off of the biggest game that the Cubs had ever played in their history. The Cubs manager had told everybody that he wanted his team not to think about the game too much and to have fun especially if they could do it with their families.

There would be plenty of time to worry and stress on Friday night, the day of the infamous game eight. Chris was curious and had to ask. "Has there ever been a game eight in baseball?"

Jack answered the question. "Not since 1922. For a few years professional baseball had a best of 9 series...owners wanted to have more games so they could make more money, but never has there been a best of 7 series where a game eight had to be played."

Chris had a learned a lot about baseball in the past year and he had figured out that there were not any other fans in the world like Cub fans...never had he seen so much devotion to one team. But for the first time since this had all happened he began to see the gravity of the situation. He saw how unique game eight was for the Cubs and he figured out like most Cub fans that only in Chicago could this happen. The common and the usual didn't apply to the Chicago Cubs. The Larson family spent the rest of the night laughing and understanding what the true meaning of family really was. They had a come a long way through all the heartache and close calls that go with being a family of players and being Cubs fans, but they still loved each other and they were still devoted to one another despite it all. That's what made the difference.

The next day, Friday night in Chicago, was crazy. Fans poured into the stadium hours early and the streets around Wrigley were crowded and filled to the brim with fans. It seemed that the entire city of Chicago was there. Large screen TV's were displayed on every street corner for the crowds in the streets to watch the game. It was anticipated that game eight would the most watched baseball game in history and they were right. It was hard to believe anybody on the Cubs actually got any sleep. Lou Pinella had put a plan together for the game and it was an unlikely plan...one that had never really been done before, but this was game eight and it just might work he thought to himself. Nobody in the media knew who was going to be the starting pitcher for the Cubs; it had been kept a secret.

Lou had, had a meeting with the team the day before and told them his plan.

He was going to use everybody for the game. Big Z would be the starting pitcher, but he would only be in there for two innings. They would rotate starting pitchers out for an inning or two to keep fresh arms in the game except for Ted Lilly who had pitched in game seven. He would be used only if necessary in the later innings especially if it went to extra innings. The Cubs would use every man off their bench for different situations to keep the Yankees on their toes and to keep them from expecting the obvious. Lou wanted to confuse the Yankees and to use batters that had not been scouted as much. It was a bold plan, but Lou wanted everybody to have a chance to contribute because this game was going to be a total team effort.

Before the game was about to start Lou gathered his team in the clubhouse to say his final words...the last words he would say to them in the 2008 season. He looked at every one of them and said. "I want you to know that I've never been more proud to take the field with a team. Nobody expected us to be here playing a game eight, but we have continually proved everybody wrong and I think tonight will be no different. We are still the underdogs, but as far I am concerned we are the better team because you have never given up and you have done everything anybody can ask of you to get here. I know it's been a hundred years since the Cubs won a World Series and I don't care if it's a hundred more. Whatever happens tonight between winning or losing doesn't matter because if we give the very best of ourselves tonight on that field then we are the champions despite what that scoreboard says and let's face it we have the most devoted fans in the world. So the only thing I am going to ask, one more time, is that you play the best that you can play and you have fun doing it because if we can do that then we have no regrets. Pure hearts, no regrets, and for the love of the game, we won't lose."

Lou smiled and said again. "Pure hearts, no regrets, and for the love of the game, we won't lose." That's when the team's quiet captain, Derrek Lee spoke up and said. "Pure hearts, no regrets, and for the love of the game, we won't lose." The rest of the team joined him in unison and said. "Pure hearts, no regrets, and for the love of the game, we won't lose." The Chicago Cubs took the field to complete the journey of this season. As they took the field they received a standing ovation from 42,000 fans. Fifteen minutes later game eight started and while most sports writers and critics fully expected the Yankees to win the Cubs were not going down without a fight. The entire Larson family was there, but Steve opted not sit with them, instead he watched the game with the Wrigley Field Grounds Crew, the same group of men that he used to work with when he was in high school, learning how to make a perfect baseball field. If he had not been a baseball player, he probably would have been a grounds keeper for Wrigley Field and been happy doing it all his life.

As the game started the FOX baseball commentators were talking about the fact that Lou had a secret plan for the game and no one knew who was going to be the starting pitcher so when Big Z took the mound it was the obvious choice. Big Z was perfect in the first inning; he struck out two and got the third batter to pop the ball up for an out. In the first inning the Cubs struck first and got a run on the board. Big Z was almost perfect in the second, but allowed a couple of hits. Great defense did prevent the Yankees from scoring and the inning ended on a close double play. The Yankees manager argued it, but the call stood. The Cubs made a pitching change and put Rick Harden in. He pitched a sold inning and gave up only one hit. Then Ryan Dempster replaced him for the fourth and fifth inning. He was perfect too, retiring the side in both innings that he pitched. The score remained 1-0 after the 5th inning, but the Cubs were stranding too many people on base. The offense wasn't slowing down at all, but they couldn't seem to get any runs. That's when Lou shook up the lineup and brought in players off the bench who were hitting well. He even took the pitcher out of the lineup to give the Cubs another opportunity. It seemed to be working, but in the sixth the Yankees tied the ball game up with a solo home run. By the 7th inning it seemed as if Lou's plan was going to backfire. In the bottom of the 7th after Ernie Banks was finished singing "Take Me Out to the Ballgame" during the 7th inning stretch the Yankees scored another run and took the lead.

It was fitting that Mr. Cubs did the 7th inning stretch, but not even that little bit of magic could hold off the Yankees. The Cubs had gone to their bullpen in the 6th inning so Carlos Marmol had started the 7th inning. While he did give up the go ahead run Lou kept him in the game just to give the other guys some time because he figured the game would go to extra innings. Ryan Larson started to warm-up in the 8th inning. Carlos Marmol got the first out, but gave up two hits and a walk to load the bases. Lou took him out and brought in Ryan Larson. Ryan had played well all through the playoffs and pitched the game of his life in game five of the National League Championship Series. Lou handed him the ball and said just one thing. "I need two outs!" Ryan responded by saying, "No problem, skipper." The only way to get out of the inning without any runs scoring was a routine double play.

Ryan did something both his grandfather and father used to do on the mound. He threw two pitches to the inside of the plate for balls, backing the batter of the plate and making him think that he was now going to throw a curveball or a slider low and away to make him miss it for a strike, but he did the opposite especially when he saw the batter not taking the bait and crowding the plate. On the third pitch he threw a breaking ball to the inside making him pound a grounder to the shortstop who could easily turn it into a double play and get both outs. Three pitches were all it took to get the batter to hit into a double play.

In the bottom of the 8th inning the Cubs threatened again. After the first out of the inning four straight hits gave them 3 runs to reclaim the lead. They now led the game 4-2 and it was more than what was expected. The next two batters both hit pop ups to give the Yankees three outs and end the inning. Kerry Wood, the closer got up and began his warm up. Now that the Cubs had the lead and a chance to win the game in the top of the 9th inning wood was expected to go in soon. Ryan Larson was sent in to start the inning, he had been perfect as a setup man for the closer all through the playoffs and tonight was no different. The heart of the Yankees lineup was coming up too so it was going to take great pitching to win. As he took the mound in the 9th inning the entire stadium was on their feet. Joe Buck, the FOX commentator, had only one thing to say, "Cub fans, you are three outs away from a World Series Championship, but the Yankees will not go away quietly."

Ryan was able to get the first batter out with no problem; a ground hopper to third base took care of him. But Ryan walked the next batter and the tying run came up to bat. After 7 pitches and hitting four foul balls the Yankee batter hit a standup-double, putting men on third and second based. Larry, the pitching coach, looked over at Lou and asked him if he wanted to go and get Ryan. Lou said. "No, leave him there for a moment. If he lets a run score then we'll take him out." All the Cubs in the dugout were on their feet. Amy was in the press box clinching her chair as tight as she could. Mary Larson couldn't even watch while sitting next to Jack, Ruth, Chris and Tara. Ryan took a deep breath and went into his wind up. He threw a changeup and made the batter pop it up over second base. Ryan pointed up in the air for Mark De Rosa, the second baseman and he caught it for the second out. The stadium was getting loud and the fans were cheering "One out away!" Lou didn't want to take Ryan out; he wanted to see what he could do. Alex Rodriguez was up next and with one swing the game could be all over for Ryan. A-Rod was a powerful hitter and could easily hit a home run out of the stadium onto Waverland Avenue. Ryan tried to go to the inside with him and the pitch was off the plate for a ball. The next two pitches were outside and off the corner putting the count 3-0. That's when Lou went out to the mound. Everybody expected him to take Larson out of the game. Lou got to the mound and Soto, Lee, and Ramirez were standing there with Larson. Ryan asked Lou. "Am I done?"

Lou responded. "No, but I do have a question. I heard a story about your dad and helping you at Tennessee with three pitches. Is the story true?"

Ryan gave the skipper a surprised look and said. "That's what you came here to talk about, probably not the best time to tell the story, but yes it's true."

Lou smiled at everybody and replied. "It's a good story, what pitches did he throw?"

"He threw a slider, a breaking ball to the inside, and then his famous sinking fastball."

Lou smiled again and said. "Sounds like three great pitches to me and that's exactly what I need right now."

"You're kidding right?"

Lou didn't say anything; he just turned around and walked back to the dugout.

Derrek Lee smiled at Ryan and told him. "It's all you baby...one more out, and we are right here with you."

Ryan stood on the mound for what seemed an eternity, rubbed the ball and warmed it up. He paused and took another deep breath. A-Rod had been given the green light to hit a home run at this point. Ryan went into his windup and threw his slider when everybody was expecting a sinker or curveball. A-Rod didn't even swing, but it was a strike. Then Ryan threw a breaking ball to the inside and A-Rod tried to crush the ball but it went foul. Strike Two! It was hard to hear anything in the stadium, but the crown chanted, "One strike away...One strike away!" Ryan clutched the ball with a loose grip and paused as A-Rod got done with his practice swings then he smiled at him with all the confidence that a pitcher could have. He went into his windup and it was like a gymnast in slow motion. The ball sailed from his hand with flawless movement – it looked as if it was a straight up fastball right down the middle for A-Rod to send into the bleachers, but by time it reached the plate the bottom dropped out from underneath it. It was the sinker made famous by his grandfather, deadly when used by his father and it was the perfect pitch to fool a batter. A-Rod swung right over the pitch with everything he had missing it by inches. Strike Three! Cubs Win! And as the team rushed from the dugout to celebrate there was a graceful line said over the airwaves by the FOX baseball commentators, "The Cubs did it...Cubs Win...after a 100 years the Cubs are World Series Champions."

Amy began to cry in the press booth, she had never been happier at a baseball game. When Soto rushed to the mound he picked Ryan up off the ground in celebration. It was a perfect ending to a game and the three pitches that had started his career brought him greatness tonight and gave the Cubs their victory. There was no more talk of the curse. The Cubs were World Champs. It was hard to contain the excitement in the stadium and in the streets, but it didn't matter because for one special night the world seemed perfect. As Steve was watching the celebration with the grounds crew Jody his old catcher came walking up and said to him. "You have to feel proud tonight."

Steve replied. "I do, he pitched a hell of a game and he has the makings of a great pitcher."

"You taught him well."

"Do you ever wonder what it would have been like if we had won it?"

Jody smiled and said. "Every day, but I also know that I played on one of the best teams in baseball. That's all that matters to me now and that's what I remember."

"Despite everything, I wouldn't want to play on any other team or have anyone else catching for me."

"It's the same with me and if you ever need a catcher for the old timer's game, just give me a call."

"If you ever need a pitcher, you know where I'll be...old friend."

Jody smiled and shook Steve's hand then walked off. Ryan and his teammates celebrated beneath the lights at Wrigley and maybe it would have been better in the day time, but nothing could take away this moment. The Cubs had struggled with their backs against the wall but they had overcome. This rag tag team that nobody ever expected to win did just that and they beat the team that always seemed to win. The Cubs played with pure hearts, no regrets, and for the love of the game to become champions – it was worth the wait.

Epilogue

A Good Dream

Amy was restless in bed, she didn't' seem to get much sleep and it was useless to try so she decided to get up and work. Baseball season was here and there was a lot to write about. Also she was in a great mood as she started making coffee at 5:30 in the morning. She had the most wonderful dream and it seemed as real as anything she knew. Amy started writing in her blog for the Chicago Sun-Times. She had had this idea to talk about what it really means to be a Cubs fan.

Chris had finally woken up and found Amy out of bed. He saw her in the living room typing away. He walked over to kiss her and said. "You're up early, hope nothing is wrong."

She smiled and said to him. "No, just couldn't sleep...I had this really great dream."

Chris walked over to the coffee pot and poured himself a cup. Then he asked her. "What was the dream about?"

"I dreamed that the Cubs won the World Series this year and that they had to come back from behind to do it."

"Wow, that does sound like a great dream, do you think they really will?"

"They've got just as much of a chance as anybody else."

Chris walked over to Amy and hugged her. He asked. "Are you going to be disappointed if they don't?"

"Of course, but it doesn't matter whether they do or not. I still love them, always will, and I will always be a fan. I'll be a fan even if they go a 100 years, or 102 years, or even 200 years without winning the World Series."

Chris smiled at her. He had started watching the cubs this year with her and had already experienced spring training, opening day at Wrigley Field, and the devotion that fans have to this team. He had never experienced that in Texas. He was amazed by it to say the least. He replied to Amy. "That's what I love about you and Cub fans...eternal optimism and devotion to a lost cause. It's a beautiful thing."

Amy smiled and said. "That's why there are no better fans than Cub fans."

She went back to writing and after thinking about it for a moment she deleted what she had written and started over. She titled her blog entry and column, *What it Means to Be a Cubs Fan*, and started with that.

I went to bed one night and had a great dream; the Cubs won the World Series. It seemed real and it seemed as if it had happened yesterday. And as real as it might be, it probably was just a dream, but a good one. Then again I have to admit, if the Cubs never won the World Series again, I would be heartbroken. But that doesn't matter because I am a fan through and through – born like this and cursed by my parents, but happy to be one because the struggles as a Cubs fan make us better. There is no greater faith than being a Cubs fan because we have devotion to a lost cause and we love it.

We are from Chicago and the journey is never easy here. As Carl Sandberg once wrote, "it is the city of Broad Shoulders" and I think sitting upon those shoulders are Cub fans. And to be a fan means we are beaten down, baptized in the fire of disappointment, but able to stand tall and get up again with ease and grace. After all anybody can be a fan of winning team, but to cheer for those loveable losers with no regrets and joyful innocence makes us better in the long run.

As fans we always tell ourselves "there's always next year," and it's the greatest metaphor in life. Show me another team that is proud to say that and I will show you a world gone mad. I cheer for this team because that which is easy is never as rewarding. I am always rewarded with joy when I cheer for the Cubs despite the outcome of the game because they never let me down when it comes to experiencing joy. Just watch a game at Wrigley Field and you will understand.

No matter all the broken dreams that surround the Cubs and no matter how cursed my reality is when I convince myself that they could win it all, I have never had a better feeling when rooting for my favorite team, the Cubs. When my heart is broken under the October Moon of the baseball season, I know that the Spring Sun over a Cubs game at Wrigley Field will make it right. I know that being a fan for someone else will never feel the same and no other fans can I call my family other than Cub fans. A thousand dreams of winning the World Series and never seeing it come true could kill just about any other fan, but the broad shoulders that I live with being from Chicago and cheering for those loveable losers gives me strength and makes me powerful beyond measure. Give me struggles and give me broken hearts so I can show you what joy really is. Do that and I will show you a Cubs fan who can withstand anything! Being a Cubs fan is what it really means to be an American because it's not supposed to be

[283]

easy. And maybe what I say doesn't really make sense, but ask yourself this. Can you devote yourself to something, completely and honestly, knowing that you will be let down? As Chicago Cub fans we know that we can and we're proud of it. That's what it means to be a Cubs fan and that's why we will never have to win the World Series to be happy....but it would nice if we did. That would be a great Story from Wrigley.

[285]

"Chicago Cubs fans are ninety percent scar tissue."

~ *George F. Will*

[286]

People ask me a lot about the values I got from playing for
the Cubs for so many years. The value I got out of it was
patience. A lot of people these days are not very patient.

~ *Ernie Banks*

Acknowledgements

I would like to thank my dad, stepmother, and grandfather for taking me to my first Cubs game; it was one of the greatest thrills of my life. I would like to thank Jack Hall for giving me my first Cubs hat before I was a month old. You told my family that I would be a Cubs fan and I have been all my life, which makes me blessed and cursed. I would like to thank my editor for her painstaking and meticulous process when working on one of my books because it helps me become a better writer...even when we disagree. Most importantly I would like the Chicago Cubs and all the players that have played for the Cubs – you have given me a lifetime of memories. No matter how much heartbreak I have gone through watching the Cubs you have also given me one of the greatest joys in my life...couldn't imagine being a fan for any other team. This is why I am a life-long Cubs fan.

Stories From Wrigley is dedicated to Chicago Cub fans.

[289]

[290]